NO ONE IS SAFE

A LUCA MYSTERRY
BOOK 15

DAN PETROSINI

Print ISBN: 978-1-960286-15-4
Naples, FL
Library of Congress Control Number: 2023903292

OTHER BOOKS BY DAN

THE LUCA MYSTERY SERIES

Am I the Killer

Vanished

The Serenity Murder

Third Chances

A Cold, Hard Case

Cop or Killer?

Silencing Salter

A Killer Missteps

Uncertain Stakes

The Grandpa Killer

Dangerous Revenge

Where Are They

Buried at the Lake

The Preserve Killer

No One is Safe

SUSPENSEFUL SECRETS

Cory's Dilemma

Cory's Flight

Cory's Shift

OTHER WORKS BY DAN PETROSINI

The Final Enemy

Complicit Witness

Push Back

Ambition Cliff

1

WE DIDN'T HAVE A BODY, BUT SOMEONE DIED.

The room was dark and the air still. What was left of Lisa Ramos was sitting across the table from us. A pervert had killed the young woman her family and friends described as vibrant.

A deadbolt, installed since yesterday's visit, reflected her intense fear. I'd interviewed parents and spouses whose loved ones were murdered. They scarred me, but this ranked as the most emotional exchange of my career.

Ramos had been unable to say much, but there was no doubt how badly she'd suffered. Twice, I faked the need to use the bathroom to regain my composure.

This time, sitting next to me, was Sophia Livoti, a counselor with Project Help. How did this woman sleep, working with the shattered women she did?

Livoti said, "We need you to be strong and tell Frank what happened. Frank and I have known each other a long time, and he's been incredibly supportive of victims of sexual abuse."

Ramos bit a fingernail.

Livoti said, "Would you like a glass of water?"

Ramos shook her head.

"Talking to Frank is the best way to get the predator who attacked you off the streets. Okay?"

She shrugged.

"It'll be okay. Frank's a good guy and knows what he's doing."

I had some training dealing with rape victims and might even have been a good guy, but I was in the deep end of the pool. I said, "Whenever you're ready. There's no rush."

That wasn't entirely true. The more time passed, the harder it was to solve most crimes. But sexual assault was in a category of its own. Though it was impossible to know the exact number, just 16 percent of rape victims reported the assault to the police.

Ramos whispered, "All right."

I leaned in, and she cowered, moving toward Livoti. Retreating, I said, "Thank you. If you're uncomfortable or need a break, just let me know. Okay?"

She nodded.

I fingered the recorder in my pocket. "Tell me what happened, starting from the beginning."

She swallowed. "Every night I take a walk in the park, and he, he just grabbed me from behind."

Had someone been watching her in North Collier Park? "You didn't notice anyone beforehand?"

"No. It was just after seven, and the park was quiet." She shook her head. "There were no games or anything."

The park was open until ten. "I see. Take your time, and tell me what happened when he grabbed you."

"I usually walk all the way to the baseball fields, but, like, by the soccer fields, I was, changing the music on my phone, and all of a sudden, a bag was shoved on my head. I was, like, stunned and dropped my phone . . ." She closed her eyes.

Livoti said, "Take a deep breath, honey."

Ramos inhaled.

"Good. Feel better?"

Ramos nodded.

"Whenever you're ready, continue."

"I tried to pull the bag off, but he, he stuck a knife in me, right here"—she touched her left hip—"and said he'd kill me if I didn't do what he said."

I said, "I'm sorry. It must have been terrifying."

She frowned.

"What kind of bag do you think it was?"

She shrugged. "Like a plastic-fabric one, kind of rough. Maybe like a reusable grocery bag?"

"That's good. Now, did you see his face?"

"No. I'm not sure, but I think he was wearing, a ski mask or something."

"What makes you think that?"

"When he was, uh, you know, on top of me, I could feel it on my neck. It was like those hats we used to wear in Michigan."

"After he threatened you, what happened?"

"He kept jabbing me with the knife and forced me off the path . . . I knew it was going to be bad . . ."

"Would you like to take a break?"

Hoping she'd say yes, she wagged her head. "I need to get this over with."

"Sure. So, you're being forced off the path, and then . . ."

"I couldn't really see where I was going but I was kind of looking down my nose, out the bottom of the bag, and I knew we were . . . going into the woods . . . by the soccer fields . . ."

"He forced you to the ground?"

She nodded. "He tore at my clothes like an animal. I just, like, shut down. Like I was there but not, you know, like, watching it."

A wave of nausea crashed over me as Livoti patted her hand. "I'm so sorry."

Ramos's lips quivered. I thought tears would flow, but she took a deep breath and threw her shoulders back. "Thanks. It's difficult to recall this, but the worst part was telling my dad what happened."

My lunch stormed up my throat. "Sorry."

Ramos sniffled. "He's a marine. I never seen him cry until this."

She reached for a tissue and blew her nose.

"I'm a father and can't imagine how upset he was."

"My father will be better if he's caught."

"It's not *if*. It's *when*."

She bowed her head. "I hope so."

"I know this was extremely traumatic, but is there anything you remember about him?"

"His breath. It was disgusting. Like water from a fish bowl you didn't change."

Familiar with the smell, I nodded. "What can you tell me about the size of the attacker?"

"He was strong and bigger than me."

A coward is what he was. "How about his voice? Anything distinctive?"

She shuddered. "I'll never forget it."

"Any accent?"

"No. But he had a drawl. And talked kind of rough."

Rough? If I didn't choke the bastard before he went to trial, he'd find out what rough was behind bars. The satisfaction of him likely getting cornholed in jail didn't quell my anger.

"Did anything that happened remind you of anyone?"

Alarm spread over her face. I said, "Please don't misunderstand me; this was in no way your fault. People, even those we know, have, let's say, twisted rationales. I'm only trying to understand if there is someone you're aware of who could be a possible suspect."

She shook her head rapidly. "No. No. It's not anyone I know."

"I hope you understand I had to ask."

She shook her head slowly. It was time to stop asking her to relive the worst day of her life. "I want to thank you again. Sophia is going to stay a while longer, and I'm going to get to work."

Hunting killers is what I usually did, but the timing was good; nailing the Preserve Killer meant I could focus on catching the lowlife who assaulted Ramos.

2

———————

HEADING BACK TO THE OFFICE, I HIT SPEED DIAL. THE SOUND of Mary Ann's voice brought some relief. I said, "Hey, how're you doing?"

"I'm fine, but bored."

"You hear from Jessie today?"

"No. She has classes. Why?"

"Just asking."

"What's going on, Frank?"

"Nothing. Just thought I'd check in."

"New case?"

Busted. I filled her in.

"I don't know how many times I have to tell you; you can't reflect every case on to our family."

"That's not what I'm doing. I'm making sure you and our daughter are okay. It's not like I just started worrying about your safety."

"I know it's hard doing what you do. There's so much evil out there. I just don't want you to get affected by it."

Affected was better than being numbed by it. "You know I'm not."

"Just watching out for you."

"It's not me that needs watching. Some lunatic is out there preying on women."

"You'll get him. Just don't lose yourself in the process."

I wanted to tell her what Ramos said about her father. Maybe Mary Ann would get my uneasiness. "I know how to separate my job from the rest of my life." As soon as it came out of my mouth, I knew it was a fib.

"Does running surveillance in the middle of the night qualify?"

"Uh—"

"It's okay, Frank. Just kidding. What time will you be home?"

"Couple of hours, around six thirty."

I called Derrick. "Hey, the traffic is crazy. I'm going to stop by North Collier Park to check out the Ramos rape scene again."

"How'd it go with her?"

"Heart wrenching. I don't know if she'll ever be the same."

"It's almost impossible. She lives alone, right?"

"Yeah. Her old man's a marine and took it hard."

"Somebody touches my girl, I'll dump a load of lead in their head."

"I know, but it wouldn't change a thing."

"I don't care. I'd blow his frigging head off."

"Something happens like that, the main thing would be taking care of her, getting her back to living her life."

"They'd never be the same."

"Of course not. Everything that happens affects your life, and something like rape . . . I can't even imagine."

"We gotta get this dirt bag."

"We will. I'll see you in the morning."

Driving along Livingston Road, I thought about recommending Dr. Bruno to Ramos. But she wasn't a specialist in dealing with rape victims. Maybe she knew the best therapist.

North Collier Park was massive. Sitting at the north entrance was the Golisano Children's Museum. They had plenty of hands-on exhibits that Jessie had loved. Across the road was the Sun-N-Fun Lagoon. Every time we'd gone, I drove home soaking wet.

It was a place for having fun, but I'd never be able to think about the park without seeing the dead look in Ramos's eyes. I circled the main building: soccer fields to the left and a wooded area before the baseball fields.

I pulled over and got out. There were plenty of places for a deviant to lie in waiting. It was hard not to think of someone watching my Jessie, earbuds in, heading somewhere. Was she carrying the pepper spray I'd given her?

We'd been interviewing visitors to the park, but no one had seen anything suspicious. Two males were said to have been near the ball fields, but the ages and descriptions of the men varied from witness to witness. It was disappointing but not unusual; eyewitnesses were unreliable.

Looking into the woods brought me back to hunting down the killer who'd posed his victims in our parks. This rapist was using the wild area to hide his perversion. He was also careful. He'd left nothing obvious behind.

The park was frequented by hundreds of people a day. Though the rapist had watched Ramos, it appeared she was an opportunistic choice. Unless he struck again, it was going to be near impossible to track him down.

Heading back to the car, I cursed the odds facing me. Ramos was living in fear. I had to do what I could, give her a measure of relief by catching the bastard.

Driving home, I couldn't shake the image of this beast

forcing himself on Ramos. To make it worse, we had nothing but his bad breath and a manner of speech.

––––––––––

I PECKED Mary Ann's cheek. "How you doing?"

"Good. You?"

I shrugged. "Poor woman is counting on us, and we have nothing."

"You just started. You'll develop leads."

I exhaled. "I hope we catch the bastard before he does it again."

"You check his MO?"

"Derrick is running through sexual assaults and near misses."

"You think it's a repeat offender?"

"It could be. It seems he was prepared, but we'll see."

"Good luck. You know, I just heard that Dana Foyle ran away."

"Dana Foyle? Who's that again?"

"She went to school with Jessica but was two years behind her."

"You talk to Jessie?"

"Yes, she's fine."

"Good. What do you know about the Foyle kid?"

"I was out walking and ran into Lee—she's close to Dana's mom—who said Dana never came home last night."

"And she's, what, sixteen?"

"Yes. She had a fight with her father and stormed out."

"Oh, she's probably throwing a tantrum. She'll come back."

"I hope so. Her parents must be worried sick."

"Kids don't realize the effect they have on parents. Argument or not, she should've called them."

"You're right."

The acknowledgment was a good place to end the conversation. "I'm going to get changed."

Walking to the bedroom, I was nagged by the belief Dana's parents had called their daughter's friends, but the kid was still missing.

3

———

I LOOKED OVER AT MY MONITOR; IT WAS TEN AFTER TEN.

"Derrick, where are those files from the sex crime unit?"

"They said they'd bring them down."

"Tell them to move their asses."

"You believe it's a repeat offender, don't you."

"I'm not sure, but it's a good place to start."

"Bunch of damn creeps. They should castrate them all, like they did during the Roman Empire."

I said, "Since it's a mental illness, and they can't be reformed, they should expand the use of chemical castration, to reduce their sex drives."

"Mandatory castration has been on the books for over twenty years, but it's way underused."

"That's because the American Civil Liberty Union fights it, calls it cruel and unusual punishment."

"What the hell do they call rape?"

It was a great point. "Don't get me started."

"Frigging irks me to no end. These bastards volunteer for chemical castration to get out of prison early—"

An intern came in with a handful of files. "Detective Luca? These are for you."

"Thanks."

I handed off half the stack to Derrick. "Let's split these up and get to work."

Collier County did a good job tracking sex offenders, but there were holes in the system. If you served time for sexual assault, we tracked you, notifying neighborhoods when you moved in.

If you came from outside the county, you were required to register. But that demanded the cooperation of an offender. If he came into the area to rape someone, we were blind.

Criminals were stupid, but driving a couple of miles to another county for anonymity was something even the dumbest would know. Believing we'd have to look beyond Collier, I flopped open the top folder. A picture of Jorge Blanco stared at me.`

It was hard to be dispassionate; shaved-headed Blanco had a smirk on his ugly face. Wiping it off wasn't what came to mind. Blowing his head to pieces did. After serving six years for sexually assaulting a North Naples woman, he was released.

Blanco was smaller than Ramos had described. But it was natural to believe your attacker was enormous. Adding to the blur of helplessness, was the blade he'd threatened her with.

What made him interesting was he'd been freed a month ago, and his original victim had been out for a walk at night. Countering it was the victim's sixty-five-year-old age.

Blanco could've thought the woman was younger, or did satisfying his deranged urge make age immaterial? He needed to be checked out. Sliding the Blanco file to the corner of my desk, I opened the next one.

John Craven. If names meant anything, he was our guy.

Craven served five years before being released eight months ago. Six foot three and two hundred ten pounds, Craven's size lined up with Ramos's claim.

His modus operandi was different but predatory. A woman had been stuck on Golden Gate Parkway near Santa Barbara Boulevard. Under the guise of trying to help, Craven pulled over. According to the report, he made a cursory attempt to start the car before offering to drive the woman home.

Instead of taking her to her house, he drove to the parking lot for a middle school and raped her. A janitor grabbed Craven's license plate number, and the pig was apprehended the next day.

Five years before he was convicted of rape, Craven was arrested in connection with a fight at The Center Bar in the Bonita Springs Promenade. The charges were dropped, but according to witnesses, Craven had been in the bar only five minutes before getting in a brawl with a man he'd had no prior contact with.

The spur-of-the-moment decision to fight had similarities with taking advantage of a stranded woman. Plus, he was armed with a knife when arrested. It was small but a weapon nonetheless.

Putting Craven ahead of Blanco, I picked up the phone and called Mary Ann. "How are you doing?"

"Pretty good. I just got off the phone with the Sheraton."

"We going somewhere?"

"No. They have a position open, and as soon as I applied, they called."

"I told you, I don't want you working. It's not good for your health."

"Sitting around isn't good either. Besides, we need to build up our savings again."

"Oh, come on. That's ridiculous."

"Ridiculous? After what we're spending on my shots and what Jessica's college costs?"

"Insurance is picking up most of it now—"

"Yes, but we have no savings. Besides, I'm bored. I feel like I'm wasting away."

"What kind of position?"

"Customer relations."

"Can you work from home?"

"It's a remote job, just three days a week."

"What did they say?"

"I think they're going to offer it to me. We'll see."

I couldn't say I was rooting against it. Her MS was in remission, but stress was a trigger. "Okay. Good luck."

"Thanks. What's going on with you?"

"Developing suspects in the rape case."

"Must be fun."

"Yeah, after reading a couple of files, I need to take a shower."

"Hang in there. What time are you going to be home?"

"About six."

"All right, have a good afternoon."

"Say, did that kid, Dana Foyle, show up?"

"No. Amy told me they filed a missing person report."

"It hasn't been that long. I'm sure the sarge is looking into it."

"Let's hope it's just a case of her getting back at her father."

"You talk to Jessie?"

"She has classes till three today."

"Okay. I'll see you later."

I hung up, sent a text to Jessie, and called Bilotti. "Hey, Doc, how are you?"

"Good, Frank. What are you working on?"

I filled him in on the rape case.

"Sounds ugly."

"It is, but I called about something different."

"Go ahead."

"Mary Ann wants to go back to work, and I'm worried the stress will screw with her MS."

"Stress could precipitate flare-ups but it'd have to be more than the ordinary stress most jobs produce. What is she looking to do?"

"Some job in customer service with Sheraton."

"Hmmm. If she's not fielding complaints, she should be fine.

"See? That's what I'm afraid of. People love to complain when they're paying what rooms go for. I'm against it."

"Is it the financial considerations?"

"We can use the money, for sure, but she's saying she's bored."

"Then she should do something. Sitting around isn't good for her either. Keeping a mind engaged is good for overall health. Is it a remote position?"

"Yes."

"Good. Just make sure she doesn't overdo it."

"I'll try, but she has a mind of her own."

He laughed. "I know what you mean. Before you go, I wanted to tell you about a value wine I bought at ABC Wines on Immokalee. It's from Montsant, Spain. It's a relatively unknown region encircling Priorat. They're turning out some nice wines."

"What grape?"

"Grenache."

"I should have known. How much?"

"Twenty-two. But drinks like a fifty-dollar bottle. I'll text the details to you."

After hanging up, I checked my phone. Jessie hadn't responded. I picked up another file and nearly gagged. With greasy hair and beady eyes, Tim Bowler was the poster child for a deviant. Reading the details of his attack, a text came pinging in.

Figuring it was Jessie, I swiped it open. Bilotti had sent the wine's name over. I thanked him and sent another text to my daughter.

4

———

THE SUN WAS SETTING, BUT MY STOMACH HAD ME GLARING through the sliders at Mary Ann. She was on the phone. After years of telling Jessie she couldn't eat until everyone was seated, all I could do was spear a roasted potato.

Mary Ann finished the call and stepped onto the lanai. "You didn't have to wait for me."

Cutting into a turkey burger, I said, "It's okay. What did Marilyn have to say?"

"That Dana took off another time, right after she went into high school."

"Oh, that's good. How long was she gone the last time?"

"Just overnight."

"But it's a pattern. They tell Gesso's men?"

"I'm sure the parents must have said something."

"They ought to know we don't have the manpower to chase ghosts."

"It's been more than two days."

"Damn, I don't like the way that feels."

"No one has heard from her, not even her boyfriend."

That bothered me. "What was the argument with the father about?"

"Something about going to visit her boyfriend's brother at FSU."

"That's an overnight trip. I wouldn't be so hot to go along with that either. The kid is only sixteen."

She sighed. "It's not easy being a parent."

"The understatement of the century."

Mary Ann said, "You want another burger?"

"No, two's my limit." I cleared the table. "I still can't believe Jessie hasn't called back."

"She sent a text."

"That could be from anyone."

She rolled her eyes. "It was Jessica. I know it was."

"Well, why didn't she answer me?"

"I don't know, Frank. Maybe she missed it or figured I'd tell you she was fine. She's busy—"

"It takes a minute. That's it."

"I'm going for a walk with Karen."

"Be careful, make sure you stay together."

"You're really something."

"You were a cop; you should know—"

"And you should know I'm aware of the dangers and know how to defend myself."

She was right. "Okay, okay, Just be careful."

As soon as she left the house, I called Jessie. After five rings, it went to voice mail. I left a message and sent another text. I headed onto the lanai, trying to rationalize my anxiety. My rapist was in Florida, and Jessie was on Princeton's campus, twelve hundred miles away.

But that meant nothing; rapists preyed on women everywhere. What was the real threat? Was Jessie in trouble or just involved in college life?

Pulling my phone out, I made a call.

MARY ANN CRAWLED INTO BED, and I shut my lamp. About to say good night, she said, "I still can't believe you called her school."

"I was worried."

"Worried is one thing. Calling the campus police to check on Jessica, borders on an anxiety disorder."

"I'm her dad; what am I supposed to do when she doesn't call me back?"

"Didn't you say something about limited manpower to run down—"

"Okay, already. I'm just concerned."

"I told you she said she was fine. You embarrassed her, treating her like a ten-year-old."

There were plenty of kids who'd gone away to college and gotten in trouble, but arguing my side wasn't going to be good. "At least she knows I care, right?"

"She's an adult and a responsible one."

"She'll always be our kid. I just don't want anything happening to her."

"You have to trust her."

"I do. It's the rest of the world I have problems with."

TURNING OFF ROUTE 41, onto Wiggins Pass, I headed east. John Craven lived in Lake San Marino, an RV community. It wasn't gated, leaving me with one less tool. An assortment of vehicles, many needing a tow to be mobile, lined the main drag. Craven lived on Sea Breeze Place. I pulled in front of an off-white Winnebago with a brown stripe running along its side.

The vehicle was at least thirty years old. Cigarette hanging from his lip, a neighbor was fanning smoke from a barbecue. There were a lot of smells, none of them from the sea.

I heard the TV over the hum of an air conditioner and banged on the aluminum door. Beer in hand, Craven came to the door. "What's up?"

His shoulders slumped when I showed him my badge. "I'd like to ask you a couple of questions."

"About what?"

"Tuesday, May tenth."

Craven shifted his weight. "I didn't do nothing."

"Where were you between the hours of five and nine that night?"

"Tuesday?"

"Yes."

"What time again?"

He was buying time. "Between five and nine p.m."

"I was fishing."

"The entire time?"

"Uh, no. I, uh, think I wrapped it up around seven. Maybe later."

The attack took place at seven. "Were you alone?"

"Yeah, my friends don't like fishing."

"Too bad, I enjoy the solitude."

"Yeah, me too, man."

"Where you keep your rods?"

"My rods?"

I ignored the ping from a text. "Yes. I keep mine in the garage, but you don't have one."

"Oh, I leave 'em at a buddy's house."

"What buddy?"

"Aw, come on, man. What's with the questions? I didn't do nothing."

"Where were you Tuesday?"

"I told you I was fishing."

"Where?"

"By the beach, at uh, Wiggins."

"What time you leave?"

"Like I said, around seven."

"Then what did you do?"

"Got something to eat."

"Where?"

"Panera."

"Who were you with?"

"Nobody. I got a sandwich and went home."

Panera had cameras. "Which Panera?"

"The one right here, across the way from Old 41."

"What did you do after eating?"

"I went home."

"You were there all night?"

"Yeah."

"You went from fishing to Panera and then home?"

"Uh-huh."

He never mentioned dropping off his fishing rod. He was lying about fishing. My cell rang. I took a peek; it was Derrick. I swiped it away and noticed he was the one who sent the text. Another text pinged in. I stiffened when I saw the preview. "The Foyles received a ransom note."

5

Sergeant Gesso was sitting on the edge of my desk when I walked in. "What do we have?"

Derrick said, "This is a copy of what the parents received. The lab is going over the original."

Gesso said, "To me, it looks like they held the pencil with their fist." He held up his hand as if holding a knife like a weapon.

Derrick said, "Not going to be easy for the handwriting experts."

I read the note: "Twenty thousand in small bills or you won't see her again."

Derrick said, "Twenty grand isn't a lot of money—"

"I bet it's a drug addict, probably a meth head," Gesso said.

"Could be. Kidnapping for twenty in ransom doesn't match the risk. It feels like a spur-of-the-moment thing."

Derrick said, "Could be a stupid kid who got in a jam and is looking for a quick way out."

A plausible scenario. "Could be."

"Either way, it's a relatively small amount to raise, especially when your kid is on the line."

Gesso said, "Hate to break the positive vibe, but whoever did it knew enough to prevent her phone from pinging. Maybe they took the girl out."

Derrick said, "You think he killed her?"

I said, "Not me. The ransom note is a net positive. He's got to figure we'll want proof the kid is alive before any money changes hands."

Gesso said, "Let's hope so. I don't think we need a professional negotiator, but I called the Fort Myers FBI office to have one on standby."

"Good idea. If this escalates, we'll get them involved."

"All right, you need anything, let me know."

"Thanks, Sarge. If you can press the lab to process the note, we'd appreciate it."

"You got it." As Gesso disappeared, I said, "Let's go to talk to the parents."

Heading to the parking lot, I said, "I think this kid is going to be all right. If the parents survive the scare, it's going to be okay."

"You think so?"

"I don't want to jinx it, but it feels amateurish. The 'small bills' thing is straight out of a movie."

"You going to tell the parents to pay?"

"Ninety-nine percent. Too many people are killed for less, but with kidnappings, over seventy percent are released after paying ransom."

"Then it's worth the shot."

"Asking for only twenty thousand makes me think whoever has her is desperate to return her."

"True."

"Let's get this kid home and get back to hunting the rapist down."

———

SPEEDING DOWN GOODLETTE-FRANK ROAD, Derrick slowed, making a right into a gated community called Lemuria. I said, "I've never been here. You?"

"No. But Lemuria means a lost continent that sank under the Indian Ocean."

"When was this supposed to have happened?"

"About eighty million years ago."

"You get that from the Discovery Channel?"

"No, my mom told me when I was a kid, and I never forgot it."

"Pull behind the patrol car."

The Foyles' coach home backed up to a lake, like the others in the small community. I sized up the property. "What do you think these are going for?"

Derrick said, "Who knows? I'd say five hundred, but the run-up in prices—"

"Too low. It's more like seven to eight hundred now."

"I don't doubt it."

Before I could hit the bell, a uniformed officer opened the door. "Detectives."

"How are you, Bennett?"

"Good." He leaned forward. "They're in the kitchen, but they're pretty shaken up."

"Are they alone?"

"Yeah, I booted the neighbors, like you said."

"Okay, but as soon as we're done, make sure they have people around. They're going through hell."

We breezed into an open floor plan. Mrs. Foyle was

blowing her nose. Her husband shot out of his chair. "You've got to get Dana back!"

"We're working on it." I introduced ourselves and said, "Tell me how you received the ransom note."

Mr. Foyle said, "It came in the mail. It could've been there yesterday; we never got the mail. We've been going nuts since she was taken."

"It came in an envelope?"

"No. The note was loose."

"Did you notice anyone by your mailbox?"

"No, nobody."

"Was there any other mail in the box?"

"Yeah, like I said, it was from yesterday."

"What time does your mail usually get delivered?"

"Around twelve."

"Does the handwriting look familiar?"

"You think somebody we know did this?"

"Not particularly, but we want to narrow down who might have done—"

"Look, that's all good. I want them to rot in jail, but right now, let's pay these people and get our baby home."

"I know it's difficult. I have a daughter a bit older than Dana, but to ensure her safe return, we need as much information as possible."

"Okay, okay."

"I understand there was an argument that originally was thought to have caused Dana to take off."

"Oh, that was nothing."

"What was it about?"

"She didn't run away; she was kidnapped."

The father's cell phone rang. He looked at me. "It's okay. Keep cool and answer."

"Hello?"

His face relaxed. "Yeah, it's fine, come in. The police are here." He hung up. "It's *WINK News*."

"You shouldn't be talking to the media."

"Look, I have to to let whoever has her, know we're going to pay."

"It's not a good idea."

"We can't just sit here and hope they contact us. I got to do something."

"We're investigating—"

"We can't waste time. The internet said the clock is the enemy in kidnappings; the more time passes . . ."

That was right, to an extent. Hiding a hostage was risky. Sometimes the abductors would fold under the pressure, harming or killing their prisoner. "I understand your concerns, but it's best if we follow protocol—"

"With all due respect, sir, the police didn't save Jessica Lundsford. Did they? They botched it."

He was wrong. There was no sense in arguing about the murder that led to legislation named Jessica's Law, making it harder for sexual offenders to reoffend. The thought it was a sexual predator turned my stomach.

"I have two more questions before you talk to a reporter."

"Go ahead."

"Has your daughter ever mentioned anyone approaching her or watching her? Someone creepy?"

"No, we tried to think of something, but there's nothing. This came out of the blue."

"Okay, keep thinking about anything unusual."

"Believe me, we're wracking our brains."

"If, uh, when they make contact, are you prepared to have the money? In small bills?"

"Yes. We have a friend at Bank America. He's getting the money together and said he'd be here this afternoon."

6

A WOMAN LED A CAMERAMAN AND LIGHTING TECHNICIAN INTO the house. Derrick said, "I think that's Emma Heaton from the six o'clock news."

"Yeah, that's her. Look, we can't waste time. We need to canvas the neighbors, see if anyone saw or heard anything."

"The note was probably dropped off late at night."

"I'm sure it was under the cover of darkness, but we can't assume that."

"Yep."

I surveyed the outside of the Foyles' home. "They don't have cameras."

"Maybe one of the neighbors do. Some of these doorbell cameras capture cars going down the street."

"I don't know how people live with the chiming, every time a car passes."

"I guess you tune it out."

The palm trees swayed as a gust of wind blew through. "We need to take a look at Mr. Foyle."

"You think he's involved?"

"Just covering bases. He's the one who found the ransom note and claims an argument made Dana take off."

"That's why you asked about the argument."

"As emotional as this is, we need to be methodical."

"I didn't consider him planting the note."

"I'm not saying anyone is covering up a homicide, but we can't be caught flat-footed if this takes a turn."

"I'll go to a couple of houses, then dig into the parents."

"Okay. I'm going back inside."

Hands on hips, Mr. Foyle said, "Just choose one!"

His wife raised a picture frame. "She looks good in this one, right?"

"It's perfect."

Studying the couple, I reminded myself of the danger of making assumptions. If they had nothing to do with their daughter's disappearance, the pressure of a missing child would turn a statue into jelly.

Blinking as the photographer turned on the lighting gear, I stepped to the side. He held a monitor up. "It's good."

Emma Heaton nodded and faced the camera. "*WINK News* is coming to you live from the Foyle home. Dana Foyle has been missing for three excruciating days. Her parents wanted to speak directly to our viewers in the hope it will speed her return home."

She turned toward the Foyles. "We know these are very trying times for you. What would you like to say to our viewers to enlist their help in Dana's safe return?"

As his wife sniffled, Mr. Foyle stared into the camera. "We're going to pay the ransom. You don't have to worry; all we want is Dana back home."

"You received a ransom note?"

"Yes."

"When? How much are the kidnappers demanding?"

Shaking my head, I stepped forward and drew a finger across my neck. Foyle said, "It was twenty thousand dollars, but I can't say anything further."

"Do you believe Dana will be released?"

"Yes. We trust whoever took her—and don't care who it was—as soon as she's released, we're going forget this ever happened."

He might, but there was no way I was going to give a pass to a kidnapper. The father would change his tune as well. Everything was relative. If his daughter was freed, his focus would shift to the abductors.

"But don't you want justice?"

"All we want is Dana home. Thank you." Foyle pulled his wife out of the camera's view.

I rushed over. "I know you're doing what you feel is right, but kidnappings are a, uh, delicate matter. We need as much control as possible."

"I understand, Detective, but if they're true to their word, they'll let Dana go after we pay."

He was placing his trust in a dangerous mixture of gullibility and hope. Or was he acting desperate as a diversion? The reporter said, "We'd really like to cover the ransom story. How was the contact made?"

I threw up a hand. "I'm sorry, ma'am, but the Foyles have said all they can at this point. Any more may endanger their daughter."

"But—"

"The detective is right. We've said our piece," Mr. Foyle said.

It was good he agreed, but it was at odds with talking to the press in the first place. He wanted to go public but only to a degree, which never worked with the media. Throwing a chin toward a crying Mrs. Foyle, I said, "Tend to your wife. As soon as they're are out of here, we'll talk."

The warm air was soothing. About thirty neighbors were gathered across the street. A reporter made a beeline for me. I waved him off as my phone rang.

"Detective Luca."

"Sorry to disturb you, sir. This is Felix Ramos, Lisa's father."

"Hello, Mr. Ramos. What can I do for you?"

"Lisa said you're in charge of the investigation into, uh, what happened to her."

"Yes, I'm heading it up."

"What's the status?"

"I can't discuss an active case."

"Do you have a suspect?"

"It's early, but we're developing leads."

"Developing? With all due respect, sir, it sounds like you haven't done anything."

"That's not the case, sir. My partner and I are working it, but I have other responsibilities at the moment."

"It's clear her case isn't the priority it should be."

"It certainly is."

"Then show it—ramp up the effort to catch the thug who, who, uh, accosted my daughter."

"I understand you're a military man."

"Retired Lieutenant Colonel, Marine Corps."

"I appreciate your service, sir."

"Thank you."

"With your experience, you're aware that to the public, nothing seems to be going on, but behind the scenes, things are in action. It may take more time than you're comfortable with, but we'll bring whoever it was to justice."

"It's unfortunate, and with all due respect, I don't have the confidence you do."

"I understand, sir. Just give me an opportunity to prove it."

"I will."

"Thanks. I've got to go."

I scanned the street. The crowd of people were chattering among themselves. They were upset and shocked one of their own had gone missing. They sympathized with the Foyles, but they had no clue what Dana's parents were going through. As close as I was, I couldn't imagine being in Mr. Foyle's shoes.

A reporter answering his phone brought back the conversation with Lisa Ramos's father. Only his military training kept his anger in check. Who could blame him for pressing for an arrest? With no way of reversing what happened, it was the only thing he could focus on.

Shaking the thoughts out of my head, I headed back to the Foyles' house to face another father in distress.

7

———

THE SMELL OF GARLIC HAD MY STOMACH GURGLING. MARY Ann saw me and finished her call. I pecked her cheek. She said, "Hungry?"

"Yeah. What did you make?"

"Spaghetti and clams. I figured after the day you had, you'd need some comfort food."

For some reason, she thought it was one of my favorites. It was good, but when it sat, it clumped together as if glued. "Sounds good."

"Where'd you leave it with the Foyles?"

"It's a waiting game. Gesso has a couple of officers with them. As soon as they make contact, I'm in motion."

"I hope it's soon. I can't imagine what they're going through."

"A parent's worst nightmare."

"Twenty thousand is a strange amount to ask for."

"Yeah. Something is off."

"You think they said yes too soon? And they're going to ask for more?"

"No doubt that's a risk, but I don't think that's going to happen."

"You don't think she might be . . ."

There was no point in worrying her. "No, no. It'll probably work out; we just need to get past handing over the money."

The microwave beeped, and Mary Ann took out the bowl of pasta. Dousing it with olive oil, she said, "Do they have the money ready?"

"Yeah, they have a friend at a bank."

"You're going to mark the bills with UV?"

"No, even though I told them you couldn't tell, Foyle said it could endanger his daughter."

She put the clams and pasta in front of me. "It's invisible."

I forked the linguine and twisted it around. "I know. He gave me a hard time when I told him we had to record the bills' serial numbers."

"He's uptight."

My phone rang. Before answering, I said, "Maybe."

"Hey, Derrick. What's going on?"

"You busy?"

I put my fork down. "No, it's okay. What's up?"

"You need to see the video from a Ring doorbell across from the Foyles' house."

DERRICK GOT out of his car as I parked behind him. Before I pulled the keys out, the door of the *WINK News* vehicle across the street flew open. As they approached, I said, "We're not commenting."

I followed my partner to a gray stucco home, diagonally across from the Foyles' home. The owner logged into his

Ring account, pulled up the footage, and handed his phone to Derrick.

Derrick put it in full-screen mode and hit play. You couldn't see the Foyles' front door, but their walkway to the curb was visible. Twenty seconds in, a man appeared, walking down the Foyles' paver path toward the street.

I whispered, "Looks like Mr. Foyle."

He hit pause and zoomed in. "That's what I think."

"The time stamp says it's nine fifty-five p.m. Is it accurate?"

Derrick resumed play in slow motion. "Appears to be."

"He's heading to the mailbox."

"Yeah, but wait."

A second later, a UPS truck came down the street. It slowed, obstructing the view of Foyle and his mailbox. When it passed, Foyle had turned toward the house.

"Jesus! We don't have him going to the mailbox."

"He could have planted the note then."

"Play it again."

I stared at Foyle as he tread down the path. "He's looking around."

"Could be checking if the coast is clear."

"But why not go out in the middle of the night? Instead of taking a chance?"

"Maybe he didn't want his wife to get suspicious."

It was a good point. "Ask the neighbor if he'll give us authorization for a copy of the video."

The man was agreeable, and Derrick told him he'd get the paperwork in motion. I said, "Let's talk to Foyle."

An officer I'd worked a vehicular homicide with, let us in. The Foyles were sitting around a glass-topped kitchen table.

Mrs. Foyle's eyes searched my face. "Did you find Dana?"

"Not yet, ma'am. We'd like to talk to your husband."

Mr. Foyle stiffened before rising. "Sure. What's going on?"

I stepped into the family room. "Tell me what you did last night."

"Last night?"

"Yes."

"Nothing, I was here, with Judy. We were worried sick about Dana."

"Did you go anywhere?"

"No. We were in the house the whole time."

"Are you sure?"

"Yeah, I'm sure."

"We have reports of you leaving the house."

"Reports? What the hell does that mean?"

"Easy, sir. We're only trying to piece together the events that led to your daughter's—"

"What? You think I had something to do with it?"

"We didn't say that, sir."

"Maybe not, but you're sure acting like it."

"Did you leave the house or not?"

He hesitated. "I mean, I might have gone out for some air or something. Or, you know, I think I went outside to check the street, see if Dana was out there."

"Did you go to the mailbox?"

"The mailbox? Why would I get the mail?"

"Out of habit . . ."

Foyle's phone was ringing. He dug it out. "It's restricted."

"Could be a burner phone. Answer it."

Foyle said, "Hello." He nodded quickly, mouthing, *It's them.*

I leaned in, and he pulled the phone away from his ear for me to hear. He said, "They hung up."

"What did they say?"

"To put the money in a shopping bag and start driving. He said I had to be alone, and if there were any cops or helicopters, they'd kill Dana."

"Where'd they tell you to go?"

"They said they'd call again."

It was debatable whether he was on the phone long enough for all that. "Get the money together."

Foyle left, and I turned to Derrick. "That was a smart way to play this. Call Gesso, and have him get a couple of unmarked cars in the area."

"Okay."

"Stay with the missus. I'm going to try and tail him."

Foyle came back holding a Whole Foods bag, loaded with money. I said, "You have to be extremely careful here. We don't know who we're dealing with."

"I realize that."

"Don't try and be a hero. As soon as they call you, call me."

"They said no police."

"They won't know—"

"Yes, they will; they'll hurt Dana."

"I'm not going to be anywhere near you, but if things get out of hand, I have to be in a position to help."

"You're putting my daughter at risk."

"We don't know who we're dealing with. You could be putting yourself in danger."

"I don't care about me. I just want Dana back."

"Look, we have to do this my way. I'm not going to be noticeable, but I have to be close by when the drop off happens. Something goes wrong, I've got copters standing ready. We'll close off the streets and grab the bastards."

"They said no planes or helicopters—"

"They're grounded until they take the money. All you have to do is call me when they give you the drop location and when the handover is completed. All right?"

He nodded.

"Good. Let's go and bring Dana home."

Sliding behind the wheel, I figured we had a good chance of catching whoever was behind the kidnapping. Most extortion plans, especially ones concocted by amateurs, led to their capture.

As Foyle backed out of his driveway, scenarios flashed through my mind. I had to nail whoever took one of our community's kids.

Whether tonight was a success or not depended largely on Foyle making the calls. But his fear of antagonizing the captors would make him wait until after they made contact. He'd delay it until he dropped the bag of money. His focus was on getting his kid back.

As Foyle's taillights disappeared, I reminded myself what was at stake. Pulling away, my shoulders tightened. Dana had to sleep in her own bed tonight.

8

FOYLE'S TAILLIGHTS WERE RED PINPRICKS. HE WAS HEADING north on Goodlette-Frank Road. There were two other cars on the road. I kept my headlights off. Foyle's car approached the stoplight at the Immokalee Road intersection. It was green. He'd probably turn left to get to Route 41.

Foyle turned right. Before the light. He was going into the strip mall that housed the Bone Hook Brewery. I gripped the wheel. Was someone going to commandeer his car? Was the ransom note a ruse to rob twenty grand?

A flash of Foyle's headlights suggested he turned in the lot, toward Landmark Hospital. I tried to recall the setup by the specialized facility. Veteran's Park was close by, as was the Arthrex complex, and a couple of office buildings.

He'd gotten the call but didn't let me know. Picking up the radio, my pee-pee alarm rang. Again. Now was not the time to play it safe with the bladder my doctors had made. "This is Detective Luca; patrol cars needed in the Airport and Immokalee area and around Mercato. Tell them to keep their strobes off and to stay out of sight. I'll call when ready."

Foyle shut his lights. He parked at the far end of the hospital's lot. I went left, pulling into a spot at BurgerFi.

Hugging the building, I poked my head around the corner. Foyle was getting back in his car. Had he dropped the money?

I punched in his number as he approached Goodlette-Frank. "Did you meet them?"

"No. They said to leave the money in the last parking spot."

"What did they say about Dana?"

"That she'd be home in an hour, after they were sure I didn't bring the police."

"Okay. Go home, I'll meet you there."

Keeping my eyes on the empty parking lot, I considered whether to set up roadblocks. Someone was coming to get the money or was in the woods, waiting to grab the bag. Either way, they'd need to get away.

I scanned the surrounding area. A pinpoint of light caught my eye. It was descending. It took a second to put it together. It was a drone.

I snapped two pictures of it and called Gesso. "Sarge, they're using a drone to make the Foyle pickup."

"Damn."

"I need one of our drones to follow it."

"It'll take us ten minutes to get one in the air. What about a copter?"

"No. They'll see it."

"They have to get the drone down somewhere. You want to block streets?"

"No, forget it. I'll track down the bastards as soon as the kid is back home."

"You sure?"

"Yeah. We'll talk later."

The bag of money lifted off the ground. I snapped more pictures as it flew east. It floated just above the tree line and disappeared from view.

9

———————

IT WAS MY THIRD CUP OF COFFEE, BUT THE JAVA WASN'T THE reason for my jangled nerves. The Foyles were standing by the front window, waiting for Dana to appear. It had been two hours.

Derrick leaned in. "You think she's going to be okay?"

"I sure hope so. But the whole thing doesn't fit."

"I know."

"Using a drone to make the pickup was a damn good idea. It doesn't match asking for only twenty K."

"Maybe it does; it weighs about twenty pounds. Easy for a drone to carry away."

"Can't be a toy one, then."

"Right. I Googled it; recreational ones only handle three to five pounds."

"We have to keep that in mind. Maybe focus on people who know how to fly these things."

"It don't take much to learn how. One of our neighbors watched a couple of YouTube videos, and in two days, he had the thing buzzing all over."

"Just great."

"I hate to say it, but this whole drone thing could be a test run."

"You looking to depress me?"

Derrick chuckled. "You always say, nothing is impossible. It may be hard but it—"

"Here she comes!"

I exhaled as the parents ran to the front door. I caught Derrick's arm. "Let's give them a minute alone. But get an EMT rolling; the kid needs to be checked out."

Mrs. Foyle wouldn't let Dana out of her grasp, and her father keep kissing the top of her head. It looked genuine. I reminded myself the job was about examining every possibility. The father was fair game, and it was a relief an ugly situation wasn't getting uglier.

Mrs. Foyle had her arm around Dana's waist. "You want something to eat?"

"No. I'm good."

"Did they hurt you, baby?"

She shook her head. "No."

"They treated you okay?"

She nodded.

"I was so worried about you."

"It's okay, Mom. It's over."

Dana saw me and averted her eyes. I stepped forward. "Hi, Dana. We're glad you're safe."

She cast her gaze down, as her father approached. "Not now. She just got home."

"It's best if we talk now, while everything is fresh in her mind."

"I don't know."

"It'll be a quick chat. We'll do a full interview in the morning."

Dana frowned. "Do I have to?"

Mr. Foyle said, "It'll be fast. No more than ten minutes. Right, gentlemen?"

"That's works for us."

"Okay. We can use the den."

I didn't want Mr. Foyle in the room, but he was in protection mode. We'd have a shot at her alone tomorrow.

Foyle took out folding chairs for us before sliding behind a small desk. Dana flopped into a low-backed chair.

I said, "I'm sure you're tired, but memories tend to get foggy, even after a day."

Dana picked at a seam on her jeans. "I'm kinda tired."

"We'll be quick. Tell us where you were taken."

"I don't know where I was."

"Where you were when they kidnapped you."

"I was walking home from Carmen's house. And I had, like, just crossed Goodlette, by the church."

"What church?"

"The one on the corner, by Vanderbilt."

Mr. Foyle said, "It's the Naples Christian Church."

"Okay, what happened?"

"I don't know. It-it happened so fast, and this van—it pulled over, ahead of me, and as I was walking by, I just got dragged in, and that was it."

Mr. Foyle reached out, squeezing his daughter's shoulder. "I'm sorry."

"The van was ahead of you? Pulled over?"

"Yeah, kinda of like in the cutoff to get to the church."

"Did you see the license plate number?"

"No. But I think it was from Georgia or something."

"What color and make was the van?"

"Uh, white. I'm pretty sure it was white, but I don't know cars."

"But it was a van?"

"I think so."

"It had a side door?"

"Yeah. It was a van."

"How many people were inside?"

"How many people in the van?"

"Yes."

"Uh, two, I think."

"Male or female? What did they look like?"

"They were guys. But I didn't see them. They, uh, put a bag over my head."

Exhaling, Mr. Foyle shook his head. "Bastards."

"It's okay, Daddy. It's over now."

"Do you know who might have done this?"

"No. No idea."

"What did they say when you were put in the van?"

"To keep quiet, and if I did, nothing would happen to me."

"Did they have any discernible accent?"

"No."

"How about their ages? What can you tell me about how old they might have been?"

"Umm, they were definitely older. One guy had, like, a gravelly voice."

"Did they talk among themselves?"

"No."

"They drove silently?"

"Yeah. Except one time, one of them called the other guy Frank."

"One of the men was named Frank?"

"Yes, I'm all confused, but I think he said the name twice."

The kid went through a traumatic experience, but why didn't she lead with the name of one of her abductors? "What about the other man? Did you get his name?"

"I don't know. I'm all confused. I just want to lay down."

"We understand. Get your rest. We'll go over this in detail tomorrow."

Standing, I said, "You don't have to worry. We're going to keep a patrol out front, to be sure."

Mr. Foyle said, "You think these people are a threat?"

"No. At worst, it'll keep the press from hassling you."

Derrick closed the car door. "The kid's been through a ton, but it doesn't add up."

"I hear you loud and clear."

10

—————

REMIN APPROACHED THE PODIUM. THERE WASN'T A WRINKLE in his suit. "Good morning."

The roomful of reporters quieted down. "Thank you for coming. We're pleased to report that Dana Foyle has been released and is home with her family."

Applause rippled through the room.

"Before I take questions, I wanted to thank all of you and members of the press not here today. Your cooperation, following our guidance, on covering this kidnapping is appreciated. I'm hopeful we can build upon this success and work together to keep Collier County residents and visitors safe. Now, who has a question?"

Nearly every hand shot up. Acknowledging *WINK News* had played ball with the sheriff's office, Remin pointed to the reporter who covered the ransom letter. "Emma Heaton, *WINK News*. What is the status of the investigation into the kidnappers?"

"I can't comment on an ongoing investigation, but I can tell you, no resource will be spared in capturing those responsible. The men and women of this department will make sure they face justice."

"Do you have a primary suspect?"

"I'm sorry. As much as I'd like to, I can't answer that."

Remin moved to a man wearing a yellow jacket. "Earl Hening, the *Naples Daily News*. Given the short period of time between the abduction and ransom payment, are you concerned kidnapping will be used by some as a quick way to make a buck?"

"No. Extortion is neither a quick nor easy way to make money. And I can promise you, this department will remain vigilant as it confronts all threats to the safety and well-being of our citizens and those visiting.

Remin was a politician by nature, saying a lot without saying anything. Remin rambled on for ten more minutes before closing the press conference.

I followed him into the anteroom. He said, "I'm counting on you to wrap this one up quickly."

Instead of saying, then why'd you waste my time listening to you bloviate, I said, "I'm interviewing Dana Foyle in an hour, and Derrick is conducting background checks."

REPLAYING THE PRESS CONFERENCE, I turned onto Vanderbilt Beach Road. Was the reporter right, insinuating paying ransom would motivate others to snatch people off our streets?

This was the United States, not Mexico or Nigeria, where a couple of people a day were abducted for ransom. I squirmed in my seat; the wealth in Naples did make it easy for cretins to plan get-rich-quick schemes. A fast solve would make sure any seeds along those lines wouldn't get watered.

Turning into Lemuria, I spotted the satellite dishes of news vans. I hoped the Foyles would respect our instruction and only speak to the media after we interviewed Dana.

A handful of reporters converged on my car. Stepping out, I said, "I'm not going to make a statement today, so I'd appreciate you giving me and the family space."

Humming to block out the questions being shouted, I waved to the officers parked out front and hit the doorbell.

I shook Mr. Foyle's hand. "How is Dana today?"

"She's not herself. I guess it'll take time to get over what happened."

"You may want to get her some help. It might be good for her to talk to a professional."

"I don't know about that."

"Trust me; a therapist can do a lot good. I know someone excellent, if you're interested."

"We'll let you know."

I nodded. "How's the missus?"

"She's good, but believe it or not, she's still sleeping. I guess the stress got to her."

"No doubt. You're not immune to it yourself, you know."

"I'm fine. Don't worry about me."

"I used to say the same thing. Be careful."

"I will. Let me get Dana. She's sitting outside, been on the phone nonstop."

I smiled. "I know all about that. We have a daughter older than Dana."

"These kids are glued to their phones."

I nodded. "Look, you have the right to sit in, but I think it's best if we talk alone. She may hold back if you're there."

He hesitated. "You think so?"

"Trust me on this."

He nodded and left. A minute later, Dana, in flip-flops

and cutoffs, trailed behind her father. She barely said hello, and I followed them into the den.

"Dana, just the two of us are going to talk."

Her eyes darted to her father, who said, "It's okay. Detective Luca is here to help."

"We want to make sure you and your family are safe. If you're uncomfortable at any point, you can stop the interview."

"Okay."

I took the same folding chair as last night. "Good to be home, isn't it?"

"Yeah."

"Where did they keep you?"

"Uh, I think it was a basement or something."

There were less basements in Southern Florida than Martians. "You sure it was a basement?"

"Uh, maybe not. I got confused, 'cause they had a bag on my head."

"Was it a paper bag or fabric?"

"Some kind of material. It was real scratchy."

"Did they keep it on you all the time?"

"Yeah. They didn't want me to see them."

Her face didn't exhibit signs of irritation. "Let's go back to when it happened. I know you told me last night, but I'd appreciate you going back over it."

She stuck to her story, but it felt scripted. "And you're sure it was a van? A white one?"

"Yeah, I thought about it, and it definitely was white."

"And the men, they were older, you said."

"Definitely. I was scared they were, you know, going to, uh, you know?"

I did know. I couldn't tell her about the rape I was working. "Thank God, they didn't't."

She shrugged.

"Where did you sleep?"

"Uh, on a couch."

"What color was it?"

"Blue. It was—"

She caught herself, but it was too late. "Go ahead."

"I saw some of it, you know. I lifted the bag off my head. I mean, it was hard to breathe."

"What else did you see?"

"Uh, nothing. It was dark."

"You were alone?"

"Yeah, but I think they had cameras or something."

"What makes you think that?"

"I don't know. It felt like they were watching."

"Were you tied up? Restrained in any way?"

"No. But I couldn't get away, I wanted to but . . ."

"You were afraid?"

"It was real scary."

"Did they ask you if your parents had money to pay a ransom?"

"It wasn't that much money."

"They told you the amount?"

"I, uh, I don't know if they did or my dad did. But it was like thirty thousand dollars, right?"

"Twenty."

"Oh, right."

"What did you eat while you were held?"

"Eat? What do you want to know that for?"

"I know it's a stupid question, but they make us ask."

"We had pizza."

"They ate with you?"

"No. They just put it in the room I was in."

It was curious she used "we" if they didn't eat together. "How do you know they had pizza?"

"I just figured they did."

"Where'd they get the pizza from?"

"Rosedale . . . I think. I'm tired and getting mixed up. I really want to end this."

"Just one more question, okay?"

"All right."

"You said one of them was named Frank."

"Yeah, the guy slipped and said his name."

"Do you know anybody named Frank?"

"No. Nobody." She stood. "I'm really tired."

My experience with kidnappings was limited, but either way, this was a strange interview.

11

____

WAITING FOR A CHANCE TO PULL OUT ONTO GOODLETTE-Frank Road, I took my phone out to call Derrick and noticed a voice mail. I hit play: "Detective Luca, this is Felix Ramos. You said you'd keep me in the loop. I'm looking for an update. Please call me."

I stared at the phone. My promise was more a figure of speech. I hoped he wasn't expecting me to check in on a daily basis. As a car pulled around me, I called Derrick.

"Hey, Frank. How'd it go?"

The kid deserved the benefit of the doubt, but I put my fatherhood aside. "Her story had more holes than a macaroni strainer."

He chuckled. "What'd she say?"

I filled him in and said, "The fact she didn't mention the name Frank right off the bat, and claims not to know anyone named Frank? I don't buy it. She didn't even try to think of anyone she might know—the kid just spewed no."

"A canned response?"

"It sure sounded like it. The question is why?"

Derrick said, "Something is fishy."

"She referred to them as 'we,' like she knew them."

"And you said, one minute she's got the bag on and then it's off?"

"She knows whoever did it and wants to protect them."

"You think so?"

I hit the gas and pulled out of Lemuria. "Can't discount it."

"I talked to her friends. Nobody could think of anyone. They seemed like nice kids and spoke highly of Dana, except nobody seems to like her boyfriend."

"What they say about him?"

"Bradley Richter is his name. He's a year older than her, and they said he's controlling."

"How long they been going out?"

"About two years."

"Two years? Why wasn't he with the family?"

"Good question."

"Did her friends mention anything about the two of them having a fight or something?"

"I asked, but they said no."

"Either way, he needs scrutiny."

"I'm heading to see him now. He lives by the Golden Gate Middle School."

"Okay. See what he has to say. Text me his info; I'll run a background on him when I get back."

"Talk later."

I hung up and made a right onto Vanderbilt Beach Road, pulling onto the grass. This call couldn't wait for a red light. "Mr. Foyle, this is Detective Luca."

"Oh. Something the matter?"

"Not particularly, but Dana's boyfriend, Brad Richter . . ."

"What about him?"

His tone changed. "I understand they've been in a relationship for two years. You'd think he would've been around the house, with you and your wife—"

"Bradley is not welcome in this house."

"I understand. May I ask why you feel that way?"

"He's not good enough for Dana."

It was a common lament from parents. One I was guilty of. For the longest time, I cold-shouldered anyone Jessie had a date with. She wouldn't bring anyone home, which made it worse. I still didn't trust her judgment a hundred percent, but Mary Ann commented I'd made progress. "Is there anything particular about him?"

"No. It's everything."

"Was there an incident that made matters worse?"

"From day one, I didn't like the way Dana was with him. She changed since meeting him."

"Would you say he's controlling?"

"I don't know what goes on between the two of them, but he's no good for Dana."

"I understand. Sorry to bring him up."

"It's okay. As much as I don't like Brad, I don't think he had anything to do with the kidnapping."

I couldn't tell anyone I was disappointed it wasn't the boyfriend. A quick solve would get my sole focus back on the Ramos rape.

AFTER UPLOADING the pictures I'd taken of the drone, I called the lab. "Hey, Charlie, I just sent you cell phone images of the drone used in the Foyle kidnapping."

"Hang on. Let me check."

He tapped on a keyboard. "Yeah, I see them."

"I need help making an ID on the type, and where they're sold."

"My son has a similar one. I'll blow it up and run comps."

"I don't have to say it's priority, do I?"

"Isn't that your middle name?"

I hung up. This was going to be a long day, and I needed a pick-me-up.

The cafeteria was empty. I pulled the lever down, and as steaming coffee trickled into my mug, I heard footsteps. "Hey, Frank. How are you?"

"Good, Brian."

"Hey, how's the Foyle kid?"

"She seems okay."

"Good. Look, we had an attempted rape early this—"

"Ow!" I let the lever go and shook the coffee off my hand.

Brian passed me a handful of napkins.

"Thanks." I wiped my hand and the counter. "Tell me about the attempt."

"I don't know much but knew you were handling the one at North Collier Park when you got pulled into the Foyle case."

Maybe Ramos's father had a point. "I'm working both of them. Up in Jersey, I had ten cases going at the same time."

"Man, I can't imagine that."

"What happened?"

"This woman, Joan Samus, is in town visiting her mother and was attacked going to her car."

"What time was this?"

"After one a.m."

"Where did it happen?"

"She was parked off Third Avenue by the middle school."

It was a challenge getting a parking space near Fifth Avenue. "How'd she get away?"

"Guy was dragging her to the track and tried to put something over her head when she bit him. The creep let go, and she took off for the CVS store."

"It might be the same guy; he covered the last victim's head too."

"That's what I remembered."

"I'll talk to the sarge, but do me a favor, and get the report to me ASAP."

12

———

THIRTY-EIGHT-YEAR-OLD JOAN SAMUS WAS FROM LAKE George, New York. Visiting her mother, she'd been out late, hanging at Vergina's bar until their 2:00 a.m. closing time.

The streets were deserted at that hour. Most of Naples already had four hours of sleep by the time Ms. Samus left the Fifth Avenue restaurant. We'd responded to a couple of alcohol-inspired brawls there but never a serious crime.

Considering if a patron had been casing her, Derrick strode into the office. "Guess who I think did the kidnapping?"

"What did you find out?"

He grinned. "Guess. You're not going to believe it."

I wasn't sixteen, nor did I have the patience I once had. "Just tell me what you found out."

His smile faded. "Dana and her boyfriend, Bradley Richter, made up the whole thing."

I jumped out of my chair. "What makes you think that?"

"The boyfriend was lying and inconsistent. I asked him where he was when Dana disappeared, and he said he was home. But his mother said he didn't get home until late and had missed dinner."

"You spoke to the mother separately?"

"Yeah, and you know what the best part was?"

"She baked you cookies?"

"Sorry, can't help myself."

"Trust me, I know. What about the mother?"

"Bradley denied having a drone, but his mother said they bought him one a month ago after he expressed a sudden interest in them."

"What kind did they get?"

"She didn't know and said it's usually in the garage, but she hadn't seen it for a couple of days."

"We need to find out what they bought."

"She was going to ask her husband. Said he was the one who shopped for it."

"You did some great work here. I'm proud of you."

"Thanks, Frank. Just doing my job."

"What did you think of the boyfriend? Easy to crack, if we press him?"

"He acted tough, but he's a kid."

"I sent photos to the lab. We get a confirm of the model that lines up with what he's got, we bring both of them in."

"Sounds like a plan."

I sat down. "Did you hear there was an attempted rape downtown?"

"Yeah. Was going to tell you, but I guess I got excited after talking to the boyfriend."

"No worries." Ugh, I hated using that phrase. "I'm thinking it's related. The attacker tried to cover her head."

"Could be."

"She bit him."

"Serves the bastard right. I hope she took a chunk out of him."

"Me too, it'll be something to look for in a suspect."

HEADING EAST ON 41, I made a right on Thomasson Drive, on the opposite side of the Tamiami Trail. It was called Rattlesnake Hammock Road. It was another road that changed names, confusing visitors and residents.

I slowed, approaching the East Naples Community Park. I'd heard about the sixty-some-odd pickleball courts there. Naples was the American capital for the growing sport. With ten minutes till my appointment, I hooked a left into the park.

After a quick tour, I pulled out of the park. It was surprising most courts were occupied. It looked like fun. Maybe Mary Ann and I could give it a shot.

Joan Samus's mother lived in a new community of rental apartments near the park. A six-foot fence surrounded the property, but the unmanned gate was up.

I rang the bell of the ground-floor unit. "Who is it?"

"Detective Luca, with the Collier County Sheriff's Office."

"You got ID?"

"Yes, ma'am."

"Put it up to the peephole."

I did as requested, and the door opened. "Sorry. Got to be careful these days."

"You did the right thing."

I was amazed at how easily people let someone purporting to be a police officer or official into their homes. Ninety percent of the time that I showed my badge, the person took a quick glance. With the quality of fakes these days, that was a mistake.

Countless times, we told Jessie if someone came to the door claiming to be an officer, or if she were pulled over by an unmarked car, to call the police to verify the situation.

"Joanie's in the spare room. She's been in there since it happened. Scared to come out."

I followed her to a closed door. The mother knocked. "Honey, the policeman is here."

The door slowly opened. Wearing a fleece, Joan Samus was birdlike. It was a wonder she was able to fend off her attacker. "Hello, Joan." I extended my hand. "I'm Detective Frank Luca."

She didn't take my hand. "Hi."

"I have some questions about what happened to you. I realize you're shaken, but it's best if we talk today."

"Okay." She sat on the bed, hugging her knees.

"Tell me as much detail as you remember. You were at the bar in Vergina, so start there."

She swallowed. "I was just enjoying the music and having a drink."

"Were you alone?"

"Yes. I mean, a couple of men came up to me, but it was nothing."

"Anyone who might have been the attacker?"

She wagged her head.

"Did you notice anyone there who might have been watching you?"

"No, I mean, there were a lot of people in there. But I was into the music; the DJ was good."

"What time did you leave?"

"When they said 'last call.'"

"How much did you drink?"

"I had two drinks the entire night."

It was probably four, and at her size, anything more than two would affect her. "When you left, were you aware of anyone following you?"

"No! I wouldn't have gone to my car if I was."

"Which way did you walk?"

"Straight across, through the plaza."

"So you passed to the left of the Sugden Theatre?"

"Yeah, by that restaurant, Truluck's."

There was a valet stand on the street she came out on. Maybe someone saw something if they were there that late. "Then what happened?"

"I was walking and checking my phone, and next thing I know, this man grabs me from behind."

13

———

Everything was set. But instead of tingling with anticipation, I was conflicted. I didn't monkey with the temperatures of either room. There was no use in making a bad situation worse for both sets of parents.

Derrick met me in the hallway. "Be nice to convince the parents to let us interview them without them in the room."

"I'm okay with it. It might work to our advantage."

"How so? They're not going to admit to anything in front of their fathers."

"I don't know. They may open up with daddy in the room. It may be embarrassing if they did it, but with their father there, they may feel protected. It's scarier being alone and admitting something to a cop."

"I hope you're right."

"Me too. Look, I want to do this myself. With two of us in the room, it may be too frightening."

"No worries. It's intimidating enough."

Glad he didn't take offense. I let the stupid, "no worries" phrase pass.

"All right, let's see where this goes."

I knocked on the door to interview room 1. "Good Morning, I'm Detective Luca."

Nudging his son as he stood, Mr. Richter extended his hand. "Frank Richter."

Bradley offered a chin nod.

I set a thick file on the table and squared it. "This isn't a formal interview, but I'm still bound by rules, forcing me to record it."

His son picked at a cuticle as Mr. Richter said, "We understand."

Hitting the record button, I stated who was in the room. "All right, let's see if we can clear up what happened to Dana."

"I told you, I don't know anything."

Flipping open the folder, I took a handful of images out. Laying them tile-like, Mr. Richter said, "That's our house. You've been watching our home?"

"Your son knows Dana well. It's standard procedure."

I laid down the pictures of the drone that picked up the bag of money. Next to them, I positioned web photos of the model Richter had bought his son.

Tapping the drone carrying the ransom, I said, "Here's the pickup being made."

Mr. Richter shook his head. "It's crazy." Brad squirmed in his chair.

"And Bradley, this is the drone you have. It's the exact same one."

"So? There's a ton of them out there."

"It's less than that. To be exact, a hundred and forty-eight of these were sold in Collier County, and just thirteen at Tech World, off Naples Boulevard."

"Excuse me, that must be a coincidence. I hope you're not trying to say, because we have a drone like the one used, my son was involved?"

"I don't believe in coincidences."

"You think my son had something to do with it?"

"From what Dana has told us, it looks like he did."

Bradley bolted upright. "What did she say?"

"I can't disclose that until the agreement with her is finalized."

Mr. Richter said, "What kind of an agreement?"

"A cooperation one. It'll absolve her of any—"

"That's bullshit! I want a lawyer."

"Bradley! Watch your mouth!"

"But Dad!"

"No buts. Keep quiet." Mr. Richter turned to me. "Do I need to get a lawyer for my son?"

"I can't answer that, but he has a right to legal counsel."

He pursed his lips. "Can I have a few minutes alone with him?"

I stood. "Sure." Hitting the stop button, I said, "You don't have to worry; no one is listening. I'll give you a half hour and get something to drink for you."

Derrick was outside the door. "Two to one he gets a mouthpiece."

"Probably. I'm going to take a run at Foyle."

REMIN STRAIGHTENED HIS TIE. "Frank, are you sure you don't want to answer questions from the press?"

"I'd rather get root canal."

Remin chuckled. "It's not that bad. You have to know how to deal with them. Give them what you want people to know and they can be an asset."

"This one is going to get more attention than it deserves. There's more interest now than when the kid disappeared."

"It'll vanish in a couple of days. Let's go."

Remin pushed through the door to the press room and headed for the podium. I held the door open, scanning the crowd of reporters. Emma Heaton was sitting in the front row, another prime seat.

"Hold up, Frank."

"Hey, Sarge. What's up?"

"Mr. Ramos is here. I told him you're tied up, but he won't leave."

The good feeling I had passed as quickly as a fortune cookie's positive message. "Let Derrick handle him."

"He refused to talk to Dickson. Said he'd only speak to you."

"All right, show him to my office."

Seeing Ramos made me pull my shoulders back. This guy must have a plank running down his back. Wearing shiny shoes, he was bouncing on the balls of his feet but had bags under his eyes.

"Mr. Ramos."

"Detective Luca. Sorry to be firm on seeing you but—"

"That's okay. As I said, your daughter's case is a priority."

"What's the status of it?"

"There's no change, but don't take that as a negative. We're developing threads that will lead to persons of interest."

"Meanwhile, this cretin is out on the streets; my daughter is barricaded in her home, and I can't sleep."

"I'm sorry. I feel for her and you."

"You have no idea the toll this is taking on us."

"You're right. But I have a daughter as well, and I know it's got to be—"

"If it was your daughter or another cop's, I'm sure everyone would be out there hunting this bastard down."

"That's not true. We treat all victims of crime with the same urgency and care."

"No disrespect, Detective, but from what I've seen, that's not good enough. I can't rest knowing he's out there."

"Trust me, Mr. Ramos, we're on it and I can tell you, I'm committed to finding the culprit and bringing him to justice."

"Bring him to me. I'll show him justice."

14

—————

Coming into the house, I was engulfed with the aroma of onions and garlic sautéing. They should make an after-shave like it. It didn't matter what was for dinner, I was opening a nice red wine.

Looking through the sliders, the table on the lanai was set with wineglasses. This woman had a sixth sense. Mary Ann came out of the bedroom. "Hi."

I kissed her cheek. "Smells great."

"Me or dinner?"

"Both." I rubbed her shoulders. "What are you making?"

"You're grilling shrimp. Publix had jumbos, and I splurged, since we both have something to celebrate."

"What's going on?"

"I start the job on Monday."

"Great. Just don't overdo it."

"I won't. Tell me what happened with Dana. I saw the press conference, but it was light on details."

"Let me get a bottle of wine first."

"Oh, hold on."

"What?"

"Jan's father, Freddie, died today."

"He was way up there."

"Ninety-four."

"What happened?"

"Died in his sleep."

"He was a good guy, who did it right."

"Did what?"

"Living long and dying fast."

Bottle in hand, we went onto the lanai. Mary Ann set down a Tupperware of marinating shrimp. I put the grill on and grabbed the corkscrew.

"Beautiful night. What kind of wine is it?"

"It's from Spain. Bilotti said the 2020s are real good."

"Expensive?"

I popped the cork. "No. Not at all. Here, try it."

"Just a little, to celebrate."

I filled her glass halfway and gave myself a generous pour. I clinked her glass and swirled mine around. "Look at the color; it's dark purple." I inhaled, "Not much of a nose."

"Nose?"

"The aroma."

"You're really into this, aren't you?"

"It's fun. Plus, it makes me frisky."

I kissed her neck.

"Hey, not now."

"Later?"

"If you're a good boy."

"I promise. I'll even do the dishes."

She laughed. "Put the shrimp on, and tell me what happened with Dana. I still can't believe it."

"We had Dana in one room with her father, and the

boyfriend and his dad in another. I laid out a bunch of photos of their houses and them. It made it look like we had surveillance on them."

"I don't know if I like that. Where'd you get that idea from?"

"Remember that French crime series we were watching?"

"The one with the subtitles?"

"Yeah, set in Paris."

"Captions make me fall asleep."

"Anyway, the boyfriend wouldn't come clean, but Dana didn't last long. She said Brad came up with the idea of faking her kidnapping to make some money."

"But she was stealing from her own family."

"I know. She said he got the idea from a YouTube video from England where dogs were taken from their owners for ransom."

"Why'd she go along with something like that?"

"According to her, she was afraid of him and couldn't tell him no. He said he needed the money for a car and promised her they'd take a trip."

"It's unbelievable. He's got her under his thumb. I read an article online, said a quarter of high school girls were in abusive relationships."

"Disgusting, but I believe it. I felt bad for her. She was crying like a baby, and her father was in shock."

"Terrible, but the good thing is that's the end of Dana and Brad."

Putting the shrimp on the grill, I said, "I hope you're right. These relationships are stickier than Krazy Glue."

"Are charges going to be filed?"

"Mr. Foyle wouldn't file a theft complaint, and the guys in juvie have it now. It looks like they'll both get community service, if they make the county whole for the costs we incurred."

"How embarrassing for the Foyles. I'd have to move, if it happened to us."

"Teenagers aren't the brightest of God's creations."

"I can't imagine what either of the parents are going through. What did Remin think about it?"

"He was just glad it had a good ending for the department. Remin doesn't have kids and doesn't get the emotional end of it."

Turning the shrimp over, I thought of Ramos. The father was trying to keep it together, but the strains were apparent. If there was no solve, he might put a bullet in his own head.

I wanted to tell Mary Ann about the Ramos case but needed a break from negativity. Plus, I wanted to keep my chances alive for bedtime. I took a sip of wine. "You're feeling good, right?"

"Yeah, why?"

Kissing her cheek, I said, "Just making sure. You know you made a promise before."

She laughed. "You have a one-track mind."

"I'm a man. What did you expect? So, tell me about the job."

Not wanting to spoil my chances for lovemaking, I agreed to watch another Hallmark movie, even restraining from making snarky comments. As it ended, I said, "All right, let's go to bed."

"Wait a couple of minutes; the news is about to start. I want to see what they say about the Foyles."

She scrolled to *WINK News,* and the anchor said, "Good evening. Tonight we have a report on the happy but bizarre ending to the disappearance of Dana Foyle."

A split screen had Dana on the left and the Foyles' home to the right.

"Sheriff Remin, of Collier County, held a press conference today, confirming the report the disappearance was a hoax. Dana Foyle and her boyfriend, Bradley Richter, staged the kidnapping in an attempt to extort twenty thousand dollars from Dana's family.

"Though unconfirmed, sources tell us, Richter planned the caper, pressuring Dana to go along with the scheme. Instead of being taken off the street by two men in a van, as originally claimed, Dana was hiding out in the home of Bradley's grandmother, who was on a two-week cruise.

"Neighbors, who came out in support of the Foyles, were shocked to discover the truth. We spoke with one, who used to babysit Dana, who felt betrayed.

"The case has been referred to Florida's Department of Juvenile Justice, and we'll bring you further details as they emerge."

The picture behind the newscaster changed to two masked people running from a home. "In a brazen theft in Livingston Estates, two people broke into a secluded home. But it wasn't jewelry or cash they were targeting. If you'll look closely at the person to the left"—the camera zoomed in—"these burglars took a beloved terrier belonging to the owners of the home."

Mary Ann said, "Oh my God. They're stealing dogs?"

"The last Interpol report I read, mentioned a rash of pet thefts in England. With the prices of some of these breeds, they're selling the stolen ones on the black market."

"It's felony theft."

"Yeah, but I'm sure courts aren't doling out harsh penalties."

"Not unless the judge is a dog lover."

"Talking about lovers . . ." I got off the couch and put my hands on her shoulders. "Can we stick to the human kind?"

"Ah, that feels good."

"I'm just getting started."

15

The Foyle kid was as stupid as they get, but she was safe and home. It made for a great night. Sleeping six hours was a bonus.

The sun was shining and the humidity low. It was close to perfection, but there was a dark cloud: the Ramos case.

Crossing the parking lot to the office, I told myself, with the Foyle case out of the way, we'd focus on the rape. I pushed through the door and stepped into my office.

Derrick peered over his monitor. "Morning, Frank. How you doing?"

"Good." I grabbed the coffee he bought me. "Thanks."

My partner held up the *Naples Daily News*. "You see the paper? It's all about the Foyles."

"I saw the news last night."

"Where do they get these headlines? 'Kid's Drone Caper Crashes.'"

"I know teenagers make mistakes, but I can't imagine my Jessie doing something like that. I'd resign and move to Idaho."

"I'd like to think that doesn't happen to guys in our line, but remember McKloskey?"

"Anytime drugs are involved, everything goes out the window. Someone hooked will steal from their grandma."

"This country better get a handle on fentanyl or it's gonna kill us."

"Most of it comes from Mexico and China. We should be forcing them to shut it down."

An older officer, pushing a trolley of mail, stopped by the door. He picked up a rubber-banded stack, and came in. "Here you go, gents."

"Thanks, Judd. How you doing?"

"All right. Fifty-six days until permanent vacation."

"Nice."

"No more of the bullshit, like tracking down dognappers."

"Nuts, ain't it?"

"I hear they made a ransom demand."

"What?"

"Yeah, Tommy D told me."

I shook my head, and he said, "I'll see you tomorrow."

"Derrick, check if that's true."

"You think we're going to get the case?"

"No way. But I'll bet these guys are copying from the Foyle kid. The parents paid the ransom a couple of days ago and now this?"

"It's got to be a coincidence."

I raised my eyebrows.

He said, "I know you don't do coincidences, but did you ever see the video *The Dog Detective*?"

"*The Dog Detective*? No, never saw it."

"It's on YouTube. It's pretty good. One of those British inspectors tracks down people stealing valuable dogs and selling them."

"Something like that was in the Interpol feed. They're selling them at a discount to the crazy prices some breeds go for."

"They'd get more, ransoming the owner. People love their pets and will pay anything. Lynn took our dog to get his teeth cleaned, and it was four hundred bucks, more than what they charge for our toddler."

"I know. A neighbor paid nine grand for a hip thing with their dog. I think it had cancer."

"People are nuts. How many you see at restaurants these days? It's getting out of hand."

"Thieves are good at one thing—identifying a weakness. If the owners pay, we'll see more of it. Find out if it's true, and then let's get on the Ramos case."

Derrick picked up the receiver. "I got a couple more names from the Sex Crime Unit when I got in this morning."

He wasn't waiting for my direction as much as he used to. I was proud of him, but it wasn't easy seeing my importance slowly fade. I stretched my fingers and inhaled; there was a rapist on the loose.

It was time to read the notes on John Craven. Not only had he lied about fishing, he did it poorly. It wasn't like me to give credit to a criminal, but they usually worked up an excuse to cover their tracks. Craven didn't, which was a negative in the suspect game.

However, in this case, we were dealing with a rapist. Experts said rapists don't have a behavioral or mental disorder. They also claimed no condition existed that could compel someone to commit rape.

In their world, they were probably right, but I was a cop not a psychologist. It may not be the best approach, but for me, what worked was viewing rapists as people with a mental illness. That meant rational thinking was out. It was about the need for power and failure to control their animal urges.

It was a perspective devoid of nuance but hard to argue it was off base.

Craven was the natural place to start. But there was the other sex offender, who'd surfaced immediately: Jorge Blanco. Tripped up by the Foyle hoax, we'd hadn't dug into him.

I was staring at the sexual predator when Derrick hung up. "It's true. The owners received a call asking for a three thousand dollars."

"What kind of dog?"

"A mutt."

"That's crazy."

"You don't have a dog. It doesn't matter the breed. They're part of the family. Especially with people whose kids moved out; they're something to mother over."

"I guess you're right. I never had a dog, growing up, but I like them."

"You're definitely a dog person. Every time you come over, Prince goes right to you."

"He's cute. What kind of breed is he?" My desk phone rang. "Detective Luca."

"This is Felix Ramos."

This guy was a pit bull. "Hi, what can I do for you?"

"You know why I'm calling. I want to know what the hell is going on with Lisa's case."

"We're working on it. And, as a matter of fact, we're leaving to interview two persons of interest."

"Where do they live?"

"I can't tell you that, sir."

"Oh, just asking to see if they live where it, uh, happened."

"We've got to get moving. Have a good day, Mr. Ramos."

"That Lisa Ramos's father again?"

"Yeah. I feel for the man. His only daughter went through the most traumatic and dehumanizing experience you could go through, and he can't do anything to make it better. The worst thing for any father is feeling helpless."

"We got his back. We'll get him some justice."

He was more confident than I was. It did no good to remind him that, in two-thirds of the rapes reported to the police, no arrests were made. "Take a good look at each of the names you got this morning and work up a priority list. I'm going to see this turd, Blanco."

16
___

I TURNED OFF ROUTE 41. IT WAS A GOOD THING IT WAS TEN in the morning. Otherwise, it would have been a stop into LowBrow Pizza for a couple of slices. Contemplating naming an eatery something with negative connotations, the phone rang. It was Derrick.

"What's up?"

"Can you talk?"

"Yeah, I'm a few blocks away from Blanco's place. What's going on?"

"Gesso just came in, said another young girl has gone missing."

"Where did this happen?"

"They're not sure. The father called in this morning, and Gesso sent a car over. The kid went for a bike ride and never came home."

"How old?"

"Sixteen."

Same as Dana Foyle. "What neighborhood?"

"The kid's name is Debbie Holmes. She lives in Briarwood, off of Livingston. She was last seen near Wyndemere, about three miles north."

"It's quiet on that stretch at night."

"That's what I thought. But you know, it could be a copycat thing. Another kid who thinks they can get quick money."

"Did the parents get a ransom note?"

"Not yet."

"It's early. She'll probably turn up. I'm surprised Gesso came to you. He wants us to look into it?"

"Not yet. He wanted to let us know, given we handled Foyle."

"He thinks it's another hoax?"

"Didn't say, but that's the message I got."

"Another set of parents whose aging process just sped up."

"You want me to do anything?"

"Not at this point. Stay on Ramos."

"All right, talk later."

"Hold on a sec."

"What?"

"Did they find the bike this kid was supposedly riding?"

"No. It's missing at this point, but you know, if this is a scam, they would've taken it."

"Not necessarily. An abandoned bicycle could strengthen the case it was an abduction."

"Somebody could've been passing by, saw the bike, and grabbed it."

"True. Let's see what the next twenty-four hours brings. She'll probably show up."

Even a quiet county like Collier, had over three hundred missing kids a year. Most were runaways, who either came back or were located. Chasing them took valuable resources from the fight against crime.

I turned onto Bamboo Drive and took it to Mango Drive. Jorge Blanco lived in a large house. The metal-roofed home was built in the eighties but in good shape. A lone palm tree anchored the landscaping. It was sparse but well-maintained.

Gravel crunching beneath my feet, it looked like someone moved away from the window. I rang the bell and scanned the street. It was quiet. I counted to thirty and pounded the door.

A second later, it opened. There was Blanco. A small scab marred his shaven head. "Sorry, man. I was on the phone with a customer."

I held up my badge. Blanco inhaled. "What's the matter?"

"I need to talk to you. Can I come in?"

He hesitated. "I'm working."

"What kind of work?"

"Customer service for Southwest Airlines. It's all remote."

Mary Ann was starting the same type of job. My stomach dropped. One of her coworkers could be a sex offender? "This should only take a few minutes. If you have a call to make, I'll wait."

He frowned. "We're graded on our response time."

Stalling, or was it a legitimate concern? "We can do this at headquarters, if you prefer."

He stepped to the side. "Come in."

The front room acted as his office. The main room behind it was furnished with a plaid-cushioned couch and a yellow corduroy recliner. Not only did he live alone, but whatever taste he had was in his mouth.

He tapped his keyboard. His hands had no bite marks. "Take a seat."

I sat in an old wicker chair. Blanco swiveled around. "I signed out for a bathroom break."

"Nice place you have here. Job must pay well."

"Not really. My daddy left the house to me, used to be his parents. We moved in with them after Mom took off."

His mother leaving was his excuse to dominate women? "Where were you Tuesday, May tenth, around seven p.m.?"

"Home."

He answered too quickly. "How do you remember that?"

"I don't go out much. Especially, during the week."

"What about Saturday night. May fourteenth."

"I was with a friend."

"Where?"

"We got something to eat and then had a couple of drinks."

"Downtown?"

"No. At The Cabana at Bayfront."

He made like it wasn't within walking distance of Fifth Avenue. "What time did you leave?"

"I don't know. The place closes at eleven. We hung around for, like, fifteen, twenty minutes and left. Did something happen?"

"There was an attempted rape in the area."

"It wasn't me. I swear!"

It couldn't be him. He swore it wasn't. "Who were you with?"

He shrugged.

"Give me the name of the friend you were with Saturday night."

His head glistened with sweat. "I wasn't with anybody."

"Why'd you lie about it?"

"It's not fun saying you don't have anyone to hang out with."

It was easy to understand why a convicted sex offender found it hard to make friends. "Where did you go after The Cabana closed?"

"Nowhere. I walked around a little and went home."

"How'd you get home?"

"I drove."

"You drove after drinking?"

"I had one, one and a half drinks. That's all, I swear."

"Where'd you get that cut on your head from?"

"That? Oh, I nicked myself shaving."

I couldn't imagine shaving my head. Keeping my face clean was enough of a chore. "All right. Thanks for your time."

He shot out of his chair. "Sure. Anytime."

Joan Samus had fought off her attacker. I needed to ask if she might have scratched him. We also needed to show pictures of Blanco in the downtown area when the attack occurred. Maybe someone would recognize Blanco.

17

THE SUN BAKED MY FACE AS I WALKED TOWARD THE OFFICE building. Before ducking in, I noticed a dark mass of clouds on the horizon. If it rained, I wanted it to come now. By dinnertime, it'd be sunny, and we'd have the normal Fifth Avenue crowd to run Blanco's mug shot by.

Derrick said, "How'd it go?"

"Not sure. No bite marks, but I caught him lying. He had a scratch on his head. We need to see if Samus could have scratched him."

"That'd be huge."

"Saturday, he claimed to be a couple of blocks away at Bayfront. Said he was by himself and left for home after a couple of drinks at The Cabana. Get some pictures of him to Gesso, and ask him to get a couple of guys down to Fifth, and see if we can get an ID."

"I'll get on it. What about when Ramos was raped?"

"Said he was home, that he didn't go out during the week."

"You buy that?"

"We'll ask his neighbors. And I want to show his picture

to the regulars at North Collier Park. We find out he goes there, we'll press him."

"Sounds like a plan."

"What about the Panera video?"

"I called again. They said the legal department didn't sign off yet."

"What the hell are they afraid of?"

"Damn lawyers got everybody scared."

"Stay on them."

"Will do."

"How's that list going?"

Derrick got up, holding a piece of paper. "Good. I have three new names."

He handed me the sheet. As I read the names, Delvin Cooper, Ricky Shaw, and Bernie Lyle, Derrick said, "All of them are convicted sex offenders. Cooper and Shaw were released from prison within the last three months, and Lyle moved from Orlando, registering with the county a week ago."

"Lyle? The guy with the beard?"

"Yeah. Sex Crimes is pulling the files on these sleazebags. I'll stop by after I get Blanco's photo to Gesso."

Logic was out with men like these. Which one to start with? Was it the inability of Cooper or Shaw to contain them-selves any longer, or did Lyle move to Collier, where he was unknown and struck before information on him was widely spread?

We had laws mandating a sexual-offender register when they moved. The problem was disseminating that vital infor-mation to the community. It was simply impossible to knock on everyone's door to warn them. You could sign up for an email alert but if you didn't, and most didn't, you were blind.

The county posted the information to a website, but nothing more was done.

It was a tough balance for someone who'd served time, supposedly paying his debt to society. My problem was the belief sexual predators were essentially unreformable, unless castrated.

My inbox had thirty-eight emails. I knocked out ten before Derrick came back with a couple of folders. "Just heard that the dog was returned."

"They paid the ransom?"

"Yeah. They found the dog in a neighbor's yard."

"Don't be surprised when we see more of this."

"Could've been worse. They could've taken the money and sold the dog."

"At least somebody is happy today."

"For sure. Gesso said he'd get the photo shown."

"Good. Whatever happened to that Holmes kid? She show up?"

"Not yet. But my gut's telling me the parents will get a ransom note by the end of the day."

"Okay, Sherlock, we'll see." I chuckled. "As long as she's safe, I'm good."

He held up the files. "Which ones you want?"

"The first one, and you take whatever you feel like."

He handed me the Cooper file. I flipped it open. Cooper's middle initial was B. "Cooper has the same name as the guy who hijacked a plane and got away with it."

"I never heard that one."

"I think it was in 1971. A man named Daniel Cooper boarded a flight from Portland to Seattle. After it took off, he showed the stewardess a bag with red sticks and wires, saying he had a bomb."

"Man, that would never happen today."

"Maybe. So, Cooper tells them he wants a couple of hundred grand in cash and four parachutes. The pilot radios the request, and when they land, Cooper gets what he wanted and lets the passengers off. Then he tells the pilots to fly him to Mexico City but to stay under ten thousand feet."

"Sounds like he knew what he was doing."

"He did, because somewhere between Seattle and Reno, he puts on the parachutes, grabs the cash, and jumps out."

"Holy shit."

"Yeah. And despite a massive manhunt, they never found him or his remains."

"Wow. He got away with it."

"Looks that way. I think the FBI still has it as one of their top unsolved cases."

"What a story."

"Yep. All right, let's buckle down and see what we have."

I was rereading the Cooper file when Derrick's desk phone rang. He answered it and said, "It's the Samus lady."

I picked up the receiver. "Hello, Ms. Samus. This is Frank Luca. Thanks for calling me back."

"I wasn't feeling good earlier."

"I'm sorry. You better now?"

"A little bit."

"I have a quick question. When you fought off your attacker, do you think you might have scratched him?"

"I could have. It was instinct. I'm not sure what I did."

"Did you notice any blood on you? Even a trace amount?"

"My nose bled a little; he hit it trying to put the bag on me."

"How about under any of your fingernails? Was there any blood?"

"I-I don't know."

"That's okay. Why don't you give it some thought. There's no pressure at all."

"Okay."

"If you think of anything, let me know."

"Okay."

"Have you decided you're going back home?"

"Thursday. I'm on a ten o'clock flight."

"Going home will be good for you."

"I hope so. I-I'm afraid something is going to happen. It's silly but . . ."

"It'll be fine. Don't worry, I promise."

I hung up. "This poor woman is scared out of her mind."

"We need to nail this bastard."

"Amen. But I don't think it's Cooper; as a condition of his parole, he agreed to be chemically castrated."

"So did Shaw."

"We're starting with Lyle."

"I got a bead on him, he's busing tables at Iguana Mia."

I tossed him the keys. "You drive. I want to read the transcripts."

18

———

As we approached Iguana Mia, Derrick said, "You ever eat here?"

"A long time ago. Not a big fan of Mexican."

"Why not?"

"Can't find a wine that goes with it."

Derrick pulled into the parking lot for the lime-green restaurant. He backed into a spot by their cactus-shaped sign. "That's why I drink beer. It goes with anything."

"No way I could have a brew with pasta."

Derrick laughed. "You're right. A Chianti and Italian food. I'm getting hungry thinking about it."

"It's more than that. The food and wines are regional in Italy. Bilotti tells me that each area has their own foods and wines that go with it."

Spinning around, I scanned the lot.

"What's the matter?"

"Feels like someone is watching us."

He surveyed the area. "I don't see anything."

"All right. Let's go."

The entrance was lined with benches for people waiting to

be seated. They didn't take reservations. The place was half-full of people enjoying a late lunch. The hostess went to get Bernie Lyle.

I said, "This place sure is festive."

Derrick pointed to a sombrero hanging from the ceiling. "I bought one when we went to Cancun. I don't know what I was thinking. What a waste of money."

"Too many margaritas?"

"Guilty. It was the first trip Lynn and I took."

Wiping his hands on the apron hanging from his hips, Bernie Lyle looked our way. He slowed, recognizing we were cops.

Lyle had two days' worth of stubble and wouldn't meet my eyes. "We'd like to talk to you. You want to step outside?"

He looked over his shoulder. "I'm working, man. I just got this job."

I pointed to a woman. "Is that your boss?"

"Please, man. I don't need no trouble."

"It's okay." Lyle moaned as I left.

"Ma'am. I'm real sorry to disturb you, but we need to have a quick word with Mr. Lyle. He didn't do anything; we're looking for information on somebody who lives near him."

"We always cooperate with our friends in law enforcement." She smiled. "Besides, it's between lunch and dinner."

"Thank you, ma'am."

I gave the okay sign to Lyle, and Derrick led him outside. The hum of traffic on Route 41 had me raising my voice. "What are you doing in Collier County?"

"What do you mean?"

Hands clean, he had a scratch running down his right forearm. "Why'd you come here?"

"Got tired of Orlando. All the frigging kids and tourists up there. It gets to you, man."

"Why Naples?"

"My bro lives here. Been here for ages."

"Where'd you get the scratch?"

"This? Uh, was working on my car."

"You sure?"

"Uh-huh."

"Where were you Saturday night? Late, say eleven to two in the morning?"

"I work Saturdays. It's frigging chockablock at this place."

"What about Tuesday, May tenth, between six and ten at night?"

His eyes flashed fear. "I was here, working, man. It's a new job. I need the dough."

"Sure. What were you fixing on your car?"

"My car?"

"Yes. You were working on it."

"Oh yeah. Nothing big. I was changing the wiper blades, it was like, the rubber was shredded, man. Couldn't see shit."

"You've been behaving yourself?"

"Oh yeah, man."

"Make sure you keep it that way."

He nodded. "You know, I ain't got a problem like they think I do, but I'm going to those counseling things, like two times a week. It helps, man."

Counseling was great, but perversion couldn't be fixed. If he was working those nights, he wasn't our guy. We could check now, but it would undermine what I told the manager, and there was no sense ruining our reputation. Plus, Lyle might run if he knew we were onto him.

We hopped into the car. Derrick said, "What did you think?"

"When we get back, you call Iguana Mia and vet Lyle's story he was working."

"I hope he was. I know he's a predator, but he seems to be trying. I mean, busing tables at forty-two can't be easy."

"Or enough to pay your bills these days."

"Maybe his brother is helping him."

"Could be. Let's head back. Before we waste time on Cooper and Shaw, let's make sure they're getting the maintenance injections to keep 'em castrated."

———

WE GOT out of the car and headed for the office. The sun felt good on my back. My cell rang. "It's Mary Ann, go ahead. I'll meet you inside."

"Say hello for me."

He disappeared as I answered. "Hey, Mary Ann."

"Hi, can you talk?"

"Sure, what's up?"

"Nothing, I just wanted to let you know I was going take the training webinar for the job in a little while. My phone is going to be off. When you come home, I'll be in the den, so please be quiet."

"Sure. No problem. You want me to pick something up for dinner?"

"No. I made escarole and beans already."

One of my favorites. Was the rest of the day about to go downhill? "Sounds good."

"Is there an update on the Holmes girl who went missing on Livingston?"

"No. Why?"

"I was watching the news, and there was a report they found her bicycle."

My chest tightened. What did it mean? If it was staged, would the kid sacrifice her bike with how much they cost these days? We needed to know how old the bicycle was.

"Frank?"

"Oh, just thinking."

"You think it could be another fake kidnapping?"

"It turns out Debbie Holmes and Dana Foyle are good friends."

"Really?"

"Yeah. They may have planned them together. Derrick said we could have a rash of them."

"Oh my God. Who would've thought?"

"You can't make this up. Say, did you talk to Jessie today?"

"No. Wednesday is her busy day. She has classes till five."

"Oh yeah. Okay, good luck with the training. I'll see you later."

I walked out of the sunshine into our building. There was a low hum of activity but nothing like the way TV depicted police stations. Derrick was on the phone. I stared at my email box. Where was Debbie Holmes?

Derrick stood up and put the receiver down. "Lyle lied. He worked Saturday but was off Tuesday."

19

———

I POPPED OUT OF MY CHAIR. "THEY SURE ABOUT THAT?"

"Yeah. He lied; it's tantamount to covering for the crime."

"Tantamount? Is that your word of the day?"

He smiled. "Yesterday's. I didn't have a chance to use it."

"I'm no English major, but you didn't use it right."

"Really?"

"Back to Lyle."

"Well, he only gets one day a week off and it's Tuesday."

"But he was working Saturday?"

"Yeah, manager said it's all-hands-on-deck Saturday nights."

"What time they close?"

"Ten on Saturdays, but people linger doing cleanup. She said they were out of there by midnight."

"Lyle too?"

"She didn't know what time he left but said nobody leaves before eleven."

"That time of night, he could've made it downtown in twenty minutes."

"Plenty of time to attack Samus."

"For sure. Even had time to change, though he wears black, working."

"Maybe some girl at the restaurant turned him on. He got worked up and—"

Gesso walked in. "How are you doing with the Ramos case?"

"We're getting there, Sarge. A person of interest lied about his alibi, fitting the time of the Ramos rape. And got off work with enough time to attack Samus."

"Bring him in. It'd be perfect if you could wrap this one up. I want the both of you on the Holmes kid."

"I heard they found her bike."

"Yeah, but it wasn't us; we missed it. The parents' search party came up with it."

I knew the answer but asked anyway. "The sheriff is looking for something to feed the press?"

"Oh, come on, Frank. That's out of line."

Gesso was a straight shooter, but his dodge told me all I needed to know. "It doesn't matter. It's a missing kid. We'll do our best, but we can't rush the Ramos investigation."

"Of course not."

"Get us in the loop; we'll help out."

"We're getting a warrant for the kid's phone records."

"Good."

"You going to bring that rape suspect in?"

Shrugging, I said, "Have to think it over. May be better to fish around first."

Gesso left and Derrick said, "You see the Holmes parents on the news last night?"

"No."

"It was heartbreaking; neither of them could keep it together. If it turns out to be an inside job . . ."

"They'd need to send her to a military school for a dose of reality."

"It's crazy thinking your own kid would do something like that. Don't they know the toll it'd take on their mother and father?"

"They're not thinking of anything but the money."

"You should have seen the mother. Dressed in a housecoat, looked like she hadn't showered in weeks."

I checked the time. "I'm going take a ride to see Foyle. Maybe I can get something out of her on Holmes."

"Okay. I'll see you in the morning."

"I'm going to be late tomorrow. I have something to do."

<hr>

MRS. FOYLE CALLED HER HUSBAND. "Okay, you can speak to Dana, but only about Debbie."

"Thank you, ma'am."

"Dana!"

Wearing an oversized Miami sweatshirt and shorts, Dana slunk into the kitchen. "Detective Luca needs to ask you about Debbie."

She rolled her eyes. Her mother said, "Dad said you have to talk to him."

"Okay, okay, already."

As she collapsed into a kitchen chair, I asked the mother to leave us alone.

"Dana, I'm trying to locate Debbie Holmes. I understand you two were good friends."

"She's not my BFF, but I like her."

"Did she know about what you and Bradley were going to do before you did it?"

"No."

"Are you sure?"

She hung her head. "Bradley said we couldn't tell anyone."

"You're popular at school, right?"

A smile appeared and disappeared.

"Is Debbie the kind of girl who'd follow you?"

"I don't know, maybe. But everybody wants to fit in, you know?"

Peer pressure was an enormous factor. "Sure, I do. I was kid once."

She looked at me as if I said I used to be a horse.

"Do you think it's possible Debbie saw what you and Brad did and copied it?"

"I guess she could've." She lowered her head and voice. "I know she needed money."

"She told you she was in need of money?"

She nodded.

"Did she say what it was for?"

"A car. Everybody wants a nice one, you know. But they're, like, crazy prices now. Even the used ones, they jumped up, like, way up, overnight."

She was right. Inflation was impacting everything. "Let's say Debbie wanted to fake her kidnapping. Who would she ask for help?"

She frowned. "Jason."

"You don't like him?"

"He's bossy. Thinks who he is."

"What's his last name?"

"Reedy."

"Is there anything you can tell me about where Debbie could be?"

"I don't know. Jason probably does."

In front of the Foyles' house, I sat in my car. It was hard

to understand if Dana was telling me everything she knew. Was she holding back because she shared her scheme with Debbie Holmes before doing it? If so, her reputation would take another hit.

The way she said Jason probably knew where she was had me leaning toward it being a repeat hoax. Except, there had been no ransom note or contact.

What happened to her? I pulled away, and nearing the entrance, I slowed, gripping the wheel. Though Debbie Holmes was younger than Ramos or Samus, I needed to check on her frame and coloring. The two previous victims, weren't twin-like, but they were both petite and had short brown hair.

Could this poor kid been targeted by the same animal who'd attacked Ramos and Samus?

20

FINISHING THE LAST SIP OF COFFEE, I MADE A RIGHT OFF Route 41. Two minutes later, I pulled to the curb. Walking toward a building, I spun on my heels. Scanning, I couldn't pick up anyone following me.

Shaking it off, I knocked on the door. "Who is it?"

"Detective Luca."

The door swung open. "Why are you here? Did you catch the man who did it?"

"Not yet, Mrs. Samus. I know your daughter is concerned we haven't yet apprehended him."

"She sure is."

"I thought if I drove her to the airport, she'd feel a bit more comfortable."

"Really? You'd drive her?"

"Yes, ma'am. I figured it'd give her and you some peace of mind."

"Come in. Joan? Detective Luca is here. He's going to take you to the airport."

I TOSSED my jacket onto a chair. Derrick said, "Everything good?"

"Yeah, I took Samus to the airport."

"What?"

"She's scared out of her mind and hadn't left her mother's apartment since the attack."

"Some vacation."

I shook my head. "Pull up the file on Debbie Holmes. I want to check her against Ramos and Samus. See if there are any physical similarities."

Tapping on his keyboard, he said, "You think it's the same guy?"

"I don't know, but we can't discount anything."

"Here she is. She looks older than sixteen. Brown hair, like the others, and is small framed."

I came around his desk. "Hmmm. They're not that close."

"They all happened at night."

"True, but she's twenty years younger."

"He might have thought she was older."

"But Holmes was on a bike."

"I don't know. Let me see something."

Derrick scrolled down. "She was wearing jeans. I thought maybe she could've been in exercise clothes."

The thinking was the mark of a good detective. "Good try. Let's talk to Lyle. We'll press him on lying about working and check where he was the night Holmes disappeared."

"Sure. Maybe we can grab lunch while we're there."

I wasn't a fan of Mexican food, but that wasn't the motivation to say, "Let's wait until lunch is over. I have the public appeal to film at one. It won't take long. We'll go at two, and if we don't get anything major out of him, he'll be clearing tables during dinner."

I STOOD in front of a screen with the Collier County sheriff's emblem. The cameraman was adjusting the lighting. I said, "What have you guys been busy with? I wanted this out days ago."

"Uh, yeah, we've been busy."

"Doing what? This only takes five minutes."

"Umm, they had us doing, some, uh—"

"I get it. Remin didn't want the publicity."

He shrugged.

"Pretending it's not happening, is what got New York and California in trouble."

He nodded. "You ready?"

I filmed the appeal for help. The hotline would get calls from people saying they had information on who attacked Ramos and Samus and we'd sort through, hoping one would pay off.

APPROACHING OLD 41, I said, "Keep your eyes on that Hyundai. He's been behind us since Immokalee."

Derrick swiveled. "The white one?"

"Yeah. One driver, looks like a female."

"You sure? Yeah, unless it's a dude with long hair."

"I keep getting the feeling we're being tailed."

"Next time we go out, we'll do separate cars. See if anyone is."

"Forget it. Let's stay focused."

Derrick frowned pulling into Iguana Mia's lot. We entered. The manager was behind the podium. Her smile disappeared. "Can I help you?"

"We'd like to speak with Mr. Lyle again. But remember, we're just looking for information he might know."

Lyle trudged toward us.

I put my sunglasses on. "Let's step outside."

Lyle said, "Man, I don't why you're up my ass, man. I didn't do nothing."

Derrick said, "You lied. You weren't working Tuesday. I wanted to call your probation officer, but my partner, he said to give you another chance to come clean."

We hadn't rehearsed the good-cop, bad-cop routine. "He wanted to bust you for obstruction. You don't start telling the truth, I won't be able to help you anymore."

Lyle shook his head. "I didn't hurt nobody, man. I don't wanna go back in."

"If you didn't hurt anyone, then tell us where you were on Tuesday from six to eight at night."

"But I'm gonna get bagged for it."

"Was it violent?"

"No, no, man."

"Was it sexual?"

"No, no."

"Tell me."

Blanco hesitated, and Derrick pulled out his phone. "That's it. You're going back on a parole violation."

"Hold on, man. I was . . . at a club in Fort Myers."

"What club? Doing what?"

"It's a gambling place. You know, Johnny Griffin? He runs it."

Griffin was a character who had his fingers in gambling and prostitution. He was also an informant who fed Lee County information to avoid going to prison. "Griffin? No. Where's his place?"

"On Unity, in back of Popeye's Louisiana Kitchen."

"Who was there that night?"

"A whole bunch of people."

"If you're lying again, I swear, I'll drive you to jail myself."

"I ain't. You can check it out."

"What were you doing there?"

"Playing craps. I had a good night."

We would check out his new alibi, but the problem was the people he claimed to be with. Upstanding citizens they weren't. Getting ten of them to back up Lyle was worth less than a suitcase full of carnival tokens. Griffin was an informer, but known to play both sides of the street.

"We're going to check this out. But don't get any ideas. I'm calling in; we're going have eyes on you, twenty-four seven, so get used to the company."

"That's cool, that's cool with me, man. I don't want no trouble."

"Get back to work."

As Derrick and I walked to the car, I whispered, "Don't be obvious. To the left—it's the Hyundai."

"I'll grab the first three on the plate, you get the last ones."

"They're taking off."

The car screeched out of a spot. I aimed my phone and took shots of the rear of the vehicle.

"You get it?"

Spreading my fingers on the screen, "Yep. Call the plate number in."

21

———

THE LIGHT AT WIGGINS PASS TURNED GREEN AND I HIT THE gas. Derrick was on the phone and asked, "Are you sure?" before hanging up.

"You aren't going to believe this one. Guess whose car that was?"

"Just tell me!"

"Felix Ramos."

"What the hell is he doing tailing us?"

"Maybe he wants to make sure we're on his daughter's case."

I swerved into a turning lane. "This guy is planning to take matters into his own hands."

"You think so?"

"We can't wait until it's too late. He's on the edge."

I pulled into Piper's Grove. They were in the midst of changing the colors of the old community from peach to white. Ramos lived in a coach-home section, without garages. I spotted his car.

The sun was high in the sky, but that wasn't the source of the heat coming off the hood of the Hyundai. A bag was sitting on the floor of the passenger footwell. It probably contained the wig Ramos wore while tailing us.

As Derrick rang the bell, I told him I'd handle it, drawing another frown. The door swung open. Ramos's face faltered. "Uh, Detective Luca. Do you have news?"

"Why are you following us?"

"Following you? What makes you say—"

"Cut the nonsense. We saw you at Iguana Mia and ran your plate."

"I just wanted to see that something was being done. For Lisa's sake. She's falling apart."

"I understand your concern. Really, I do, but I'm telling you, stay out of the way. Let us do our jobs. You take care of your daughter."

"I'm sorry. You're right."

"We'll get him, I promise. Just give us a little more time."

"Is it Bernie Lyle?"

"I can't discuss that."

"The bastard thinks he can move here and get away with—"

"You've been checking into him?"

"It's public information."

I looked into his eyes. "I'm assuming, as a marine, you own a firearm?"

"I do."

"Do you have a carry permit?"

He hesitated. I added, "I can look it up."

"Yeah. Why?"

"Do yourself a favor and keep it locked up at home."

Before he could respond, I turned around, and we walked away.

MARY ANN WAS TOWELING OFF. I stepped onto the lanai. "You did your laps?"

"Yes. It was so busy today, I had to work two extra hours."

"Don't overdo it."

"How was your day?"

"The usual, but at least I found out I wasn't going crazy."

"That's up for debate."

"Ha ha, very funny."

"What happened?"

"The father of the poor girl who was raped in Livingston, was tailing me."

"What? Why?"

I shrugged. "He's a father and a marine."

"And a control freak."

"I hope that's all."

"What's going on with his daughter's case?"

"I have to go up to Fort Myers later to vet an alibi."

"Tonight?"

"Yeah, sorry."

"It's okay. I'll grab another hour of work."

"You know stress is no good for you."

"It's not stressful. I'm enjoying the job."

Denials always sounded convincing.

A FORT MYERS contact said there was no use getting to the club before nine. Double duty and late nights made the years piling up more apparent than necessary.

A dozen youths were hanging out in front of Popeye's. Half were smoking and the others were pulling fried chicken out of buckets. Cardiologists would have a steady supply of patients. Pulling into the lot of a green building, I took a sip of coffee and got out.

I banged on a black metal door. A slab of granite opened the door. "Whatchoo want?"

My badge was inches from his face. "I need to talk to a couple of people about Bernie Lyle."

"Nobody's here."

The lot was full of low-riding vehicles. "And this is for the valet?"

"Place is closed."

"I don't care what's going inside. You either let me in, or I get the Lee County sheriff to shut this place down and keep it that way till you're on Medicare."

"Hold your shorts."

He disappeared, and a minute later, a skinny Black man with a cross bigger than my hand, hanging from his neck, appeared. "What can I do for the poo-leze?"

I took a step forward. "Let me in, now."

"Sonny don't want no trouble."

"He won't get any. Step aside."

The place made the Immokalee Casino look like Vegas's Bellagio. Six Costco tables were filled with gamblers playing poker and blackjack. The dealers wore T-shirts and shorts, instead of black vests and slacks.

A roar from a table, surrounded by bettors slapping each on the back, caught my attention. Somebody threw seven or eleven. I took out a picture of Lyle and headed for the craps table.

Heads turned but went back to the action at hand. The shooter crapped out. The crowd whooped it up. He must've had a hot hand. A Hispanic man with a lightning bolt etched into his hair walked away from the table.

I held the picture out. "You know Bernie Lyle?"

"No."

"He comes here a lot."

"It's the first time I'm here." He walked away.

I asked seven others, all denied knowing or seeing Lyle. They couldn't be seen helping a cop. The guy with the cross was keeping an eye on me. I approached. "I need to speak to Sonny."

"He ain't here."

"Look, I know he is. You don't get him, I'll drag the both of you in for running an illegal gambling operation."

His eye twitched. "Hold up, man."

Sonny Griffin bounced out of the back room. He hiked a thumb at me. As I closed in, he shut the door and leaned against it. His purple silk shirt was the only sign he was a gangster.

"Nice place you have here."

"It ain't mine. I just hang out every now and then."

I lowered my voice. "Detective Luca from Collier. You have nothing to worry about. All I want to know is if Bernie Lyle was here Tuesday, May tenth."

"That boy in trouble again?"

"Could be. Said he was here that night."

"I hear y'all think he raped that girl up in Naples."

We relied on him for information. Was somebody feeding him? "Who told you that?"

Sonny smiled.

"Look, Lyle said he was here, playing dice the night of Tuesday, May tenth. Was he?"

"I was in the back that night. Had meself a sweet date."

"And you didn't see him playing that night?"

"No, but that boy, he likes craps. Problem for him, he ain't good at it."

22

———

Derrick's cologne wafted into the hallway. I stepped into the office.

"Morning."

"Hey, Frank. I thought you'd call last night. How'd it go?"

"It got late, and there was nothing to report."

"What do you mean?"

"Nobody, including Griffin, would vouch for Lyle."

"He lied again?"

"Tough to say. These people don't like talking to us."

"It's a conundrum."

He seemed to use the word correctly. "Yeah, one that Lyle's ass hangs on."

"If he wasn't there, he did it. Otherwise, why lie?"

"Not having a good alibi hurts him, but we need him at the scene."

"Unless we get him to confess."

"I don't see that at this point. He'd be going away until he qualifies for the octogenarians' club."

"We could try and offer a deal."

"As much as I want this one solved, I'm not giving a pervert a deal."

"I hear you. Just brainstorming."

"Did you know brainstorming doesn't work?"

"Really?"

"Yeah, I read something a week ago, said, personalities, peer pressure, and groupthink make it less effective. People get influenced by dominant personalities and can their ideas, going along with what others say."

"Never thought about it that way."

"Don't matter. We don't brainstorm anyway. We brain drizzle."

Derrick laughed. "More like misting."

I sipped my coffee. "Anything on the Holmes kid?"

"Gesso said she's still missing."

"I don't like this."

"Me neither."

"Why don't you see what calls came in from the appeal?"

He stood. "I'll be right back."

Sixty-four emails filled the inbox. It seemed like every day there were more than the day before. Technology had provided law enforcement with incredible tools, but we couldn't solve crimes sitting in the office. Answering emails took time away from hitting the streets.

Clicking the trash icon, I wondered how much diversity training could anyone take? I opened the next email. It concerned the possibility detectives would have to wear body cams.

Documenting the interaction with the public had merit but not for the job I did. It would make anyone we talked to, especially informants and witnesses, refuse to open up.

Not one complaint had been filed against a detective since

I'd been here. I snapped the pencil in two. Where the hell was this coming from?

Derrick bounced into the room.

I said, "You see this nonsense on wearing body cams?"

"Yeah, it's bullshit and counterproductive."

"The lack of trust burns me up. I can't see this being put into play."

"So why aggravate us?"

"If something happens, Remin will be able to say he's ready to roll body cams as soon as funding is available."

"He's covering his ass."

"He might have invented the term."

"Unreal."

"Anything worthwhile come in?"

"Most were the usual callers. Including our buddy Bruce Noon, who called in twice."

People wanted to help, but they didn't realize having us chase down their imaginations hindered an investigation. "You got to love him."

"Oh, and that psychic from Everglades City said the man who took Holmes is on page seven of the *Daily News*."

I shook my head.

"I checked it anyway; it was Alfie Oakes."

"Geez. Were there any interesting calls?"

"One lady said her son was at the park and saw a man that scared him. Said when he saw the kid, he ran into a wooded area."

"What time was this?"

"Supposedly a quarter to seven."

"Hmm. What else might be something?"

"A guy who goes to the park regularly, sails one of those remote-control boats, called in. Said he was there the evening of the rape and saw a car parked in a weird spot, like it was being hidden."

"Did he see anyone?"

"The report don't say."

"We need something to work with. Grab a map of the park, and let's go see the kid, and boat guy."

<hr>

MIKE SAMUELS LIVED in Livingston Lakes. The community was steps away from the park. Samuels lived in the ground-floor unit of a neat building housing eight units. My estimated value of four hundred thousand felt right when Samuels opened the door.

In his sixties, Samuels was nerdy-looking, with slumped shoulders. "Do you want to come in?"

"Thank you." The place had an open floor plan. An interior unit with light flooding in from the sliders and a window in a dining area.

He walked to a kitchen table. "This okay?"

"Perfect."

Derrick pointed to the lanai. A pair of toy sailboats sat on their cradles. "You make those yourself?"

"They're kits, but I customize them. You see the keel? I've extended it for greater stability and I built the cradles myself."

"Nice. You sail them often?"

"Four, five times a week. That's why I called."

I said, "Tell us what you saw."

"There was a car parked out of view, like they were trying to hide it."

"What makes you say that?"

"It was parked in a place you're not supposed to be, squeezed beside a building."

I unfolded a map of the park. "Show me."

"You see, here's the lake I sail on. And these are the parking spots for it." He moved his finger. "And here is where the car was. It was shielded by this building, and they have a mobile unit; I believe it pumps water for the waterslide, right here. The driver would have had to circle around it to get where he was."

"What kind of a car?"

"I'm not good with autos. I'd say it was foreign, likely Japanese."

That did nothing to narrow it down. "What color?"

"A tone of silver."

"SUV? Two door, four door?"

"Not an SUV, but I couldn't say more; maybe it was a four door."

"You saw the rear of the vehicle?"

"Yes."

"Florida plates?"

"I think so. It would have stood out if not."

"Okay. Look, I'm sure you did, but can you try to recall what you saw?"

"I didn't give it much thought, but when I saw you on the news, it hit me and I called the hotline."

"Are there any details about the car you recall . . . a dent, or decal?"

Samuels shook his head. "You have to realize I wasn't being attentive. I saw it when my boat got hung up in the reeds, and I walked to the left, around here."

"What time was this?"

"Six twenty."

"That's a precise time. How sure are you?"

"I leave my home at five forty-five, and my boat is in the water no later than six. I circled the lake several times and began practicing maneuvers when I pushed the limits, skirting the border."

"Was there anyone else in the area?"

"No. I think the forecast may have kept people away."

We asked a couple more questions before leaving. Derrick said, "Nice neighborhood in here."

"Yeah, I like it. I wonder what impact the overpass on Immokalee Road might have on this place."

"They need to do something, but it'd be a shame if it affected this place."

My cell rang. Before swiping it away, the exchange rang a bell in my mind. "This is Detective Luca."

"Hello, Detective, this is Lieutenant Morris with the Lee County Sheriff's Office."

"Hi. What's going on?"

"You went to see Sonny Griffin last night, asking about a Bernie Lyle?"

"I did. What about it?"

"I manage that source; he doesn't talk to anyone but me."

"Okay."

"He said that Lyle was there Tuesday, the tenth of May but came in late, and he thinks he could be the guy you're looking for."

"What makes him think that?"

"Sonny said Lyle told him he needed an alibi, and Lyle was acting strange."

23

___

I hung up. "That was a lieutenant from Lee; he runs Sonny Griffin. The snitch told him Lyle asked him to be his alibi and came in late the night Ramos was raped."

"Unequivocal proof it's Lyle."

I let the latest word-of-the-day go by. "There's no hard evidence, no firsthand knowledge. A snitch's word isn't enough for a courtroom."

"You're right. You want to go see Lyle?"

"What kind of car does he drive?"

"A gray Ford."

"The color is close. Samuels thought it was Japanese, but we can't rely on that."

"We should bring him in. Squeeze him and see what comes out."

"We need more. Let's talk to the kid who saw something at the park."

"Why? We could get lucky."

"The harder we work, the luckier we'll get."

Sereno Grove was set deep off Livingston Road. It was a low-key, single-family community with no amenities.

"This place is quiet. Not a soul on the streets."

"It's secluded."

The sprinklers were on at the Kirk home. We waited for an opening and dashed to the front door.

Derrick hit the Ring doorbell, and Carol Kirk qualified us before opening the door.

She was fair-skinned with red hair and hazel eyes. I expected an Irish lilt but it never came. Kirk led us to a light-filled kitchen and said, "Let me get Tommy."

Barefoot and wearing a Lightning baseball cap, twelve-year-old Tommy had his mother's freckles. "These policemen want to hear about what you saw in the park."

I extended my hand. "Thanks for helping out, Tommy. We appreciate it."

He squared his shoulders and took my hand. "Hello, sir."

"That's some grip you have there."

"My dad told me to give a strong one and to look someone in the eye when you shake."

"Your father is right. Now, tell us what you saw on Tuesday, May tenth."

He hopped onto a kitchen stool. "I was riding my scooter on the path, the one that goes by the boardwalk."

"Were you alone?"

"Yeah, Jimmy went home; he cut through the path to his neighborhood."

"He lives in Wilshire Lakes?"

"Uh-huh."

"What time was this about?"

"Like, a little after six. I got to be home for supper, and we usually eat at, like, six thirty. Right, Mom?"

"That's right, honey."

"So, your friend leaves, and you were on your way home?"

"Uh-huh. I was, like, past the boardwalk part, and I see in the woods, this man. He was, uh, scary. As soon as I seen him, he turned away, like he was trying to hide."

"What did he look like?"

Tommy slipped off the stool and held his hand up. "He was, like, this tall. And had a hoodie on."

"What kind of pants?"

"I think jeans."

"How about his face? What did he look like?"

He scrunched his nose. "I don't know."

"Did he have a beard or facial hair?"

"No. But I think, maybe he was bald."

"What makes you say that?"

"You know, with a hoodie on, you can see some hair but I didn't see any."

"How old d'you think he was?"

"Younger than Dad. Maybe thirty or something."

"How far was he from you?"

He pointed out the window. "Like, where the palm in back of the pool is."

About fifty feet. "What about the way he walked? Any limp or something that stuck out?"

"No, but he hurried away. At first, I thought he was going to come after me . . ."

"Why did you think that?"

"He looked at me and I felt, like . . . I don't know, but like he was mad I was there or something."

"Do you think you saw this man before?"

"No, first time."

I wanted to show the kid a picture of Lyle, but we needed to present it with others, or it'd be thrown out as prejudicial. "Do you think you'd recognize the man if you saw him again?"

He looked at his mother before saying, "I don't know. Would he see me?"

"No. You wouldn't have to meet him. It would be done secretly, if we did it at all."

"I don't want my son dragged into this."

"I understand, ma'am. Tommy, you've been very helpful. We really appreciate your cooperation."

The kid beamed. I turned to his mother. "Ma'am, could we have a word in private?"

Tommy left, and I said, "I understand your reluctance in getting your son involved, but the young woman who was raped is traumatized. And the person who did it is still out there."

"I know, everyone in the neighborhood is staying indoors."

"We can catch him and put him behind bars so he'll never hurt another soul, but we need help."

"I have to talk to my husband first."

"Sure. Let me know." I handed her my card.

As soon as the car door closed, Derrick said, "Sounds like it could've been Lyle."

"Same height and no hair, on top of what Sonny Griffin said."

"And the car the boat guy saw is close in color."

My cell rang. It was Gesso. "Hey, Sarge. What's going on?"

"Two things: Deborah Holmes's phone last pinged off a tower south of Golden Gate, and the Holmeses just had a press conference. They're claiming we don't care their daughter is missing and we're not doing enough to find her."

"That's bull."

"I hear you, but Remin wants more focus on it, so get ready."

"Thanks for letting me know."

"How're you doing with Ramos's case?"

"We're about to bring in our top suspect."

"You have enough to get an indictment?"

My phone vibrated with another call. "Not yet, but we're closing in on him. I got to run, it's Remin calling."

24

———

I TRUDGED INTO THE HOUSE. THE DOOR TO THE DEN WAS closed. Mary Ann was working. Again. I cracked the door open to let her know I was home.

Lunch had been a vending-machine sandwich made when bell-bottoms were in style. Nothing was on the stove or in the oven. I opened the fridge, grabbed a can of peaches, and slammed the door shut.

The fruit didn't cut it. Where was the comfort food Mary Ann always seemed to have ready when I needed it? She wanted to work. I understood the need to be engaged, but retirement wasn't far off for me. My vision of the two of us, kicking around, going to the beach, and taking short trips was getting muddy.

Mary Ann came out of the den. "Sorry."

I pecked her cheek. "It's okay. You all right?"

"Yes. The system's been up and down all day. You look exhausted. Bad day?"

"Remin is giving me twenty-four hours to wrap up the Ramos rape. He's assigning me to the Holmes case."

"I saw the parents on TV. The mother was inconsolable."

"I heard."

"Where are you on the rape?"

"We need something putting Lyle at the park when the assault happened."

"Is there anything promising?"

"I'm hoping to do a photo lineup with a witness tomorrow. He's only twelve, and the mother didn't want him involved. She's checking with her husband."

"I hope they agree."

"Me too. If not, I'm going to have to bring in Lyle and see what we can get."

"You'll get the sleazebag."

"We'll see."

"Oh, did you hear about the other dognappings?"

"No. It just happened?"

"Yes. I got a breaking-news text, and there were two in Port Royal."

The thieves were upping their game by targeting the wealthy enclave. "Expensive breeds?"

"I think both were mixes, Malty-poos or something. But it doesn't matter, people love their dogs."

"If they're going to sell them, it matters."

I remembered what Derrick said about the rash of pets being taken in England. None were ransomed. Selling them was less risky than interacting with owners to return the dogs.

"I guess so. I feel bad for the people. Remember when Carol's dog died? It took her months to get over it."

"Carol? Who's that?"

"She used to patrol as part of the school unit. She retired a few years ago."

"Oh yeah." I was battling bladder cancer when it

happened, and it was tough to focus on a dog dying while fighting for my own life.

WE LOOKED at the video feed. Lyle was biting his nails. I said to Derrick, "Right now, all we have is him lying twice about his alibi."

"I wish they'd let the kid do the lineup."

"Wishing isn't going to solve any case. We'll work with what we have."

Another frown sprouted.

"Let me start this alone. You wait outside. When you see an opportunity to be the good cop, come in."

"He's sweating already. I'd be a savior, turning down the air."

I smiled, putting my hand on the doorknob. "More power to you."

Lyle took his finger out of his mouth as I slid into a chair opposite him. I hit record and recited the formalities, including his right to an attorney.

"I don't need no lawyer. I didn't do anything."

The number of people we questioned who denied the opportunity for counsel, was amazing. I was grateful, but it made no sense, especially as a person of interest in a crime.

Most figured not asking for a lawyer made it look like they were innocent. Others were arrogant, believing they could outsmart someone trained to interview.

"We've given you several opportunities to clear yourself but you keep lying."

"No. I told you, the first time was a mistake. I was afraid if I told you I was gambling, you'd bring me in."

"Lying to a law enforcement officer, could be construed

as obstruction. I don't have to tell you that qualifies as violating your parole."

"It was a mistake, man. I'm sorry, man. I was gambling at Sonny's place, like I told you."

"You sure you want to stick with that?"

His eyes widened as I stood.

"It's true. I was there."

"You better call Iguana Mia and tell them you won't be in for a long, long time."

"What do you mean?"

Before I got to the door, it swung open. Derrick said, "Let's take it easy here. We can settle this." He handed a bottle of water to Lyle.

"Thanks, man."

I said, "You're wasting time. This guy's nothing but a liar. He's going back to prison."

"No, it's not true. He won't believe me. I was playing dice."

Derrick said, "You seem like an okay guy, and I want to believe you. But there's a problem. Can you clear it up for me?"

"Yeah, sure. What?"

"We went there, and nobody we spoke with verified it."

"That's bullshit, man. They don't wanna get involved, that's all. Talk to Sonny. He'll tell you—I was there."

"Here's the thing, Mr. Lyle; Sonny Griffin said you were there but you came late."

"It wasn't late. He don't know what he's talking about. He can't remember, that's all."

"And you know what else he said?"

Lyle's eyes widened. "What?"

"He said you asked him to be his alibi."

"Stop messing with me."

"We're not. That's what he said."

"Why would he say that?"

I said, "Because it's true."

"No, man. Look, I'm into him for ten grand. He's just trying to fuck with me. You got to believe me."

25

———

Derrick said, "What do you think?"

"That all we have is a bad alibi. Lyle has zero credibility, but Griffin isn't the Dalai Lama."

"Yeah, but if Lyle is behind bars, how's Griffin going to get his money?"

"He might be sending a message: you don't pay, he's going to screw you."

"I don't know."

"Griffin said Lyle was a bad player; owing money fits. The other thing is he said Lyle was there."

"Yeah, so?"

"I talked to a few people, and not one said Lyle was there. I think Griffin may have said something."

"I don't know, that's a pretty big conspiracy to keep together."

"You were up in DC. Gangs killing people left and right and nobody says a word on who did it."

"They're scared to cooperate."

"Let's hold Lyle. We have a day to try and sort this out."

"We need someone to put him in the park."

"Exactly. I'll go upstairs and tell Remin where we're at with Lyle."

SOUTHWEST FLORIDA INSURANCE was housed in a two-story building in Vanderbilt Collections, an upscale shopping center that was expanding.

Taking my sunglasses off, I stepped into an office. Everyone was on the phone. I waited for the receptionist to pass the call she was on, to an agent. I introduced myself and took a seat.

A neatly groomed man in a white shirt came into the lobby. "Detective Luca."

"I'm sorry to bother you at work, Mr. Kirk."

"No problem. How can I help you?"

"Can we step outside?"

"Sure."

We stood in the shade of a royal palm tree. "That's one busy office."

"The insurance market down here needs reforming. Too many lawyers allowed to sue for anything. Companies pull out to limit their exposure, and we scramble to find reasonable coverage for clients."

"I'll keep you in mind."

"Thanks. How can I help you?"

"We'd really like to have your son look over a lineup."

He shook his head. "He's only twelve. We don't want him pulled into something like this. It could scar him."

"I understand, Mr Kirk, but there's another family—actually, two at this point—who are looking for justice."

"I feel for them, really I do—"

"Sir, we're holding a man but don't have enough. He may be the one responsible for the attacks."

He pulled his lips in. "I'm sorry, but I don't want my son involved."

"We can do this with photos, and I'll come to your home. There'll be no pressure on your son. We need to know if we have the predator. I'd hate to release him and find out he's raped someone else's daughter."

"He won't have to testify, will he?"

We might need him, but I said, "No. No way. I need to know if we should keep holding this man."

"All right, I'll agree, but I want to be there."

"That's fine. Can we do this later today?"

"Sure."

I called Derrick. "Hey, good news; the father agreed to letting the kid do a photo lineup."

"Excellent. We're getting close."

"I hope so." My phone vibrated. "I got to go, it's Mary Ann."

"Hey, everything all right?"

"Yes. I just wanted to congratulate you on catching the rapist."

"What? We didn't—"

"It was just on breaking news."

"Damn it."

"What's the matter?"

"Somebody, and I'm betting it was Remin, leaked we brought Lyle in." My phone vibrated again; it was Felix Ramos. "Hon, I got to go. The victim's father is calling. I'll talk to you later."

"Hello, Mr. Ramos."

"I see you caught the bastard."

"That's not accurate."

"But it was on the news."

Why did people believe everything the media said despite countless examples they couldn't be trusted? "That's unfortunate. At this stage we're talking to a person of interest."

"It's Lyle, isn't it?"

"I can't discuss an ongoing investigation."

"You have to tell me, is it Lyle?"

"I can't say anything more than, once we know, you and your daughter will be the first to know."

"That's bullshit! You brought him in and you didn't say a word to us."

"Trust me, Mr. Ramos, you don't want to be involved in the details of the case."

"Well, I want to be."

"That's not going to happen. I've got to go, Mr. Ramos. Have a nice day."

I jabbed in the sheriff's number but didn't hit call. Bad as a leak was, getting into it with Remin before knowing if Lyle was our man, was wasting energy I didn't have.

I GRABBED the envelope containing the six photos the lab generated. As required, they were identically shaped and sized. Five were police officers and Lyle. All had shaved heads or were naturally bald. They were also within ten years of each other.

Mr. Kirk answered the door, and I caught a whiff of sautéing onions. "Thanks for agreeing to this."

"My wife isn't happy about it."

I followed him into the kitchen. "I understand. This will just take a few minutes."

"I'll get Tommy."

Barefoot, the kid bounded into the room. Tom Sawyer came to mind. "Hello, Tommy. It's good to see you again."

He gripped my hand. "You too, sir."

"I'm going to show you a couple of photos. Take a careful look at them, and see if you recognize any as the man you saw in the park."

"Okay. I'll try."

"There's no pressure here. If you do or don't see the man, that's perfectly fine. No problem. You got that?"

"Yes, sir."

I unclipped a sheet from the outside of the envelope. "Before we look at the pictures, I have to let you know that the man we're looking for may or may not be in the lineup of pictures you're about to see.

"Don't assume I know which one is the man. I want you to focus on the pictures and don't ask anyone in the room for help in making a possible identification.

"If you do make an identification, I'll ask how certain you are about that identification.

"You should know that whether you make an identification or not, our investigation is going to continue. Whatever help you may give us, it's only a small part of the work we do. Do you understand everything I've said?"

He looked at his father. "Yes, sir."

"Good. I'm going to ask your father, as your legal guardian, to sign the consent and instructions form."

Mr. Kirk scanned the form and signed it. I broke the seal on the envelope and put my fingers on the photos. The lab had shuffled the images. Procedure dictated I had no idea which one was Lyle, and I took a mental guess he would be the second one.

Spreading the pictures in front of Tommy, I was struck how Lyle, the fourth one, stood out as evil. It was another example of our biases at work and the reason law enforcement developed protocols to prevent them from leaking to a witness.

Tommy bent over the lineup, his head slowly moving as he scanned the faces. He picked up the first one and put it down. Then repeated it with the third photo. He lingered over Lyle's. I rooted for him to say it was him but he moved on.

"Can I look at them again?"

"Sure. Take your time. There's no need to rush."

After two minutes, Tommy pointed to a photo. "I don't know for sure, but this one—he looks like the man I saw at the park."

26

———

REMIN WORE A LONG-SLEEVED, WHITE SHIRT AND FROWN. DID the news get to him? "What's on your mind?"

"I wanted to let you know that we're releasing Lyle."

"That's disappointing. What happened?"

"We don't have more than a bad alibi and the insinuations of an informant Lyle owes money to."

"I see. Are you clearing him?"

"We have no evidence Lyle was at the park. The witness, who saw the man we believe was the attacker, was unable to pick him out in a lineup."

"That witness was a minor, and the suspect is a sex offender."

"Yes. But we don't have anything more on him."

Remin picked up a pen and drummed it on the desk. He set it down, saying, "I need you and Dickson on the Holmes case."

"We can work both cases."

"I know you can. The public seems concerned about how serious we've been about the Holmes case. It's nonsense, but

I'd appreciate if it was known you and Dickson are working the disappearance, to reassure the public."

"I understand. A statement from the department might be the way to get the word out."

"That's what I'm planning."

"Good."

"Okay, get back to work."

I took the stairs down, stopping by Gesso's office to pick up the latest reports on Debbie Holmes. Derrick was staring at his screen when I stepped into the office. He said, "O'Rourke picked up the Panera video."

"Finally. You see Craven?"

"Not yet. I'm in the middle of the time zone but no sight of him."

"It felt like he was lying, but we'll see."

"What's with these people thinking they can give us a bullshit alibi?"

"They're counting on us not checking."

"Better off saying they were home alone than making up something we can check."

Blanco said he was home. Was he the smartest of the predators? How could we verify Blanco's alibi?

"Maybe. Truth has a way of showing up. I just wish it didn't take so damn long."

"Maybe with technology, we'll be able to move past lie detectors and get a truth meter that works. Something out of *Star Trek*, when someone is lying, a bell would go off."

"We might be out of a job with something like that."

Living in a world where even white lies would be exposed? People would have to thicken their skins when asking opinions of friends and families.

"I'm not seeing Craven. Do they have a drive-up?"

"Not that I know of."

"I'll go back over it and slow it down. I might have missed him."

"All right. I'm catching up on Holmes."

It was hard to keep thinking the kid was kidnapped for ransom. There'd been no contact from anyone saying they had her. The interview with Jason Reedy, Holmes's boyfriend, didn't jibe with what Dana Foyle had said about him.

Sara Gullo was Debbie Holmes's best friend. She didn't have much to say but did mention an older boy who expressed what she said was an unusual interest in her a year ago. The kid, Javier Lopez, had gone off to college shortly after pursuing Holmes despite her telling him she wasn't interested. There was nothing in the file documenting that anyone followed up on him.

"Frank, I went over this three times. Craven fed us a line of crap. He wasn't at Panera."

"And where he lives, they don't have a gate."

"I always wondered whether criminals factor that in."

"If they were smart they would, but they're usually not." I stood. "I'm going to see him."

I handed Derrick the Holmes file. "Do me a favor and check into this kid, Javier Lopez. It doesn't look like anyone spoke to him. He was trying to date Holmes, but she rebuffed him."

"I'll check with Gesso. If no contact was made, I'll track him down."

AN IMPRESSIVE RV was parked two lots down from Craven's home. It reminded me of one I'd seen in a magazine. People were selling their homes and buying mobile homes that had all the creature comforts. It wasn't for me, but the idea you didn't have to pay property taxes was compelling.

Craven's eyes were bloodshot. He stiffened when he saw me. "What's the matter?"

"You lied."

"Whaddaya mean?"

"You didn't go to Panera."

"I-I-I could've mixed things up or something. Tell me again what the dates were."

"Tuesday, May tenth."

He pawed his stubble. "Oh yeah, I was fishing."

"Without a fishing pole? Look, get your shoes on. You're going with me. I'll let your parole officer—"

"Oh, come on, man. I didn't do nothing to nobody."

"Where were you?"

His shoulders sagged. "Key West."

"When?"

"I left Monday afternoon."

"You drove?"

"No, took the ferry out of Fort Myers. I can get the receipt."

"When did you get back?"

"I went to see my sister."

"I'll find out anyway, so you better tell me when you got back."

"I was supposed to come back, I got a ticket for Wednesday, but my sis, she was real sick, throwing up an' all."

"When did you come back?"

He mumbled, "Thursday night."

"And you lied because you didn't register with Monroe County?"

He nodded.

They had forty-eight hours to register. Getting video from

the ferry was easy. "You show me the tickets, and I'll talk to your sister. It checks out, I'll give you a pass."

"Oh, man. You will?"

"I'm going to keep an eye on you. You so much as roll through a stop sign, your parole officer will know about your trip."

"I got it, man. Hold on, I'll get the tickets."

I pocketed the tickets, took his sister's information and left. Pulling onto Route 41, the radio squawked, "Ten Thirty-Two. Ten Thirty-Two."

A man with a gun.

"Any and all units in the vicinity of 111 Ozark Lane needed to respond."

The address rang a bell. A loud one. I picked up the radio, hit the siren, and floored the gas.

27

SIREN BLARING, I SPED DOWN OZARK LANE. MY MEMORY hadn't failed; the address was Bernie Lyle's place. Houses away, it came into focus: a man was banging the front door with his left fist. In his right hand, he held a pistol.

Pulling to the curb, I leaned on the horn. It had no effect. I drew my revolver and opened the car door. Ramos kept screaming, "Get out here, you bastard!"

"Mr. Ramos! Put the gun down."

Ramos fired a shot into the air.

"Mr. Ramos, it's Detective Luca. Put your weapon down!"

He stepped away from the door and moved to a window.

"Felix. Put your hands up!"

As a patrol car screeched to a halt, Ramos fired a shot. The front window exploded.

Taking cover behind a clump palm, I shot a round into the air. "Ramos! Drop it, or I'll shoot."

I aimed my gun as Ramos turned. "You! You let the bastard go!"

"It wasn't Lyle—we cleared him. He had a solid alibi."

The gun fell from his hand. Rushing toward him, I kicked the pistol away and shoved Ramos to the ground.

THE TV WAS ON. Mary Ann met me halfway in the hallway. "I'm sorry you had such a bad day."

"It was rough, but I'm okay."

"You want a glass of wine?"

"I do, but if I have one, I'll fall asleep."

"I can't believe it. Ramos lost his mind."

"A rapist is like a volcano, spewing destruction everywhere."

"I know. We focus on the victim, and we absolutely should, but like any crime, it effects the people around them as well."

"It's a frigging mess."

"The news said you cleared the man he went after."

"We did. I feel about as bad as you could for a sex offender like Lyle. He's going to have to leave town now. Not that that's a bad thing."

"I hope he goes to Russia."

One less predator was a good thing, but there was no sense reminding her there were a million sex offenders on the streets. And those were the ones we knew about.

"He's as low as they get. Just saying—"

"I know what you mean. But the poor girl who was raped, now her father is behind bars."

"It's sad as it gets. The guy was a marine. He lost his wife seven years ago and then his daughter. It's depressing. No wonder he lost it."

"Taking matters into his own hands made it worse—by a lot. He should've gotten help."

"People think they have it handled, you know. Especially us men."

It wasn't easy talking to somebody about your feelings and the situation you were in. I was glad I forced myself to go. It could have been the stress hitting me after recovering from cancer, but the decision to become a father had paralyzed me. Having someone like Dr. Bruno to talk with was a lifesaver.

"And where'd that macho bull get him? Now his daughter has to deal with this?"

"I'm hoping they go easy on him."

"He fired into a house. He could've killed somebody."

"I know but, you know what? I'm fried, I can't talk about this anymore."

"I'm sorry. You want something to eat?"

I shook my head. "Derrick picked up a couple of burritos, and my stomach is acting up."

"Okay. Get changed so you can relax a little."

MARY ANN WAS SNORING SOFTLY. It was time to process the day's events. Crazy as it was, understanding what Ramos did was easy from a father's viewpoint. His little girl had been violated in the most grotesque way.

What he did was irrational, making matters worse for her. His anger and frustration forced him to act. Marines were trained to be stoic, but that didn't mean they were emotionless.

The hardest thing for anyone, marine or not, was feeling helpless when a loved one was in trouble.

Ramos made a mistake, hurting the person he thought he was helping. He'd pay a price, but I hoped his lawyer could wrangle a plea, limiting jail time. Agreeing to go for anger counseling might help. The legal stuff wasn't up to me. All I could do was hope for a deal that would be easy on Lisa Ramos.

But whatever happened in the courtroom, my job was to get a measure of justice for a woman who'd suffered more than anyone should have to.

Every lead we followed smacked into a dead end. Trying to find a way to move forward, I drifted off to sleep.

The *bbzzztt* of my vibrating cell woke me. I reached for it. It was Gesso. "Hello?"

"Frank, sorry to call so late, but the Holmeses got a call from someone saying they have their daughter."

28

─────────

Driving along Livingston Road, it was hard not to think of Lisa Ramos. The rape occurred in a park off this main drag. It was the same road where Debbie Holmes was last seen. I turned into Briarwood, driving to Tivoli Lane.

Two patrol cars sat outside the Holmeses' house. It was the first time I'd been inside the community. An officer was playing with his phone outside the home's white double front doors. Despite the reason I was here, I estimated the value of the home.

After a ten-year hiatus, real estate was back as the number-one subject in Naples. Factoring in the rapid rise in prices, I pegged it at nine hundred thousand as an officer opened the door.

It was late, and the beige tile sucked up the light. I smelled coffee as he led me to the kitchen.

The Holmes couple had mugs in their hands. Introducing myself, the husband stood. "I'm Fred Holmes, and this is my wife, Laura."

Athletic looking, Mr. Holmes towered over me. Scars ran

across both knees. College basketball? We shook. "Nice meeting you."

Makeup-less, Laura Holmes offered a quick smile before saying, "I've seen you on the news."

I shrugged. "Just doing my job, ma'am. Now, tell me about the call."

Her voice cracked. "We were starting to lose hope, you know . . ."

Mr. Holmes put his hand on her shoulder. "Sit down, hon." He turned to me. "I got the call."

"On your cell?"

"No, the houseline."

Fewer and fewer people had them. "Do you have caller ID?"

"No."

"How long was the call?"

"A minute, maximum."

No way to trace it. "Tell me everything he or she said."

"It was a man. He asked if I was Mr. Holmes. I said yes, and he said he had Deborah and that she would be released if we paid one hundred thousand dollars. I agreed. Then he said he'd give me a day to get the money and would call back tomorrow with instructions. I asked him how Debbie was, but he hung up."

"Is Deborah your daughter's official name?"

"Yes, but nobody uses it. Not even our family."

"Was there anything in the background that could define where he was calling from?"

"No, but it sounded like he was in a tunnel or something."

"Was he young or old?"

"I'd say young, but with a deep voice and some kind of British accent."

"Do you or your daughter know anyone who speaks like that?"

"No. But I've heard it. I just can't place it. It's not Australian or English though."

"Did he say what time he'd call back?"

"At three. What should we do? We have to get Debbie home."

"Do you have the means to pay the ransom?"

"I will do what I have to, to get the money. If a hundred thousand gets her home, I'll be happy to pay it."

"It's a lot of money."

"I'll get it. Don't worry."

"Okay, but I wouldn't pay until we're comfortable whoever called has her and that she's well."

He looked at me like he'd read a Big Tech disclaimer. "What do you mean?"

"We need to be careful; this could be a scam."

"You mean he doesn't have Debbie?"

Mrs. Holmes cried out, "Oh no!"

"Please, let's not get ahead of ourselves. All I'm trying to say is we have to take it slowly—"

"Slowly? She's been missing eight days!"

"I was referring to the demand for ransom. Generally, especially, with large sums of money, the protocol is to require proof they have the hostage and they're in good shape, before paying."

"I get it. I really do. We just want Debbie home, and I don't know what to do."

"I understand. I'm a father of a daughter and feel for you as a parent, but we need to keep in mind the potential this is a scam. That's all I'm saying."

"That's the second time you said that. You know, it's funny, a couple of days ago, you people were telling us there was no proof she was kidnapped, no contact or ransom demand. Now we have it, and you're not believing it?"

"Let's take a step back. I got out of bed to be here. That's not a complaint; it's my job. And I take it seriously, including the call you received. We have to work together. Does that make sense?"

Holmes nodded. "Yeah, I guess I'm too worked up."

"I get it. We both want Debbie home where she belongs. We just need to be sure whoever is calling, actually has her."

"What would you suggest?"

"That he let you speak to her."

"And if they won't? What then?"

"We should insist. That way we know she's okay."

"I don't want to get these people mad. What if they refuse?"

"We need them to tell us something that a scam artist wouldn't know."

"Like a family secret?"

"It could be."

Mrs. Holmes said, "She has a birthmark on her rear end. It looks like a rabbit."

"That's perfect."

"You think so?"

"Yes. Now let's put together a plan for the call tomorrow."

29

DERRICK ARRIVED AT THE HOLMESES AT NINE. HE WAS GOING to run accents by Mr. Holmes to see if we could narrow an infinite world of suspects.

Having both of us there all day was a waste of manpower. Standing around waiting was something my body didn't tolerate well. Being in the house with both parents was too much to bear, and there was ground to cover on the Ramos case.

Derrick confirmed Craven's trip to Key West. He was off the list, meaning we had next to nothing. Blanco was another liar, but nobody we'd shown his photo to could place him near the attempted rape. I couldn't eliminate him totally. It was back to basics.

It took fifteen minutes to get to Bamboo Drive. Jorge Blanco lived a quarter of a mile past LowBrow Pizza. None of the homes had cameras. It was disappointing, but there was a bright side.

Saliva filled my mouth at the smell of pizza. T-shirt streaked with flour, the kid behind the counter recognized me. "Hey, how you doing?"

"Good."

"What can I get you?"

"A margherita pie. Make it well done."

"You got it."

"I need to check your outdoor surveillance footage from May tenth. It's a long shot, but it grabs the intersection of 41."

He slid a pie into the oven and said, "No problem. Johnny's in the back. He'll get it for you."

It only took ten minutes, but the car smelled of pizza, and it was glorious.

Jim Haney had called in after the public appeal. He was the first of two stops before heading to the Holmeses'. Haney looked like a sideways U. He must have suffered from a spinal condition.

"Mr. Haney, you contacted the hotline regarding the rape in North Collier."

"Yes. What took you so long?"

"We have to prioritize, and you claimed you saw a woman."

"It was a woman."

"Are you certain? Could it have been a man dressed as a lady?"

"I know what I saw. She had boobs and all. It was no disguise."

He described what she looked like. I thanked him for calling and got back in the car. It wasn't easy keeping my hands off the pizza, but I couldn't show up at the Holmeses' house with sauce on my shirt.

The next call would also be quick. Bruce Noon had called in to almost every appeal we'd ever made. Noon lived in a tiny apartment in Wild Pines. His eyes lit up. "Detective Luca! I mean, how are you doing? Catching bad guys?"

"Hello, Bruce. All is well. I wanted to ask you about your hotline call regarding the rape in North Collier Park."

"Uh, I, uh, oh yeah. I remember. You see, there was this man; he was spooky. I seen him there."

"What were you doing there?"

"I was visiting somebody who lives there."

It was the same thing he said on every call. "I see."

"Why did you go to the park if you were visiting?"

"They have the cut-through. They live in Wilshire Lake. It's real cool to be connected to the park."

Maybe he did see something. "Tell me what you saw."

"Well, I saw on the news . . . I watch *WINK*. I really like it. You watch it?"

"Yes. Please tell me—"

"Oh yeah, so, I saw you on TV." He smiled. "You were all dressed up."

"What did you see?"

"Well, like, when I saw you, I started trying to figure out if I saw anything. You know me. I like helping the police."

It wasn't help. "We appreciate it."

"Was it a woman?"

"No, a man. He was, like, this big." He raised a hand three inches over his head.

"What did he look like?"

"I don't know, kinda normal."

My cell vibrated. Derrick wanted to know where I was. "We're going to need more than that."

"It's hard to describe him. If I could work with one of those police artists, we could get something and catch this guy."

We'd wasted resources going down that road with Noon twice before. "I'll check on availability. When you saw this man, how far away was he?"

"Not that far."

"Where was he?"

"Kinda, like, near where the boardwalk starts. And you know, I just remembered; there was this lady. Right after I saw him, she walked by me—"

Ramos hadn't mentioned being at that side of the park. "Was it this woman?"

He held my phone. "No. I don't think so. The sun, it was in my eyes and it was hard to see."

"Can you give me the contact info for who you were visiting?"

"Why? They weren't in the park."

"Come on, Bruce. You know, the police have protocols we have to follow."

30

The pizza box was still warm. I handed it off to Derrick. He said, "Thanks. Foyle couldn't narrow down the accent more than it wasn't British English."

"How they doing?"

He lowered his voice. "They're wrecks."

"Frigging shame."

Stepping past the kitchen, the Holmeses came into view. They were sitting in the family room, staring at the phone on the cocktail table.

"How are we doing today?"

Mr. Foyle stood. "Two o'clock can't come soon enough."

"I picked up some pizza if you're interested."

"Nah, I can't eat."

"Me neither."

"All right. I'll be in the kitchen."

Derrick was tearing sheets off a paper towel roll. "You get anything on Blanco?"

His detective skills were sharp. "You put that together from the pizza?"

"Sure, it's from LowBrow."

"We need to rule him in or out. I have a DVD in the car that grabs the intersection. It's not foolproof, but if he left his house, the most direct way to 41 is past LowBrow."

He folded a slice and took a bite. "Good thinking."

"I stopped by to talk with a Jim Haney who called in, but it was nothing. Also went to see our buddy Bruce Noon."

"How's he doing?"

"Same old story; he was visiting somebody and saw something."

"He needs a new line."

"Yeah, but he said he saw a man in the same area where the kid did."

"By the boardwalk?"

"Yeah. It could be a lucky guess because he also saw a woman there."

Derrick smiled. "Covering all the bases."

At ten to two, the phone rang. Holmes looked at me. "You think it's him?"

"Stay calm and answer it."

Holmes inhaled and picked it up. "Hello."

He shook his head and said, "I'm not interested. Goodbye."

"Some guy in India trying to sell me a car warranty. Why can't the government do something about this?"

It was a great question. "Don't worry about it now—"

The phone rang again. Holmes answered it. "Hello. Are you kidding me? Leave me alone."

He hung up. "Same frigging guy."

"Unbelievable. Can you imagine the guy making all these—"

The phone jangled again. Holmes said, "I miss the call, I swear I'll find this guy and strangle him."

"Answer it."

"Yeah? It's me. Okay." He put his hand over the receiver. "Get me a pen and paper."

Derrick handed off his pad and pencil.

Holmes spoke into the receiver. "Okay. I'm ready." He wrote two lines and said, "Got it. Yes. I can do that."

I whispered, "Tell him you want to speak to your daughter."

Holmes said, "I want talk to Debbie. Wait . . . Hello? Hello?"

"He hung up."

Mr. Holmes handed me Derrick's pad. He'd scribbled down two long series of numbers: the First Caymanian Bank, and Robert Smith.

"He wants the money wired to the Cayman Islands?"

"That's what he said." Holmes pointed to the top number. "This is the account number, and that's the routing number."

"His name was Robert Smith?"

"I guess so, but he never said."

"Did he say anything else?"

"No. That was it. Just to wire the money and that it had to be today."

My stomach tightened. "I don't like this."

"Me neither, but I want my daughter back."

"I understand, but we don't know this person even has her."

Derrick said, "It's unusual for a kidnapper to ask for money to be wired."

Holmes's wife said, "Not in today's world. They could be turning it into that electronic money thing or something, so it ain't traced."

It was a theory, but the part about not being able to trace digital money was wrong. The feds could track it down and recover it if they wanted to. "That may be the case, but we still don't know if they have your daughter."

She sniffled. "What are we supposed to do? If we don't pay, we'll never know."

Her husband said, "We're wasting time. We have less than two hours."

"You're taking a huge chance by paying, Mr. Holmes."

"Maybe, but I'm taking a chance they have her and will do something if we don't pay."

"I get it. Would you consider sending half the money now and the other half once we know they have her, and she's fine?"

He looked at his wife and said, "You think it'll piss them off?"

"Maybe, but if they have her, they'll take the fifty and know they'll get the rest."

"I'm afraid it'll—"

"You can set up both wires. Get the bank to give you a document showing they're set up."

"Okay, okay. Let's get going." He turned to his wife. "Honey, stay here."

"No, I want to come."

"What if he calls again?"

"What would I say?"

"That's okay, ma'am. Derrick is going to keep you company while we're at the bank."

"Okay, okay."

I held up the notebook. "Derrick, take a picture of this and get ahold of the feds. From what I know, the Cayman Islands have some of the toughest bank secrecy laws around."

He took two shots of it and said, "Good luck."

Relying on luck was the worst strategy. But it was impossible to reason with a parent of a kidnapped child. All parents, including this one, were susceptible to manipulation when it involved the safety of their family.

Climbing into my car, I whispered a silent prayer for the Holmeses.

31

Driving back to the Holmeses', it was impossible not to play mental ping-pong. A hundred thousand dollars was a ton of money. Sending it to the Cayman Islands without proof felt like buying a lottery ticket. It was a mistake.

On the other side, what parent wouldn't take every risk when the well-being of their child was at stake? You had to do something.

Felix Ramos came to mind. Totally different circumstances, yet there were parallels; feelings of helplessness overwhelmed your sensibilities. Ramos was behind bars; Holmes hadn't violated the law, but if this failed, he and his wife would be in a hell of their own.

Derrick stepped outside after Mr. Holmes went in. "How'd it go?"

"Too easy. Being able to move money around like that is scary."

"He sent half?"

"Yeah. Let's hope we have to send the rest."

"Amen."

"All quiet here?"

"Yeah. I feel bad, but being with her is stressful."

"Waiting and not knowing is tough."

"It sure is."

"Let's put the time to use." I pulled my notebook out. "See if you can track this woman down. Noon said he was at her house on May tenth. I'm going to the office to check the LowBrow video."

He frowned.

"What's the matter?"

"I'm getting tired of . . . forget it."

"No. Tell me."

"You get to run around, and I'm stuck babysitting."

"I'm sorry, but I'm the lead and—"

"Forget it, man." Derrick turned and went back in the house.

We had two cases to manage, and my partner was throwing a tantrum?

LEANING MY HEAD BACK, I put a drop of saline in each eye. Blinking, I kneaded the back of my neck. The time stamp on the video read 5:48. There was no sign of Blanco. Hitting play, I leaned into the screen.

The intersection was in the distance, making the cars small, and license plates, smaller. Blanco drove a light-blue Passat. Not the color or Japanese make the toy-boat sailor said was parked in a weird spot. But everything needed a follow-up.

As a pickup truck came into view, my mind drifted to Derrick. He drove one. I loved the guy, but I was the boss. He knew that. Was becoming good friends the problem? Did it blur the lines?

A car came into view. Pausing the video, it looked like Blanco's. Zooming in, the entire plate wasn't visible. But it started with PTT. Just like Blanco's did.

The time stamp was 6:09. It was a good twenty minutes to North Collier Park. It was tight, leaving a short time to canvas for a victim. But the park wasn't crowded that night.

The DMV portal had no other Passats whose plate numbers began with PTT. Blanco had some explaining to do.

Derrick answered on the third ring, "Hi."

"Hey, everything okay over there?"

"Yeah."

"Did you check out what Noon said?"

"Yeah."

"And?"

"He was with them."

"Wow. Noon didn't make it up this time."

"Nope."

"We may have to get a sketch artist to work with him."

"Whatever you say."

"What's that supposed to mean?"

"Nothing."

"You sure?"

"Yes."

"Okay. Hey, I wanted to let you know, Blanco left his house the night of the Ramos rape."

"Okay."

"You all right?"

"Yeah."

"I'm heading to see him."

"Okay."

Was it possible for a forty-two-year-old man to morph into a sixteen-year-old in an hour? "Let me know if anything develops with Holmes."

"Yes, boss."

The sarcasm was thicker than honey. "Come on, now."

"Gotta go. The phone's ringing."

"Let me know—" He hung up.

BEFORE GOING TO THE DOOR, I called Derrick to see if they'd heard anything. It went to voice mail. Was that a good sign?

Blanco came to the door, wearing a headset. He paused before saying, "Detective Luca, is something wrong?"

"You lied to me."

He waved his hands. "No, no. I didn't. I don't know what you're talking about."

"You told me you were home the night of May tenth."

Another pause. "That was a Tuesday, right?"

"Yes."

"I was home. I don't go out much. If I do, it's usually on the weekends."

"You left your house that night. I have a video feed from LowBrow; you drove your car onto 41 a few minutes after six."

He bounced on the balls of his feet. "Uh-oh. I went to get a hero at Publix."

"You never came back."

"I did. I came right back in, like, twenty minutes."

"Not according to LowBrow's surveillance camera."

"I came back through River Road. It's faster that way."

Was there a camera somewhere documenting his return? "You get one last chance to change your story because I'm going to verify it. Publix has plenty of cameras."

"That's the truth."

"Did you use a credit card to pay for the hero?"

"No. Cash. It was like eight dollars, and I didn't get anything else."

"If you're lying, I'll make sure you never get out of prison."

Blanco stood in the doorway as I pulled away from the curb. It was impossible to see if any of the homes along the way where Blanco said he'd returned, had surveillance equipment.

A stand-alone building, housing a realty company, sat on the corner of River Road and Route 41. Their parking lot was empty. Cameras hung from both corners of the building. A handwritten sign was taped to the door. The office was closed for an outing, commemorating the firm's tenth anniversary.

Why hadn't Derrick called back? The closest Publix was in Kings Lake. I headed there and called my partner.

"Hey, how's it going?"

"Okay."

"What was that call about?"

"Robocall."

"Damn. No word on the kid?"

"Nope."

"You going to stick with one-word answers?"

"There's nothing to report."

"I don't like this. If they have the kid, prove it."

"Yep."

Another call was coming in. "I gotta go. It's Gesso."

"What's up, Sarge?"

"The feds traced the ransom money."

32

The accent on the man calling Holmes made sense.
"Are you f—frigging kidding me?"

Gesso said, "I wish I was. The money hit the Cayman bank and was routed to Nigeria minutes later."

"Bastards! And there's nothing we can do, right?"

"Apparently. They said it wasn't easy to get them to say it went to Nigeria."

"It's a damn scam, and secrecy laws are letting them get away with it."

"They don't help."

"What a bunch of lowlifes, preying on the Holmeses."

"Sometimes it's a shitty world, Frank."

"It sure is."

"You going to tell the Holmeses?"

"Derrick is with them."

"All right. I got to go."

About to call my partner, I paused. Would he get worked up if he had to handle the dirty task? Delivering bad news was part of the job. He reported to me. Why the hesitancy to delegate?

I pulled into the Publix lot. They always cooperated quickly. The time to view the video wouldn't take more than ten to fifteen minutes. There'd just be time to think.

FITTINGLY, the sky darkened on the way to the Holmeses' house. Blanco was off the hook. There was no sense checking the video from the real estate company. By the time Blanco's sandwich was made, and he went through the cashier, it was 6:39.

Blanco couldn't have gotten to the park in time to attack Ramos. We had nothing. And now, we had to let the Holmeses down. A block away, I pulled over. Delivering bad news was tough. Doing it when you weren't in the right frame of mind wasn't good for anyone.

Arching my shoulders back, I tried to relieve the tension shooting up my neck. Was this a younger man's job? Retirement was a couple of years out, but if it weren't for the money and health benefits, I'd be gone already.

Leaving in the middle of a case wasn't my style. When it was time, the desk would be as clean as it could be in today's world. Derrick would be in charge. He'd be the boss, growing into the job. Whatever help he needed, I'd be there for him.

Circling my head, I stretched my neck and headed to the Holmeses'. At the curb, I sent a text to Derrick. He came outside. I flashed a thumbs-down and met him at the door.

"It looks like the Holmeses were scammed."

"Jesus Christ!"

"I know. Gesso called, said the money bounced from the Caymans to Nigeria."

He shook his head. "These poor people."

"I didn't want you to tell them alone."

"Thanks, but I can do it."

"I know you can, but I wanted—"

"I got it. The fact you came is good enough for me."

My shoulders relaxed. Did that qualify as a kiss-and-makeup? "Okay." He turned around, and I said, "Hold on a sec; Blanco isn't our rapist. We're starting from scratch."

"This shit never gets easy, does it?"

"We'll get him." It came out confidently, but that was the relief from not having to deliver bad news to the parents.

Leaning against the car, I tried to figure out the next step in the Holmes case. It was looking like something bad happened to the kid. We didn't have a body or a motive or a suspect, so it wasn't a homicide—yet. Maybe the kid was being held captive. But by whom?

My mind drifted to the Pine Ridge case and the Millers. The younger brother suffered a brain injury in a car accident and didn't have full use of his faculties.

Bruce Noon popped into my head. I didn't know what was wrong with him, but something was off. I pulled my phone out and called the lab. "Cecil, it's Luca."

"Hi, Frank. How are you?"

"I've been better."

"I heard about the ransom scam."

Bad news traveled at supersonic speed. Nothing to be gained by saying I saw it coming. "It sucks for sure. Look, I have a possible witness I'd like to work with a sketch artist."

"Sure. I can set it up. Just send me the paperwork."

"Thanks." Paperwork. The other annoying part of the job you never saw on TV.

The front door opened. Derrick beckoned with a hand. "He wants to talk to you."

"How'd it go?"

"Not good. The wife is hysterical. She's lying down."

Mr. Holmes was pacing the family room. "What are we going to do now?"

Good question. "We're going to continue the investigation—"

"Continue? Where the hell did that get us? Huh? Tell me. Am I missing something?"

"We're all disappointed, but we're not giving up. We have several lines of promising inquiries we're following."

"What lines? What are you talking about?"

"I'm unable to reveal much, but we've developed multiple persons of interest."

"Why hasn't anyone said anything? Who are these people? Where the hell is my daughter?"

The line just tumbled out of my mouth. It was the mumbo-jumbo that politicians spouted. But we couldn't strip them of hope at this point.

"As soon as we can share something, we will."

"How long is this going to take?"

Derrick said, "It's difficult to predict when a break is going to hit. But we're applying pressure."

I was thankful he jumped in.

Holmes's shoulders slumped. "I'm getting a bad feeling she isn't coming home."

He wasn't alone. The slim chance she was alive was disappearing with every tick of the clock. What could be done?

We huddled by my car. I exhaled. "What a frigging mess."

Derrick said, "Let's lean on the boyfriend."

My phone vibrated. "Okay." I held up a finger and answered, "What's going on, Sarge?"

I leaned against the car. "Damn it. Text me the address. We'll head over now."

"What did he say?"

"A five-year-old girl is missing."

33

Speeding along Davis Boulevard, we turned into the Glen Eagle Golf and Country Club. The community was gated. A minimal deterrent.

"Ask the guard if they have cameras. If she was taken out by car, we'll need every license plate number that exited."

Derrick spoke with an older man who'd have trouble walking to the mailbox. It was another example of security theater. "They take pictures."

"Good. Let's go."

The Schneider home was a single-family home on Lago Villaggio Way.

Derrick said, "What a long name for a street."

"People must get tired of spelling it out."

A patrol car came into view. Derrick pulled behind it. The home was one of several on the block who'd replaced terracotta roof tiles with sleek gray tiles. A lake, along the back of the street, was visible between the homes.

Forcing the thought of dredging the lake out of my head, we entered. Six women were pleading with the community's security patrol person to do something.

Clearing my throat, I said, "Mrs. Schneider?"

Face streaked with mascara, a thirty-year-old woman with short, blonde hair, stepped forward. "Thank God you're here."

Derrick said, "I'll join the search. You talk to Mrs. Schneider."

"Yes, please hurry."

I said, "We need a picture of her."

She pulled a framed photo off a credenza. The kid had the same hair color as Jessie. I handed it to Derrick and turned to the mother.

"Tell me what happened."

"Somebody took Mia. She was right here, and then she was gone."

"Where were you when she went missing?"

"She was on the lanai, and I went in, just for a minute. I had to get changed. I was still in my exercise clothes, and Mia had dance class."

"And when you came back out, she was gone?"

"Yes. I thought she was in the house. I checked all over . . . Oh, please find her."

"How long were you inside?"

"Like, five, maybe ten minutes. I had to use the bathroom."

"Show me where she was when you last saw her."

She walked toward the open sliders. "Right here. She was having tea with her doll. She does it every day."

The same tea set our daughter had was laid out on the lanai table. I walked onto the lanai. A screen door led to the grassy area before a long, narrow lake. The handle on the door looked off.

"Was this broken before today?"

"Yeah, it hasn't worked in months."

I stepped onto the grass. Several houses down, the lake

bent out of view. A marshy area to the right caught my attention. Were there alligators in the water or reedy area?

"Where is your husband?"

"We're separated."

"Do you think he could've taken her?"

"No. John and me, we get along. Besides, he's traveling. I think he's up in New York."

"We're going to need his contact information."

"I'm telling you; he wouldn't do something like that."

"Ma'am, I'm not saying he did. Just give me his info."

She shook her head and spit it out.

"Did you see anyone outside? Anything out of the ordinary?"

"No. It was just a normal day. I mean the landscapers were out there earlier, but that was, like, hours ago."

"No one else?"

"No. I didn't see anyone."

"Has your daughter wandered away before?"

"Mia is a good kid. She knows not to talk to strangers."

"Has she ever wandered off?"

"No, not really. I mean, one time I was in the dressing room at Bealle's, and she gave me the scare of my life. But that was it, just that one time at Bealle's."

It was impossible not to think of the waterfall of coupons the store used to attract customers. "What about her friends in the neighborhood? Could she have gone to one of their houses?"

"The kids on the block are older. They're in school."

I took my phone out. "Sarge, I need to get a drone up as fast as possible."

"You got it. Anything else?"

"We're going to need six or so more officers to conduct a grid search. This place is wide open."

"Okay, I'll send some cars your way. Good luck."

"Mrs. Schneider, call the golf club. Tell them your daughter is missing. Ask them to send golf carts out to look for her. She might be lost."

"Why would she be on the golf course?"

"Just do it."

She made the call, and I gave her my cell number. "Call me when the patrol cars arrive. Or if you hear anything."

Standing around wasn't in my DNA. Especially, when a five-year-old could be in trouble. Stepping outside, I scanned the sky. The drone was heading our way. Silently praying, I headed toward a marshy area filled with chest-high reeds.

MARY ANN WAS SLEEPING on the couch. I shut the TV off and she stirred.

"What time is it?"

"Nine thirty."

"Pretty bad day, huh?"

"Yeah, but at least one thing worked out."

"What happened?"

"The ransom thing on the Holmes girl was a big scam."

"I saw the news. What happened?"

"The wire, thank God he listened and only sent half the money. Anyway, it was sent to the Cayman Islands, and as soon as it hit there, it was redirected to Nigeria."

"Ugh, poor family. How do people live with themselves pulling stuff like that?"

"Just another kind of predator. No different than any scam preying on emotion."

"Like that case where Phil's father sent money to somebody claiming to be his grandson, for bail money."

"Yep. There better be a special place in hell for people like that."

"So, there's nothing on the girl?"

"Nope. It's not looking good."

"I can't imagine what they're going through."

"I know. Today we responded to a call about a missing five-year-old girl."

"Oh no."

"She has blonde hair like Jessie, and the kid has the same tea set Jessie used to play with. It gave me the chills."

"But it turned out okay?"

"Yeah, a boy with Down's syndrome came by. He'd caught a fish in the lake and wanted to show it off, and the two of them wandered off."

"Scary. She could have been taken or fallen in the lake. Do they have alligators there?"

It was better to avoid answering. "Life can change in a heartbeat. Remember the time we were in Marshall's, and I was trying on sneakers? We panicked when we didn't see Jessie behind the display?"

"Remember? The tension took ten years off me."

"Speaking about tension. Something weird is going on with Derrick. All of a sudden he's pushing back when I give direction."

"You're partners; you share responsibilities."

"Oh, come on, you know that's not how it works; I'm the lead. I'm the guy Remin beats on, not Derrick."

"That's not what I'm talking about. Derrick knows you're the leader. I was referring to the way you ask—"

"What are you saying?"

She crossed her arms. "Frank, don't forget we were part-ners too. I had to tell you multiple times about being rude—"

"Rude? I'm not rude."

"Will you let me finish?"

"Go ahead."

"It's the way you ask someone to do something. Instead of telling him, or anybody, for that matter, be nice about it. Everybody has feelings—"

"Hold on! I'm trying to find a rapist and a missing kid, and I got to worry about hurting my partner's feelings? This is nuts. I'm beat. I'm going to bed."

MY EYES FLASHED OPEN. I stiffened. What was that? A scratching sound? Or a prying one? In one motion, I swung my legs off the bed and palmed my revolver.

"Frank? What's the matter?"

"Get in the bathroom. Somebody's trying to break in."

"Don't go out there. I'll call nine-one-one."

"No. I got it."

It took a minute to tiptoe into the family room. The security lights on the right side of the house were on. Who was trying to get in through the laundry room?

"Get the hell out of here! I've got a gun!"

The noise stopped. "Get going!"

"Frank! Be careful!"

"Get back in the bedroom." I ran to the back of the house and hit the lanai lights. Pistol pointed out, I slid the door open. It was empty.

In the dark, a pair of eyes reflected the moonlight. I stuck my head inside and whispered, "Mary Ann, get my a flashlight."

34

RELIEVED THERE WAS A CUP OF COFFEE ON MY DESK, I SAID, "Good Morning, Derrick."

"Hey."

At least I had an icebreaker. "Take a look at this."

"What?"

"We had a visitor last night." He took my phone.

"This was at your house?"

"Yeah. It sounded like someone was breaking in through a side door. Man, I had my pistol out and all."

"It's a baby bear. Probably weighs only two, three hundred pounds."

"Maybe, but you got to see the scratches on the door. It's going to take a ton of putty to fill them in."

"Scary way to wake up."

"You got that right."

"After the day we had yesterday, I thought I'd conk right out, but I had a bad dream about Jessie."

"You did?"

"Yeah."

"And I had a bad one about Lynn."

"This frigging job might be getting to us."

"Might?"

I picked up my coffee. "At least we'll get screwed up together."

"It could be worse."

It wasn't much, but he was thawing out. "Much worse. Say, what time is Bruce Noon coming in today?"

"Eleven."

"Great. Who knows, maybe we'll get lucky."

"Luck? I thought you didn't rely on luck."

I shrugged. "Right now, if an alien came down with a lead, we'd follow it."

He laughed. "I think we should talk to Jason Reedy."

Going to see Holmes's boyfriend was already on my agenda. "Good idea."

"Let's get rolling, then."

"I'll drive, if you want."

"Nah, it's okay. I like to drive."

There were people who enjoyed driving. The question was why. Was it the traffic? The stress of being alert? Some said they did their best thinking behind the wheel. For me it was walking, though the extra ten pounds I was carrying belied it.

"Oh, it looks like another two dogs were taken?"

"Where did this happen?"

"Lakewood Country Club."

"Where's that again?"

"Across from Sugden Park, where that Indian restaurant, 21 Spices, is."

"Two dogs from the same community. This is organized. Maybe there's a ring behind all these."

"Probably. They know there's money in it."

"It's crazy. Say, you ever eat at that Indian place?"

"Too spicy for me."

"Mary Ann has been busting me to go. She likes Indian food."

"Be a good boy and take her."

"Maybe for her birthday."

Derrick turned onto Santa Barbara Boulevard. "Man, I can't believe there's so much building going on around here."

"I read something like a hundred people a day are moving to Collier."

"A hundred? That's too high."

"That's what I thought, but the article said Lee County is getting twice as many."

"That's nuts."

"Turn left on Devonshire."

The Reedy family home was beige, on a wide lot, within walking distance of a Publix. A trailer loaded with a fishing boat was parked on the garage side of the home.

Derrick held up his badge. "Mrs. Reedy? We're with the Collier County Sheriff's."

"Is Eddie all right?"

"Yes, ma'am. We'd like to have a word with your son, Jason."

"Jason? Did he do something?"

"It's regarding Debbie Holmes."

Her face softened. "Oh. Okay. He's still sleeping. Come in, and I'll get him up."

It was impossible not to contrast the difference in kids today. We'd be on our third game of something by ten o'clock, not wasting the best part of the day drooling on a pillow.

Short, stocky, and wearing thick flip-flops, Jason Reedy trudged into the room. The T-shirt the kid had on brought back images of the tie-dye craze. Derrick introduced us and said, "Ma'am, since your son is a minor, you have the right to be present if you'd like."

Her eyes narrowed. "Are you saying Jason had something to do with Debbie going missing?"

"Not at all. We're required to advise you since he's just seventeen."

"Oh, okay." She turned to her son. "Do you want me to stay with you?"

"No. That's not necessary, Mom."

"All right, then. I'll be on the lanai if you need me."

I said, "Why don't we sit?"

"Sure." He scraped a wicker chair away from the table. Derrick said, "How long have you known Debbie Holmes?"

"Approximately, a few years, I believe."

Did he have a law degree?

"How did you meet?"

"At school."

"How long have you been dating each other?"

He shrugged. "It's been a while."

"More than a year?"

"Yes. Why is that important?"

"We need your help in trying to understand what happened to her."

"I have no idea what happened. It's extremely upsetting to me."

"You know her best, and it's possible you can lead us in the direction we need to look."

"I wish I could help."

"You know Dana Foyle, right?"

He nodded.

"She said you would know where she was."

"Why'd that stupid bit— say that?"

"Easy, Jason. She thought Debbie was closer to you than anyone else. That's all."

He scoffed. "You listen to her? What did she attempt to do? Huh? Her scheme exploded in her face."

Jason had a point. I said, "Do you know anyone who wanted to do Debbie harm?"

"No."

"She have an argument with anyone?"

"Nothing major."

"Tell us."

"It was nothing. Just normal school nonsense, you know how girls are."

"It's been a long time since we were in school. Why don't you tell us what happened."

"I'm not certain for sure, but she got into a fight with a girl named Sammi. She moved here from New York and thinks she's tough. You know the kind."

"What was the fight about?"

"Something silly. I believe Debbie was going into her locker, and the door swung and hit Sammi, and she freaked out."

"And it became physical?"

He nodded as my phone vibrated.

"What's Sammi's last name?"

"Cava."

"Okay. Anything else you could think of?"

He wagged his head.

Derrick said, "What can you tell us about Javier Lopez?"

He leaned forward. "Oh, I forgot about him."

"We understand he was interested in Debbie, but she rebuffed him."

"Javier is full of himself. He wouldn't leave her alone,

constantly bothering her. Yeah, you have to look into him. It may sound crazy, but it could be he did something."

"What makes you think that?"

"He annoyed Debbie. He was very persistent, even when she said no to a date. He had some nerve; he knew we were going together. Frigging snake."

My phone vibrated again. Ignoring the call again, I asked, "What can you tell me about Mr. Lopez?"

"Not much. He was a year ahead of us but that's all."

"He was interested in your girlfriend, and you don't know much about him?"

A text pinged in, and a second later, the sound of Derrick's phone vibrating made me take a peek. It was Gesso. Someone found a body.

35

———————

Heading toward Marco Island, we drove past Fiddler's Creek, when I said, "I don't understand how nobody knows if it's male or female."

Derrick said, "Why do you say that? It's been in the water, even if only a couple of days."

The combination of warm water, bacteria, and sea life turbocharged decomposition. "I know, I know."

"You think it's Debbie Holmes?"

"Probably not," I said with false confidence.

"We haven't had a report of anyone missing out on the water."

My cell rang. It was Mary Ann. "Hi. I can't talk. I'm on my way—"

"Is it the Holmes girl?"

"How'd you know there was a body?"

"It's on the news."

Bad news spread faster than good news. "We don't know anything at this point."

"I hope to God it isn't her."

"No promises, but I'll call you later."

"Okay, hon. Try and not let it get to you."

I hung up. "The press got ahold of this already."

"What did you expect? The body popped up where people go fishing."

Nodding, I said, "Most don't know that when a body decomposes, the buildup of gases forces it to the surface. Unless you really know what you're doing, it'll pop up."

"And have the time to do it right."

"If it's a homicide, that's a factor to consider. If it wasn't submerged long, we may be dealing with something unplanned, a passion killing or something that spun out of control."

Approaching the sign for the Judge Jolley Bridge to Marco Island, Derrick said, "Who was this judge they named the bridge after?"

"I heard he was good guy, but get this: he didn't have a law degree."

"Then how'd he become a judge?"

"I don't know, but a professor at John Jay told us somebody on the Supreme Court in the forties didn't go to law school either."

We turned off Collier Boulevard by Bear Point, just before the bridge, and pulled alongside a handful of patrol cars.

Fifty feet offshore, people on paddleboards were pointing. We rounded a stand of shrubs, and I stopped short when the victim's brown hair came into view. A wave of seasickness swept over me as I recalled the hair color of Debbie Holmes.

Approaching the decomposed victim, it appeared to be a female whose size matched Debbie Holmes.

"You think it's her?"

Mouth dry, I said, "Damn it."

"The forensics van just pulled up. And Bilotti is here."

Nodding, I whispered, "I don't how much more of this I can take."

"What do you mean?"

And I thought he was a good detective? "What? How about this? All of this. Seeing kids dead or raped. Dealing with grieving parents—"

"I know, man. You want to head back? I'll handle it."

Of course I wanted to take off, but you didn't get to cherry-pick in this job. "Nah, just bitching."

The lapping water lifted the body on and off the sandy beach. Strands of seagrass were strewn on the corpse's chest. The body was missing a foot, and an arm was hanging by a ligament.

Approaching, I held my breath and knelt. What was left of her breasts ensured it was a female.

Swallowing a mouthful of bile, I checked her pockets. Empty.

"What was Holmes wearing when she was last seen?"

"Shorts and a T-shirt."

It felt like I had a lead vest on. "It's got to be her."

"Frank, Derrick."

"Hi, Doc."

He shook his head. "What's this world coming to?"

It was a troubling question. "Based on the hair and clothing, we think it's the missing Holmes girl. How soon can you make an ID?"

"I'll check for fingerprints. If not, we'll rely on dental records."

"Check for a birthmark on her behind. The mother said she has one in the shape of a rabbit."

"That qualifies as a unique marker. I'll look once we get her to the morgue."

"How long you think she's been in the water?"

"Difficult to say, but approximately five to eight days."

"Okay."

"We'll firm it. Let me do the initial examination, and we'll get an autopsy in motion."

Bilotti and the forensics team sprang into action.

"Derrick, ask the Marco guys to get a boat out there. This ain't no damn show; onlookers need to be pushed back."

The sixty-something-year-old man who'd found the body was leaning on a patrol car. Wearing shorts and a straw hat, he shook his head.

"Sir, I'm Detective Luca."

He extended his hand. "Joe Farnsworth."

"I understand you found the body."

"Yeah, I can't believe it. Just looking to do a little fishing, but before I got out there, I saw it."

"Where were you when you discovered it?"

He pointed. "I keep my boat at Marco Marina. I went straight out to the channel, and I don't even know why I looked across before turning, and I saw it. I thought it was a dolphin carcass or something and motored over."

"What did you do when you got up to it?"

He scoffed. "Almost lost my breakfast is what. I cut the engine soon as I seen it was a body. I couldn't believe it. I called the harbor and was going to wait for help, but it was drifting and I was afraid. So, I reached it with my net and that's when I seen a foot was gone. It was in, uh, rough shape. I figured I better get it to the beach."

"How far offshore was it?"

"Like a third of the way past the middle of the channel."

"Were there any other boats in the area?"

"You know, I thought the same thing, but it was pretty quiet. The tide had reversed a little while before. The fishing is better when it heads out."

"You're serious about fishing."

"Oh yeah, me and my dad used to go out when he was still around."

"If you had to guess where the body may have come from, what would you say?"

"Hmmm. Well, I'd say it probably came out of East Marco Bay. There's a ton of coves and bays by Charity Island."

I looked in the direction he pointed. "Appreciate the advice."

"Sure. But you know the tides and movement are funny things. It could've just as well come out of Tarpon Bay. There's a narrow passage leading right where I saw it."

"Would you mind showing me on the map, the places you're referring to?"

36

MUG IN HAND, DERRICK SAID, "I'VE BEEN THINKING OVER what you said about it being connected to the Ramos case."

"And?"

"Like you said, her size and hair color match Ramos's and Samus's, but if it's Holmes, she's a kid. And was riding a bike. He had to know that."

"Maybe it didn't matter to him."

"I'm no profiler, but don't perverts go after the same type?"

"We'd have to ask the experts, but don't get hung up on it. We have to keep in mind they may be related."

"Sure."

"Let's not forget Holmes was taken at night, with nobody around."

He nodded.

"Bottom line is, we don't know. But if it's not Holmes, we have to lean to a connection."

"It's not like I want another victim, but I'm hoping it's not Holmes."

"Me too."

My cell rang. "Hey, Doc. What do you have for me?"

"We have partial fingerprints to compare, but based upon the birthmark you mentioned, we're making a tentative identification it's Deborah Holmes."

A nasty burp exploded in my mouth. "It was on her rear end?"

"Yes."

Collapsing into my chair, I said, "Shaped like a rabbit?"

"Yes."

"Damn it."

"Sorry, Frank. I've got to go and get the autopsy started."

Derrick said, "It was Holmes?"

I exhaled. "Yeah."

He sat on the corner of my desk. "We have to tell the parents what we know."

"Yeah, and the sheriff."

"You go see Remin. I'll let the Holmeses know."

There was no use in pretending I should tell the parents. It was something I just couldn't do right now. "Okay." I stood and trudged upstairs.

DERRICK CAME BACK as I drove a pin into the corners of a Marco Island map. "How'd it go?"

He shrugged. "Terrible, especially the mother. But, you know, they knew she wasn't coming home."

"Reality sinks in after someone is missing more than two days."

"Kinda like a wake dulls it for a couple of days after a death."

Interesting idea, but the statement needed more thought, and now wasn't the time.

"Come here." I put a finger on the map. "This is where Farnsworth saw the body."

Derrick grabbed a pencil and drew an X. "It could have come from anywhere."

"I know, but he knows the waters and said it probably came from the east side of the bridge. He mentioned it could have come out of here"—I pointed to Tarpon Bay—"but it'd have to travel through this tight spot. Somebody else would have seen it. Or it's so narrow, it could've gotten hung up somewhere."

"Either way, we're probably looking for somebody with access to a boat."

"First thing I thought of was the Reedy kid."

"With that boat on the side of the house, I thought the same thing."

"We can't jump to conclusions, but something about Reedy; he looked me in the eye, but I don't trust the kid."

"He didn't say anything about Lopez until we mentioned him."

"I know. We need to talk to Lopez."

"He's goes to Gulf Coast U."

"Any record?"

"Not since he turned eighteen, but I checked, and there is a juvenile file on him."

That was interesting. "That could be revealing, but we'll need something concrete to ask for access."

"I'll see if he's on campus."

"I'm going up to Miromar Outlets; it'd be perfect."

"You? Shopping?"

"We have a wedding, and Mary Ann wanted me to get a new sports jacket. She saw one on sale at Brooks Brothers and bought it."

"Snazzy."

"I've been putting off getting it fitted, and she's on my back because the wedding is two weeks away."

IT WAS HARD NOT BE envious; John Jay College didn't have a campus. The criminal justice university was on Fifty-Ninth Street in Manhattan. The only greenery we had came from a couple of scrawny trees planted into holes in the concrete.

A paver path led to a string of low-rise buildings, surrounding a lake. Its sandy beach gave the place a resort feel. Maybe Derrick had the right word for what they were, because dormitory didn't fit.

Backpack slung over one shoulder, Javier Lopez walked out of the Mangrove building. He had a swimmer's build and was taller than the man Ramos described.

We settled onto a bench. "This place is nicer than I expected."

"Yeah, it's not bad."

Had the entitlement mentality passed from the millennial generation to whatever they called this one? "What are you studying?"

"Marketing, but I came here to swim. Got a scholarship."

"Nice. They have a good program here?"

"The girls' team rocks, but we're just okay."

"Got to work on it, then."

He smiled. "Heading to the pool after this."

"I understand you were interested in Debbie Holmes romantically."

"She was nice. I really liked her. It's hard to believe she's, uh, gone."

Dr. Bruno had said killers used euphemisms in an attempt to minimize what they'd done. Was Lopez doing it?

"We've been told you pursued her aggressively."

"I liked her. My dad always told us, you want something, you have to go for it."

Was he a kid who broke his own toy when told to let another child play with it? "She wasn't interested?"

"Oh, she was. But I was going to college."

Was that male pride talking? "This place is only a half hour away."

"Yeah, but you know, dating a high schooler . . ."

Peer pressure was a powerful force. "Do you have any thoughts on who might be responsible for her death?"

"That jerk Jason and his sidekick, Joey, is good place to start."

"Why do you say that?"

"He was a control freak. She complained to me a bunch of times that he was suffocating her. She said his buddy is a straight-up creep and tried to hit on her."

"Hmmm. You know, it's funny you say it could be him because he said it was you."

He scoffed. "Me? No way, but you see, you see how he's trying to distract the police?"

"Where were you the night of May twenty-third, when Debbie went missing?"

"Me? Oh, come on, man. I had nothing to do with it."

"Tell me where you were."

"What day was that?"

Was he stalling? "Monday."

"Oh, I was training. We're in the pool six days a week, minimum."

"Until what time?"

"Usually six, six thirty. Then we shower and grab something to eat."

We'd verify his alibi. "Okay, that's all. Have a good swim."

He stood. "Thanks."

"Oh, I'm curious if swimmers just use the pool or if they like the beach or go fishing."

"Oh yeah. I love being on the Gulf. My dad's had a boat forever."

37

____

Derrick peered over his monitor. "You get your suit?"

"Sports jacket. Got to say, she picked out a nice one."

"Who's getting married, again?"

"A son of a friend of Mary Ann's. Last name is McCormick; they live in Kensington."

"Don't know 'em."

"Mary Ann knows them better than me. We only went out a couple of times as couples. But Bilotti is going. I told Mary Ann to make sure we're sitting with him."

"Yeah, being at a wedding with a bunch of strangers isn't fun."

"How'd it go with Lopez?"

"His version wasn't what we've been told. He said she was into him, but he dumped her when he went to college."

"Could be."

"The kid is on the swim team, said he was swimming till six, six-thirty, the night Holmes disappeared."

"Should be easy to check it. I'll make some calls."

"You know, I had an idea. If a classmate or more than one of hers is involved, they probably didn't go to school the next day. We can see who was absent on that Tuesday and the next day as well. You never know."

"That could be great information. I'll call Barron Collier High."

"Thanks."

"Hey, the artist dropped off a copy of the sketch of the guy Noon said he saw." He handed off an envelope.

"Guy looks familiar. No?"

He laughed. "It's probably a compilation of everyone Noon ever met."

My cell rang. "Detective Luca."

"Uh, hi, this is Chris Reedy. I'm Jason's dad."

I put the drawing down. "How can I help you, Mr. Reedy."

"I, uh, may have some information for you."

"In regards to?"

"Debbie Holmes."

"Are you available now?"

"Yes. I'm home. But I'd really like to keep this as confidential as possible."

"Of course. I'll be there in twenty minutes."

Derrick said, "What's going on?"

"Jason Reedy's father said he has information on Holmes."

"Holy shit! You think it's about his son?"

"It could be."

"Why didn't he say something before?"

"Good question. Let's see how he responds to it."

"Can't wait."

Keeping in mind what Mary Ann mentioned about style, I said, "Look, he wants to keep it low-key, so let me go there alone."

THE BOAT WAS STILL on the side of the Reedy house. Pulling to the curb, the garage door opened. It looked like Jason Reedy.

He bent down, revealing much less hair than Jason. It had to be the kid's father. "Mr. Reedy?"

Hands in a toolbox, he looked up, "Detective?"

We shook hands. "Handle on the fridge needs tightening."

"Always something to do."

"It's brand new, but it's the third time I've had to tighten it."

"Everybody complains about appliances. They're made to fail, it seems."

"No doubt, and you have to wait weeks to get one."

I followed him to the kitchen. "You said you had information on Debbie Holmes."

He frowned. "Terrible what happened to her. She was a nice girl."

"That's what we've heard. What did you want to tell us?"

"Well, that night, the night she went missing, I saw something, and I think it's important."

"What did you see?"

"A young man named Javier Lopez."

"Where was this?"

"On Livingston, by Hamilton Place, it's right before where Debbie lived."

"What time?"

"It was around eight."

"How do you know Mr. Lopez?"

"Pretty good. I used to coach, or really help out the base-ball coach, and he was on the team a couple of years ago."

"And you're certain it was him?"

"A hundred percent."

"What was he doing?"

"He was in the right-hand lane, going real slow. That's how I saw him. He stood out, if you know what I mean?"

"And what were you doing?"

"I went out for a walk."

"And you're certain it was the night of May twenty-third?"

"Absolutely, my wife was away that night. You have to remember our family loved Debbie. When she disappeared, we were shocked."

"Why didn't you tell us you saw Mr. Lopez before today?"

"I know I probably should have, but I didn't think Javier was a kidnapper, but when we learned she'd been murdered, I started thinking."

"On your way back, did you see anything?"

"I'm not sure, but he could've been parked in the lot for those car condos."

Another concept unheard of ten years ago. "The ones across from Briarwood?"

"Yeah, I can't be certain, but driving by, it looked like his car."

They had to have cameras. "Can you recall which building?"

He scrunched his nose. "Somewhere in the middle?"

"Your son and Mr. Lopez were rivals."

"Oh, I wouldn't say that. It's just the normal teenage testosterone thing between boys. You remember those days, don't you?"

"What kind of a car was Mr. Lopez driving?"

"A white SUV. Not one of those big ones; like a normal size. It was Japanese."

"Where was your son that night?"

"My son? What does he have to do with this?"

"Please answer the question."

"He was home, with me."

"Was you wife also there?"

"No, I said she was away with her mother visiting her sister in Orlando."

"What do you think happened to Debbie Holmes?"

"Somebody either grabbed her off her bike, or she left it behind and got into a car with somebody."

"And you think that somebody could be Javier Lopez?"

"I don't know, but that boy was there that night."

38

"YOU SHOULD'VE HAVE SEEN THE FATHER; HE LOOKS EXACTLY like his son.

Derrick said, "It's the other way around; the kid looks like his father."

Was he going for a masters in English? "Whatever. Anyway, he said Lopez was on Livingston the night Holmes disappeared."

"He could've been, because he wasn't working out in the pool that day."

"Really?"

"Yep. Coach said they give each kid a day off every other week to rest their bodies and the twenty-third was Lopez's day off."

"The frigging kid lied so easily."

"They have a lot of practice."

"We need to dig into him. Find out if he's acted aggressive, especially to women."

"It'd be nice to get a peek at his juvenile record."

"We'll need more for that."

My cell rang. "It's Bilotti. Do me favor and find out what kind of car Lopez drives."

"Hey, Doc, how are you?"

"Pretty good. Wanted to update you on Deborah Holmes."

"What do you have?"

"We believe her death likely occurred Wednesday the twenty-fifth or early on Thursday the twenty-sixth."

So much for living long and dying fast. The poor girl missed on both. "Cause of death unchanged as suffocation?"

"Yes. The bruises she suffered weren't deep, not from a weapon."

"Related to a struggle?"

"It's possible, but with the decomposition, it's impossible to determine. However, as to being held captive, it's inconclusive as well, but the bruising around one wrist is suggestive."

"Suggestive? That's as far as you can go?"

"Sorry, Frank. I'm unable to be definitive. I wish I could be of more help."

"I get it, Doc. But it's better to apologize with a nice bottle."

He chuckled. "By the way, another wine buddy of mine is going to the McCormick wedding. We're both bringing a bottle or two to the affair."

"Now we're talking."

"I'm looking forward to it, but be forewarned, I'm not dancing with you."

"If you ever see me on a dance floor, I've had too much to drink."

After updating Derrick, he said, "Guess who drives a 2015 white Acura MDX?"

"Lopez?"

"Yep."

"It's an SUV?"

"Sure is."

"Let's get as much on Lopez as we can. We know nothing about him."

"Why don't you see if we can get a peek at his juvie file?"

"It's a long shot."

"Go for it. I'll get what I can on Lopez."

Sheriff Remin was stepping out of the elevator. "Sir, can I speak with you?"

He looked at watch. "I only have a minute. The commissioner is on his way."

"That's fine."

Remin slid behind his desk. "I'm assuming this is about the Holmes case?"

"Yes, sir."

He glanced at a note on his desk. "Get to it."

"We're taking a close look at someone. It's a passion angle, and he was placed in the vicinity where Holmes was last seen."

Remin raised his eyebrows. "Sounds promising."

"It does. But at this point, that's all we have. The person of interest is a college student named Javier Lopez."

"What do you need from me?"

"He has a juvenile record—"

"And you want to get a look at it?"

"It could be helpful. If we learn what the crime was, that may be enough."

"Let me see what I can do. I'd really like to wrap this one up as soon as possible."

That made two of us. "Thank you, sir. I'll jot down his name and social."

Derrick was on the phone, taking notes. He hung up. "Apparently, there's two juvie files on Lopez. What did Remin say?"

"He's going to get us a look or at least let us know what the charges were."

"Good. Lopez was raised by his father. The mother died three years ago."

Lopez wasn't a child when he lost his mom, but it was a blow; I knew all too well. "Only child?"

Reaching for the ringing phone, Derrick said, "Yeah."

He put the call on hold. "It's Felix Ramos. When is he going to prison?"

My shoulders sagged. "In about ten days." I picked up the receiver. "Hello, Mr. Ramos."

"Hi, Detective Luca. I'd like an update on my daughter's case."

"There isn't much I can disclose at this point."

"What is that supposed to mean?"

It was a good question. "We're working it and have developed a composite sketch—"

"You know what he looks like?"

Mentioning the drawing was a mistake. "Possibly."

"Why haven't you released it to the public?"

"We don't want him to run off."

"You know who it is but don't know where he is?"

"That's all I can say at this point. I've got to go, sir."

"Look, I know you're trying to find who murdered that poor girl. I get it, but don't forget what happened to my Lisa."

"Trust me, sir, I won't. As soon as I have something, I'll let you know."

Hanging up, I said, "Ramos lost it, but as a father, I feel for him."

"It must be exasperating."

You didn't need a newspaper subscription to get the word of the day. But most times, he didn't use it in the proper context. "Holmes is the priority, but there's a rapist out there we need to nail."

"Can you imagine? We grab the bastard, and he gets locked up with Ramos?"

"You might be watching too much TV."

"That'd be a good twist."

"It'd feel good for a minute, but you don't want your kid growing up in a place where that happens. We're the law; our justice system might not be perfect, but it's better than some kind of free-for-all."

"Of course, man. I'm just saying—"

"Forget it! We got work to do."

Derrick's chair slammed into the wall as he stormed out.

The Holmes murder had pushed the rape into the background. It was both understandable and unforgivable. Waiting on possible access to the juvie files provided a chance to get back to the Ramos case.

Staring at the sketch, I begged it to send a message. The eyes were beady. But the so-called witness was Noon. He was pulling from every movie he'd ever seen. Tossing it to the side, I opened the Ramos case file.

Reading the interview notes I had taken, my stomach turned. We had to stop this predator. Spreading out pictures of the sex offenders we knew about, my heart began pounding.

39

PAGING THROUGH THE FILES, I PULLED OUT RICHARD SHAW'S. He'd been released early, agreeing to be chemically castrated. It was why we passed him over.

Had we missed something? Grabbing the phone, I tapped in a number.

"Brian O'Leary, Department of Corrections."

"Hey, Brian, it's Luca."

"Yo, Frankie, how's it hanging?"

"Good. You?"

"Everything's cool. What's up?"

"I'm working a rape case, and I want to check up on somebody."

"What do you mean?"

"Guy's name is Richard Shaw. He was released early. The records indicate he's been getting his doses."

"Okay, what about it?"

"Just want to be sure there's been no mistake."

"We record the lot number and the date. You know, these guys got to come in person."

"Can you check?"

"Sure thing, Frankie. Hang on."

He clicked away on his keyboard. "All right, I got it right here. Shaw has made every one of his monthly appointments and received the required dose each time."

"Okay. Just wanted to check."

"No problem, buddy. Good to hear from ya."

"Be well, my friend."

It was worth checking. I punched in Bilotti's number. "Hey, Doc, you have a minute?"

"What's on your mind?"

"Does chemical castration work?"

He chuckled. "I have to say, I didn't see that one coming."

"You don't get asked that every day?"

"Never more than once a week."

"We're chasing a ghost in the Ramos case. A couple of recently released pervs are in the castration program. Should we be taking a closer look at them?"

"I'm not an expert in the field, but the drug administered significantly reduces testosterone. It effectively reduces it to as low as one percent of normal levels."

"Wow, it really reduces sex drive."

"Yes, and seminal fluids. But it doesn't mean a predator couldn't attack a woman. What drives these offenders is more than their sex drive. The majority is about power."

"I'm aware of that."

"The reality is, predators could be abusive even when unable to penetrate a victim."

Ramos had been penetrated. "It effects the ability to get an erection?"

"Yes."

"Thanks, Doc."

"Glad to be of help. Have a good one."

"Hold on a sec."

"Yes?"

"Is there a way to reverse it?"

"The effects of the pharmaceuticals used?"

"Yes."

"Well, time itself, erodes the effectiveness."

"Like what's happening to all of us."

He chuckled. "Father Time is undefeated."

It was my line, but he could have it. "Amen. What I meant was an antidote for the castration medicines."

"There might be. I just don't know enough about that class of drugs."

"Is there a way you can check into that?"

"I'll see what research is available."

"Thanks, Doc."

Derrick came in with a coffee. He didn't have one for me. My partner sat behind his desk.

It was hard to focus with a grown man acting like a twelve-year-old.

After ten minutes of silence, I said, "While we're waiting on Remin, you want to take the sketch to the kid who saw the man in the park?"

He shrugged. "All right."

"We're going to need to know if Noon is being himself or if he's onto something."

I handed him the sketch, and he walked out without saying anything.

Our approach was focusing on known sex offenders. It was an obvious thread to follow. But was it the right strategy?

We had nothing. If the kid confirmed the sketch looked like the man he saw, we'd go public with it. If not, we had nothing.

Waiting for him to strike again didn't qualify as a plan.

Increasing patrols were an option, but we couldn't be everywhere.

The idea to lure the rapist with a decoy seemed to be a reasonable option. It was dangerous using an officer as bait. Even though we'd be watching, things could go wrong fast.

That risk was real. When Mary Ann worked in the Sex Crimes Unit, she was used to drawing a pervert out. Even though it was over the internet, in a chat room, I objected.

The setup was successful, and the pervert was doing time. Mary Ann could have valuable insight on how to approach putting together a sting operation.

I called, but after six rings, it went to voice mail. She was probably working. I texted her to call when she could, and pulled out another file.

The Samus woman had barely escaped from who we thought was the same man who'd assaulted Ramos.

My phone pinged a text: "Not feeling good. In bed."

"What's the matter?"

"I don't know. I'll be okay."

She was hiding something. Derrick was going to be out for a good hour, and we were waiting on Remin. Grabbing the keys, I headed for the door.

The blinds in the den were down and the house quiet. Making a beeline to the bedroom, I slowly opened the door. I squinted.

Mary Ann was under the covers.

Sitting on the edge of the bed, I felt her forehead. It was cool.

"Mary Ann?"

Her eyes cracked open. "Frank, what are you doing here?"

"I was worried about you."

"I'm okay."

"Lying in the dark in the middle of the day doesn't line up with okay."

She closed her eyes.

"It's the MS, right?"

She shrugged.

"Where? Your face?"

She nodded. "My whole head."

It wasn't the time to rant about her job being stressful. Mary Ann knew me better than I knew her, but the fact the new job was getting to her, couldn't be hidden from me.

"Did you call the neurologist?"

She nodded.

"What did they say?"

"To give it a day."

The new drugs had kept her MS at bay. It was stress that brought it back. She didn't see the irony of working to build back our retirement savings but being too sick to enjoy the so-called "golden years."

40

———————

WEIGHING WHETHER OR NOT TO CALL THE NEUROLOGIST TO ask them to tell Mary Ann to stop working, Derrick breezed into the office.

"How'd it go?"

"The kid said the sketch looked like the man he saw in the park."

"Good work. I think we should go public with it."

"Whatever you think."

"It's not whatever I think; we're partners. I'd like some feedback."

Derrick opened his mouth but shut it. He stood there mulling what to say. It was smart, something Dr. Bruno had coached me on.

As he went to his desk, my cell rang. "It's Remin."

"Hello, sir."

"Are you in the office?"

"Yes. Why?"

"Come on up. I have a summary of the juvenile files you asked about."

"On our way."

Hanging up, I said, "Let's go. Remin has info on Lopez's juvie cases."

"You want me to go?"

One arm in the sleeve of my sports coat, I said, "Sure."

Walking up the stairs, I said, "You think it's all right to call Mary Ann's doctor without telling her?"

"What's the matter?"

"Her MS flared up. I know it's because of the job. Stress is really bad for her."

"I'm sorry to hear. She going to be all right?"

"Yeah, but I want the doctor to tell her to quit."

"Oh boy."

"What do you think?"

"I hate to throw it back at you, but you're the one who says never to get involved in what happens under another man's roof."

It was sound advice. Pushing open the door to the second floor, I said, "I'm going to call. I don't care if she gets pissed. She's putting her health at risk."

We were ushered into the sheriff's office. Remin was on the phone and motioned to the chairs in front of his desk.

He finished the call and said, "Detectives, I don't have to remind you how sensitive this data is."

"We know, sir. We appreciate you getting it."

He looked each of us in the eye. "I had to call in a favor. I'm hoping this helps."

"We understand.".

Remin picked up a yellow legal pad.

"Lopez, and another unnamed minor, were caught shoplifting at the Coastland Mall in September of 2017. In the initial attempt to apprehend the youths, they ganged up on the security guard, who suffered minor injuries. They were caught by one of our patrol cars, in the parking lot."

"Were they carrying any weapons?"

"No. They were unarmed."

"But they assaulted the guard?"

"Yes. I'm not making light of it, but the injuries appeared minor."

"What store did the theft occur in?"

"Old Navy."

"Anything else we should know about the incident?"

"No."

"Thanks. How about the second case?"

"Also in 2017, but in August, Javier Lopez and another youth were apprehended at the Crest Lawn Cemetery in North Naples. The minors had desecrated grave sites, knocking over a dozen tombstones."

Derrick asked, "Do we know who the other kid was?"

"That can't be shared."

Derrick's question was a good one. "We understand. Anything else?"

"Lopez and his accomplice had been intoxicated at the time of their arrest."

It was a disgraceful episode, but what it told us was, other than mixing teenagers and alcohol, it was a crapshoot.

"Is there anything else we'd find helpful?"

"That's it, gentlemen."

"Thank you, sir."

"Good luck."

"Um, we wanted to let you know the sketch made in the rape case was confirmed by another witness."

"Good work."

"We'd like to make a public appeal, and see if anyone can identify the man."

"Get it out there as soon as you can."

I stood. "Will do."

We headed down the stairs, and Derrick said, "What do you make of the juvie files?"

"Not much. Could just be the stupid stuff kids seem prone to do."

"I don't know about that. At the very least, it shows poor judgment and a wanton disrespect for not only the law but the dead."

Wanton disrespect? He must have watched *Law and Order* last night. "True. I just don't know how you go from damaging a graveyard and petty theft to kidnapping and murder."

"We don't know if she was kidnapped."

"True—"

"But throw some passion in, mix in male hormones, and it could get volatile."

He had a knack of squeezing in new words, but they didn't fit. Again. "I'm not discounting it. They're criminal acts but not violent—"

"How can you say that? They beat up the guard."

"You're right. It could have been something physical that spun out of control."

"Easily done, especially if he'd been drinking."

"Either way, we need to talk to Lopez."

"I say we bring him in."

It seemed early to do that. "You think so?"

"Why not? We lean on him when he's here, he might cave."

"We're running the risk he'll get a lawyer."

"It's worth doing. If he's involved, he'll be getting an attorney anyway."

"Okay. You want to reach out to him or handle the public appeal?"

"I'm going to bring in Lopez."

It felt too aggressive. "Okay, but keep in mind we don't have much—"

"Don't forget, the kid lied about his alibi."

He was right, and maybe it was style or the fact he was making a point of doing it his way, but it made me uncomfortable.

41

———

Shutting down my desktop, the phone rang. It was an old friend who worked in Port Charlotte's sheriff's office. What he said clarified a situation, but shocked me.

Pinching the bridge of my nose, I tried to understand what had gone wrong. It was the monkey wrench I hadn't seen coming. Now what?

Derrick popped his head in the office. "Come on. They're in interview room four."

"I'll be right there."

We had an interview to conduct, and what I'd learned was going to make it even more interesting.

Even though Jim Ponte was a defense lawyer, he was one of the few lawyers I truly liked. The attorney was whispering into the ear of his new client, Javier Lopez.

Derrick said, "Nothing he's going to say is going to save him."

"Ponte is a straight shooter. He's the first to cut a deal when the handwriting's on the wall."

"All right, let's go."

Filing into the room, it was fifty-fifty whether Derrick

was going to piss off one of the few good guys on the other side.

We shook hands, stated the necessary, and Derrick said, "You loved your mother, right?"

"Of course I did. She was the best."

"You miss her?"

"Every day."

Ponte said, "Detective, is there a reason you're questioning my client's relationship with his mother?"

"Give me a minute, Counselor." Derrick looked at Ponte's client. "Mr. Lopez, who is Denise McCarthy?"

"Mrs. McCarthy? Our next door neighbor?"

"Yes."

"What about her?"

"Mrs. McCarthy was a witness to another one of your angry outbursts." He let it hang for a full ten seconds before continuing, "Your mother was very ill in 2016. Wasn't she?"

"Yes."

"You loved your mother, yet threw a glass at her, seriously injuring her."

"No, that's not what happened."

"Tell us, then."

"Okay, I was mad, but Mom was saying she didn't want to continue treatment any longer."

"You didn't agree with her decision, so you hurt her? Is that what happened with Debbie Holmes?"

Ponte said, "Don't answer that."

"As a result of your violent blowup, your mother suffered a cut so bad, she needed a transfusion."

"It was an accident. She was on drugs that made the bleeding worse than it should have been."

"My client has already stated it was an unfortunate accident. Let me remind you, no charges were filed in the incident."

"Counselor, I'd suggest you have a talk with Mr. Lopez. If he cooperates, before we file charges, we'll have some latitude."

Ponte looked at me, but I averted my eyes. Derrick was going too fast, but Lopez was slowly sinking.

DERRICK SAID, "We'll be able to get a warrant, don't you think?"

"We have a decent shot if we limit it to Lopez's car."

"Good idea. So, we have him at the location and during the time period she disappeared."

"According to a few of Holmes's friends, Lopez's advances were rebuffed by Holmes."

"He lied about where he was, and he's got two juvie cases."

"You can't use them."

"I know, but I can still whisper."

"You don't like this kid, but don't make it personal."

"It's not that I don't like him. I think he did it."

"I know his lawyer, and Ponte really believes the kid didn't do it."

"You can't listen to him."

"He's a good guy. He wouldn't have called me if he didn't believe it."

"Aren't you the one who said never to trust a defense attorney?"

"There's an exception to everything, and Ponte is one."

He scoffed.

Closing the office door, I said, "We have to talk."

"What about?"

"Port Charlotte."

"Who told you?"

"A friend."

He shook his head. "Just exploring my options."

"What's going on?"

"Nothing."

"You apply for the lead detective job in Port Charlotte, and nothing's going on?"

"Just forget about it, okay?"

"No. I got to know why my partner is looking to leave."

"It's a good opportunity. I'd be running things."

It wasn't easy standing by as he used debatable tactics during the interviews, but it was good I had. "You're running with Lopez. Besides, I'm not going to be here much longer; you'd take over."

"It's not the same."

"We'll make it the same. Tell me what—"

"You taught me a ton, Frank. I'm itching to see if I can do it."

"You've done it. You have better instincts than me."

"I don't know about that."

"Let's work this out. We make a great team."

"We do, but it's more than that. They're offering a signing bonus, and the pay is better."

"Let me see what I can get from Remin."

"Thanks, but it's cheaper to live up there. Houses are like half what they are here."

Housing prices were starting to force people out of Naples. "I can't fix that. But you love it here."

"We do. Lynn, even more than me."

His wife could be a major asset. "Happy wife, happy life."

He shook his head.

I had no idea if it were true but said, "And the schools down here are much better than up there."

"Really?"

"Oh yeah. And you want to make me drive to visit you?"

He chuckled. "It's not a done deal."

"I hope not, but for the record, when they called for a reference, I told them you'd be the best in the state—after me, of course."

Gesso knocked on the door and stepped in. "Closed door? Anything I should know about?"

I said, "No. Just played a silly video for him."

"Send it to me."

"What's going on?"

"I just got an update on the hotline." He handed me a note. "This woman called in, said the sketch looks like her brother."

"Amanda Reel."

"Figured you might want to jump on it."

"Thanks, Sarge. The timing's good; we're waiting on a warrant for Lopez."

Gesso walked out, and Derrick said, "You go see this woman. I'll hang here. If the warrant comes in, I'll get a tow truck going."

"You sure?"

"Absolutely."

"You're not going to run off to Port Charlotte, are you?"

"Get going, will you?"

It was tough to imagine doing this job without Derrick beside me. He had a right to do what he felt was good for him and his family. If he left, serious consideration would have to be given to retiring early.

42

———

Standing, Lopez had one arm across his chest and was pressing that elbow into his body with his other hand.

Derrick came back from the bathroom. He peered at the video feed from the interview room and said, "What the heck is he doing?"

"Looks like a stretch. A guy I went to college with was a swimmer, and he was always stretching his shoulders."

"I wonder if the kid is any good."

"He's on a scholarship. I guess he is. How was he when you picked him up?"

"He followed me down here. I told him we just needed background."

Before I could respond, Ponte came out of the bathroom and said, "Let's do this."

We stepped into the room. Lopez had his hands around his ankles. The kid was Gumby.

"Getting your stretches in?"

"Yeah, it's super important. Anytime I'm in a car or sitting for a half an hour, I stretch. If you don't stay on top of it, your muscles atrophy."

Me and stretching were like giraffes on a surfboard. It didn't sound right, but if the kid was right, it was time to reevaluate stretching.

Derrick clicked the recording system on and recited the formalities. Abandoning the good-cop role, he said, "You said you were training the night Deborah Holmes was last seen."

Fear flashed across Lopez's face. "I wasn't?"

"No. You were off that night."

"Really?"

"Why'd you lie?"

Ponte said, "That's an unnecessary accusation at this point."

"Retracted. Why did you tell us you were training when you weren't?"

"I didn't do it on purpose. I just forget, that's all."

"This is going to be a lot easier if you stop playing games and tell us where you were."

"Probably on campus somewhere."

"We have a witness that placed you on Livingston Road by Briarwood, the night in question."

"Livingston? Oh yeah. I took a ride to see my buddy, John. Went to Baron Collier together."

"And you just remembered now?"

"It totally slipped my mind. He's taking a year off before going to college."

"This John have a last name?"

"Boyers. John Boyers. He's got an apartment in Orchid Run, on Livingston."

The apartment community was gated and had cameras.

"We'll provide contact details, Detective."

"Thank you. How long were you there?"

"Oh, I didn't, like, see him. I went there, and he wasn't

home, so I went down to Celebration Park. He likes to hang down there. I figured he might be there."

"Was he?"

"No. It turned out he went to Sarasota to see some girl."

"Let me guess; no one can verify this new alibi of yours."

"It's not new, it's where I was. I didn't know he wasn't going to be home."

"And you didn't know you didn't have swim practice that night."

"No, it's where I am every day."

I said, "As a minor, you've had a couple of arrests."

"Hold on, Detective, those files are sealed."

"Sorry, Counselor, we got permission to view a summary. Tell us about the arrests."

His shoulders dropped. "Yeah, but it was a tough time. My mom had died, and I was a mess, you know?"

Losing your mom was tough at any age, but for a young teen, it was traumatic. "What happened?"

"I mean, it was stupid and I was angry. Angry that Mom, you know, she was gone. I guess I was acting out."

Derrick said, "We want details on your delinquency."

"Well, the cemetery thing, we'd been drinking and we just started, you know, being stupid. It was wrong, and I felt really bad and we, I mean my dad, he paid to fix everything."

"But you didn't get the message, because a month later you were shoplifting, and when you were caught, you assaulted the guard."

"Assault? No, no, that's not what it was. He grabbed my arm and was twisting it. I yelled, and he wouldn't stop. Jimmy, he tried to help me and shoved the guy. He fell into a display and we ran away."

"So, it wasn't your fault?"

He shrugged. "Look, I tried to steal a stupid hat, but I didn't hit anybody. It was an accident. I said I'm sorry."

Derrick slammed his palm onto the table. "You have an excuse for everything. So, tell us how Debbie Holmes ended up murdered."

"My client has repeatedly denied knowledge of the murder."

"Mr. Lopez, what were you doing where she disappeared?"

"That's just a coincidence. I was probably driving past there."

"You took I-75 from school?"

"Yeah."

"Why didn't you take the Golden Gate exit? It's closer to Orchid Run?"

It was a good question. Taking Golden Gate wouldn't have put Lopez where Holmes lived.

"I don't know. I just took Pine Ridge, like I always do. Probably on autopilot."

"You were seen parked across from Briarwood, in the car condo lot."

"No way. I wasn't there."

"A witness saw you."

"They're lying."

"With you, it's either a coincidence, a mistake, or somebody is lying."

"If you continue to berate my client, we'll have to end this interview."

Derrick shook his head. "Mr. Lopez, you're digging yourself a deep hole."

"What do you mean? I'm being honest."

Derrick leaned across the table and lowered his voice, "Look, the best thing you can do is cooperate. Tell us what happened with Debbie, and we'll cut the best deal we can for you."

"What?"

"Tell us how you killed Debbie Holmes!"

Ponte jumped out of his chair. "This interview is over."

After they left, I said, "You might have gone a bit too hard on him."

"He was going to clam up either way."

"Maybe. We need more background on Lopez."

"Yeah, and I'd love to get forensics to go over his apartment and car."

"His vehicle is more likely to have something, but we're going to need more to get a search warrant."

"I'll get it. You'll see."

IN A ROBE, Mary Ann was taking a tea bag out of a mug. "How you feeling?"

"Better."

Her voice was weak. "Here, let me carry the tea."

"I'm not an invalid."

"I know, I'm just trying to help."

"Is that what you're doing?"

"Yeah, why?"

"And telling HR the job is making me sick, is your idea of helping?"

Her doctor wouldn't cooperate. "Come on, hon. We both know stress is no good for you."

Her face crumpled. "I-I just want to be myself again."

"You are. All you have to do is make some adjustments."

She collapsed onto the couch. "Like doing nothing all day."

"That's not true. I don't want you to get so sick, we can't enjoy our retirement together."

"Without money, we're not going to be doing much."

"We will. I don't care if we have to downsize. We don't need much to have fun."

She reached for my hand, but it was my heart that was squeezed. Back against the sofa, I sat on the floor, "Remember the first time we went to Clam Pass Beach?"

She smiled.

"And you caught me looking at your behind?"

My phone rang. "I got to get this. It's Derrick, and he's been on a mission to prove himself to me."

I answered, "Hey. What's going on?"

Derrick said, "We got Lopez. I talked to a neighbor, and bingo, we got enough for the warrant."

"What did he say?"

43

Turning into Verona Walk, I headed over a pink-and-white bridge. The setting was a reference to the ancient Northern Italian city where Shakespeare's *Romeo and Juliet* was set.

Pulling in front of Amanda Reel's home, I wondered what living on a street named Chianti Lane meant. Did they have wine parties? Were Riesling lovers allowed?

Resisting the desire to snap a photo of the street sign, I walked up the paver driveway. Reel pushed open the door. Makeup-less, she had bags under her eyes.

"Come in."

Had a storm blown by, and she'd left the windows of the second-floor unit open? Reel seemed like an honest citizen but was a terrible housekeeper.

"Thank you for calling in."

She frowned. "It wasn't easy, but if Richard did this, he needs to face the music."

"I understand."

"He's not going to know, right? I told them I wanted it confidential."

"No, he won't know you called."

She nodded.

"What is your brother's full name?"

She mumbled, and my jaw tightened.

"Excuse me?"

"Richard Shaw, but most everybody calls him Ricky."

I didn't write it down.

"Do you have a recent picture of him?"

"Hang on, I think we have something from Christmas." She went to a chest and pulled open a drawer. She fished and held one up. "Here you go."

A normal-looking family was crowded around a food-filled table. Shaw was in the foreground. It wasn't the sight of ham that made me ill; it was the fact his file was sitting on my credenza.

I knew the answer but asked anyway. "Where is he living?"

"Umm, 47908 Ninety-Seventh Avenue, in Naples Park. He's renting a bungalow there."

"Okay. We'll have a talk with him and check it out."

"I hope I'm wrong."

That made two of us. "And please don't mention anything to him."

"I won't."

"And, uh, if it's him, don't be too rough on him, okay?"

Lying was easy. "We won't."

Hustling down the stairs, I took my phone out. "Derrick, it looks like it might be Ricky Shaw."

"He's one of the offenders, right?"

"Yep. One taking the castration drugs."

"Uh-oh."

"No. I checked. They said he hadn't missed a dose."

"Maybe there's a way of reversing it."

It wasn't fair, but neither was life, so I said, "I asked Bilotti, but he never got back to me."

"We need to check."

"I'm going straight there. You want to meet me?"

The other phone was ringing. Derrick said, "Hang on, Frank."

He put the receiver down as I hopped in my car. Twenty seconds later, he said, "Frank?"

"Yeah."

"We got the warrant. I'm going to oversee the pickup."

NAPLES PARK WAS a study in contrasts: sixty-year-old bungalows needing updates, mixed in with new homes in a coastal style. The beauty of the neighborhood was its proximity to the beach.

Shaw was living in a bright-yellow block home not more than twelve hundred square feet. Walking to the door, I wondered what a knock-down like this was going for these days.

The 1990 Dodge Daytona registered to him was parked on the gravel driveway. Not an SUV like the sailboat enthusiast claimed to have seen, but it was silver.

The bell hung off the doorframe. Rock music was playing inside. I put my hand through the rip in the screen door and pounded the door.

Shaw opened the door. He had a lot less hair than in his mug shot and was missing a front tooth. "What's up?"

He had a drawl. Instead of grabbing his neck, I held out my badge. "I'd like to have a chat."

"About what?"

I didn't smell tobacco on him, but his teeth were the color

of a heavy smoker. "A couple of things. You want to do this inside or at the station?"

"Oh, come on, man." He swung open the door. A lone recliner, and a TV on a stand were the only items in the room. "I ain't got much in the way of furniture. But we can go out back. I got a picnic table in the shade."

A banyan tree half the width of the house, blocked the sun from the entire yard. Three empty bottles of beer sat on a dirty plastic table.

Medium built, Shaw sat on a folding chair. I brushed plant debris off the bench and sat. Shaw's leg was bouncing like a jackhammer.

"Okay, Mr. Shaw. Before we start, I want to warn you; you lie to me, and I'll get your probation officer to lock you up."

"Take it easy, man. No worries."

"Where were you the night of May tenth, from five on?"

"I was here."

After a month, I couldn't tell you where I'd been. "Any witnesses to back that up?"

"No. I'm a loner, man."

"How can you be sure? It was more than a month ago."

"That's my sis's birthday."

"And what about the fourteenth?"

"Oh, I don't know. Uh, I usually stay home. Them drugs they make me take, make me feel like shit, you know."

"Well, you shouldn't have assaulted those women."

"I know.".

"How often you go to North Collier Park?"

His eyes darted. "That the one on Livingston?"

"Yes."

Shaw wagged his head. "I ain't never been there."

"I told you not to lie."

"I ain't. I never went there."

"We have two witnesses that put you there."

"No way, man."

"They say you were there the night a woman was raped."

"Hey, man, it wasn't me. It can't be, I got no sex drive, man."

"Come on, now, Mr. Shaw. You know rape isn't just getting your twisted rocks off. It's all about power."

"Look, man. I did my time, and you can check. I'm taking my meds every month and seeing my probation officer. I even got a job. It ain't full time, but I got twenty hours a week."

I dug my phone out. "Hold on a second. Somebody keeps pinging me."

Shielding the screen, I opened a recording app and said, "My wife, she wants me to pick something up."

"Be a good husband, now."

"Where are you working?"

"The Auto Spa, across from Driftwood."

"You like it there?"

"It ain't easy getting a job with a record, man."

He was getting less than zero sympathy from me. "Make sure you stay out of trouble. We're keeping on eye on you."

He jumped up. "I will, I will. No worries."

44

———

Closing the car door, I pulled my phone out and opened the audio app. I hit play. Shaw's voice was clear: "Be a good husband, now."

I asked, "Where are you working?"

"The Auto Spa, across from Driftwood."

"You like it there?"

"It ain't easy getting a job with a record, man."

"Make sure you stay out of trouble. We're keeping on eye on you."

"I will, I will. No worries."

The recording would be a good start toward closing in on Shaw. Scrolling to Lisa Shaw's number, I attached the file in a text. About to hit send, I deleted the text and made a call.

"Sarge, it's Luca."

"What's going on?"

"We need to get eyes on a Richard Shaw. He might be the rapist, and we can't risk him striking again before we can build a case."

"No problem."

After giving him the address and the place where Shaw worked, I made another call before driving off.

The shades were all down, and it wasn't to keep the sun out. I sent a text before approaching the door.

I stood in direct line of the peephole. Two clicks later, the door cracked open.

"It's Detective Luca, Miss Ramos."

Slipping inside, I noticed the gray cast to her skin. Ramos searched my face. "Did, did . . . you catch him?"

"We're closing in, but we've got eyes on him twenty-four seven. He's not going to do any more harm."

She nodded.

"You said the person who assaulted you had a drawl."

She closed her eyes and nodded.

"I'd like you to listen to a recording of someone, and see if it sounds familiar. Would you be willing to do that?"

Another silent nod.

"Good." Palming my phone, I hit the play button. Ramos's eyes widened, and she stepped back. "It's, it's him. I know it is."

"You're sure?"

With a look suggesting a migraine, she whispered, "I'll never forget the sound of his voice."

It wasn't the time to inform her we'd probably need her to come in and make a formal statement. The problem was audio identification alone wouldn't put Shaw behind bars. It wasn't enough for a court or me.

Saying goodbye to Ramos, I was haunted by the fact victims of sexual assault were more than ten times more likely to commit suicide.

Nailing Shaw for the rape, or anyone, if it wasn't him, would assure Ramos she wasn't in danger, but it wouldn't reverse anything.

Her father had acted like a jerk, putting more pressure on her fragile mental state. Sitting in my car, I made a call.

"Social Services, this is Sophia Livoti."

"Hey, Sophie, it's Frank Luca."

"How are you?"

"All right. Look, I just left Lisa Ramos, and, uh, I don't know, she's not right."

"It takes a long time for victims and, often, years of therapy to get to a place where life feels normal."

"Can you make sure someone drops in on her once a day?"

"Do you think she's a threat to her own life? Should we consider the Baker Act?"

"I'm not qualified to assess her. But sending someone who could is a great idea."

"I'm going to take a ride myself. If she's in crisis, I'll let you know."

Forcing her into a psych unit wasn't something I was comfortable with, but I didn't want her hurting herself or worse.

I made another call. "Derrick, Ramos ID'd Shaw's voice."

"We'll get that bastard. What next?"

"I want to stop off home to check on Mary Ann."

"Is she okay?"

"Yeah, getting better. Can you ask Gesso to send someone to show Noon and the kid a picture of Shaw?"

"Sure. The one in the file?"

"No, his driver's license is more current."

"You got it."

"What's the deal on the Lopez car?"

"It's on the way to the garage. Forensics is going to get to it in a day or two."

"Ask them to spray luminol. We'll know right away if there's any blood."

He hesitated. "Good idea."

I wanted to say, you can still learn from me, but said, "Don't give me any awards yet."

"We close both of these cases, we should get medals."

"I know what you mean, but our job is solving crimes."

"Just saying it takes a lot out of us."

If he took the lead in Port Charlotte, the toll was bound to be higher. "It sure does. But keeping the victims in mind gives you the strength to carry on. I'll see you later."

Mary Ann was napping on the lanai. I sat on the edge of the chaise lounge and she stirred. "What are you doing home?"

Saying to charge my emotional battery would worry her. "Was in the neighborhood and figured I'd say hello."

"I'm okay."

"How's the pain?"

"It's gone."

"You sure?"

"Yes. I came outside to read."

"Good. Can't hurt getting Vitamin D."

"It's so nice today."

"It is. You talk to Jessie?"

"No."

"Let's surprise her and FaceTime her."

"Now? I can't remember if she has class. It's Wednesday, right?"

"All day."

"She just has morning classes."

"Start dialing. If she's busy, she'll swipe it away."

Mary Ann pressed a button and held the phone at arm's

length. Jessie's smiling face filled the screen. "Hey, guys, how are you?"

Blinking away a tear, I said, "You look beautiful."

"Thanks, Dad. What are you doing home?"

"Just stopped by to say hello to Mom."

"Aw, that's nice. What are you guys doing today?"

Mary Ann said, "Nothing much. Did my laps this morning, and maybe I'll go shopping later."

She hadn't said anything to Jessie about the MS flare-up. Parents liked to shield their kids from worry. Whether that was a good strategy was up for grabs.

"Mom and me are good. What have you been doing, Ivy Leaguer?"

Her smile was like being hooked up to a power plant. It was more than enough motivation to keep as many cretins off the street as possible.

45

———

Derrick was on the phone when I came in. He flashed a thumbs-up before hanging up and said, "That was Skip. He said the kid was pretty sure it was Shaw, said he picked him out right away."

"What about Noon? What he say?"

"Couldn't ID him, but you know Noon."

"He's a good guy. Just wants to help."

"The kid made the ID. What do you think, Frank? We bring in Shaw?"

"I'm not sure. Thinking of going for a warrant to go over his house and vehicle."

"What do you think we'd find?"

"Who knows? The things these nuts keep around surprises me every time."

"I'm not saying some killers wouldn't have been caught without the mementos they keep, but it sure would have made it harder."

"Shows you just how sick these bastards are."

"No doubt."

"Let's draft a warrant request."

A hour later, Derrick said, "I think it's good enough."

"Then run with it."

The phone rang, and Derrick answered. He spoke for a couple of minutes and hung up.

"That was Whitaker. Guess what he found?"

"From forensics?"

"Yep. Take a guess what they found in Lopez's car?"

"Drugs?"

"Nope. Blood."

"Where? The trunk?"

"No, he said there was a smudge on the passenger door. Said it wasn't visible, Lopez tried to clean it off."

"We need to know who it belonged to. It could be anyone's." His face clouded over, and I added, "But we might have something to work with."

"Determining the sex of blood is pretty easy. I wonder how fast they can tell us if it's female."

"They can't have much of a specimen to work with, and end of the day, we're going to need a full DNA analysis to see who it belongs to."

"I'm betting it's Holmes's blood."

"We're going to have to wait. Print out the warrant request, and I'll run it upstairs to Remin. Having him present may help."

The sheriff carried a lot of weight, but his influence wouldn't make a judge sign off if the facts didn't support it. But directly including him in the process involved was an inoffensive way to play politics.

DERRICK TURNED onto Vanderbilt Beach Road. A small squadron of patrol cars followed us into Naples Park.

Approaching Ninety-Eighth Street, I turned around. "O'Reilly is peeling off."

"You think Shaw is going to try and run?"

"He might, but he goes out the back, he'll run into O'Reilly."

Derrick nodded at the car watching Shaw's house. He slowed and parked just past the driveway.

We went up the driveway. We peeked into Shaw's car but there was nothing obvious. Heading toward the house, Derrick said, "The tow truck should be here any minute."

My partner pulled the screen door open and banged on the door. "Police! Open up!"

Shaw opened the door, and I held up the warrant. "Mr. Shaw, we're authorized to search your home and vehicle."

"But I didn't do nothing."

Catching the smell on his breath, reinforced the belief we had the right man. "Step outside. You're not permitted to be in the house. You can wait in the back with an officer until we're done."

"Oh man, there's nothing inside. You're wasting your time."

"Step outside. Now!"

He nodded. "Okay, already, but you got the wrong guy."

Shaw was escorted to the rear of the house. Pulling gloves on, Derrick said, "Let's get this going. It shouldn't take long."

"Keep your eyes out for a sack, hat, or something he might have used to put over a victim's head."

The lack of furniture meant less places to hide. An officer and I went to the bedroom. I stood in the doorway surveying the sleeping quarters.

A bed without a headboard anchored the space. A night-stand with a lamp and dresser rounded it out. Bending down,

I examined a dark-brown spot on the rug. Was the hand-sized stain, blood?

I took my phone out and snapped a couple of pictures before taking my knife out. Cutting out a three-inch square of the soiled carpet, I bagged it and handed it off.

Sitting on the nightstand was a copy of *Hustler* magazine. Even with gloves, it felt seedy leafing through the porno periodical.

The sole nightstand drawer was filled with socks, underwear, and Kirkland aspirin bottles. A chipped bowl sat on a dresser made of liner board. Two sets of keys, a handful of change, and worn wallet filled it.

The billfold held Shaw's driver's license, thirty-six dollars, coupons for car washes at his job, and a faded picture of him and a teenage version of his sister.

The top drawer was filled with papers, including the lease for the house. Was fourteen hundred the right price for the one-bedroom place? Or was it an inside deal?

After asking the officer to bag the entire drawer, I rummaged through the other drawers. Nothing but ratty shorts and T-shirts.

The yellow bathroom was original. A razor and comb sat on the single-sink vanity. The medicine cabinet contained deodorant, shaving supplies, and box of Just for Men.

Opening the doors of the vanity, I peered in. A plunger encrusted with who knew what, toilet paper, and a pack of soap filled the space. I headed into the kitchen.

Derrick spilled the contents of a drawer onto the counter. I said, "Find anything?"

"Not yet. You?"

"There was a stain on the carpet. Not sure what it was but an outside chance it might be blood. I cut a piece out."

Fishing through the spilled items, he said, "Nothing here."

He opened a cabinet door and unloaded mugs and glasses. Taking out the last mug, he said, "He's got a box of macaroni and cheese with his cups?"

He grabbed the box and said, "Looky here. Our man Shaw enjoys his weed."

He held up a dime bag of pot. "Unless he's got a license for medical use, he's going back to prison."

That was possible, maybe even likely, but not enough to get him to confess to rape. "Put it back and take a photo before bagging it. I want to check something."

Going back to the bathroom, I opened the vanity doors. Two-fingering the plunger, I laid it on the bathroom floor. There was nothing inside the bell.

Moving the toilet paper aside, I looked under the sink and came up empty. Pulling my head out, I saw something taped to the back of the drain piping.

46

AFTER TAKING PHOTOS, I CUT AWAY THE TAPE. IT WAS A small, white bottle with Chinese characters on the label.

I opened the childproof top and peered inside: half full of small, pink pills. Tipping the bottle, I spilled out a few.

The hexagon-shaped pills were marked with an L and X. Placing one in the cap, I zoomed in and took a picture. What were these? A pill form of the fentanyl coming in from China?

Shaw smoked pot. Was he doing harder stuff? His teeth were terrible but not meth-head bad. It could be fentanyl.

Being high on something a hundred times more powerful than heroin made it hard to rape someone. Maybe Shaw wasn't using when he attacked Ramos but had been when he went after Samus.

Opening my phone's Chrome browser, I plugged in "drugs with an X and L on them." There were plenty of hits. But they were all for either L or X.

Bagging the bottle, I headed to the kitchen. "Look what I found taped to the sink trap."

"Drugs?"

"Maybe something to reverse the chemical castration? They're from China."

"Figures."

"You know a way to translate Chinese into English?"

"You'd need a keyboard with Chinese characters. We can probably find one online, but send it to Cindy Chen; she reads and writes Chinese."

"Good idea. I'll see what she says."

"We'll need the lab to confirm it."

"Man, I wish we didn't have to wait on everybody."

"Forensics is involved in almost every case."

"Yeah, but they're going to have to expand their capabilities by a factor of ten, to handle everything coming in the door."

"No doubt, they're besieged."

It was hard to argue with practicing new words but saying the lab was swamped made more sense. "Let's have a quick word with Shaw before we wrap this up."

Sitting in the same folding chair, Shaw was biting a fingernail. He stood when he saw me. "See, you didn't find anything, right?"

Wagging the bag with the pill bottle, I said, "What's this?"

"I don't know."

Derrick said, "Come on, Shaw. We're going to find out anyway. Don't piss us off."

"I swear, I don't know what that is. You found it inside?"

"Taped to a pipe underneath the sink in your bathroom."

"I didn't put it there."

"Then whose is it?"

"I don't know, man. Maybe you planted it."

"Stop the bullshit and come clean."

"I swear, man. It's not mine. I don't do drugs."

Derrick scoffed. "Yeah, right. We found a bag of marijuana in the kitchen cabinet."

"Marijuana? Can't be."

"It was in your house, and you live alone, right?"

"Yeah, but it's not mine." He pointed at us. "You know, I think it must have been there when I moved in. Yeah, that's got to be it."

"It'd be a lot easier if you just admitted to it."

"No way, man."

He was adamant. A rape charge aside, the threat of going back to jail for a drug violation of his parole would produce an Oscar-worthy performance from most people. "Would you submit to a blood draw?"

"You want to take my blood? Why?"

"To check for drug traces."

"You're going to put my blood somewhere to say I was there?"

"No. Mr. Shaw, despite what Hollywood says, that is rarer than a politician telling the truth."

"Okay, then. Do it."

"We'll call for an EMT unit."

It could prove he used, but the threat it would be negative wouldn't amount to much.

Waiting for a paramedic, Derrick said, "We should bring this bastard in."

"I don't know."

"We lean on him, he'll crack. We got the marijuana as leverage."

"It'd be better to wait. We'll keep eyes on him and see how it plays out."

The pot wouldn't help us prove anything. But we had the unknown drug, Shaw's tablet, and his vehicle. All we needed was one to come through.

Back in the office, Derrick said, "Now comes the hardest part: the waiting."

"You got that right."

"You said the sheriff was going to push things."

"He's under a lot of pressure on the Holmes case. But jumping the line isn't easy. Every case is important."

"That's not the way it should be."

He was right. "That's the official line. He'll get it moving. Believe me, Remin doesn't want to keep getting pestered by reporters. You know he said something about Naples losing the number-one spot with the lowest crime rate in the country."

"It wouldn't reflect well on him."

My cell rang. It was Mary Ann. "Hey, how are you feeling?"

"Good. I feel a hundred percent."

"Great. What's going on?"

"Uh, nothing much."

That meant something was coming. "We just got back in the office, after executing a warrant on a rape suspect."

"Discover anything?"

"We're waiting on processing, and we found some pills we need to identify."

"You'll get there. You always do."

Her confidence in me belied the fact nobody had a perfect record. "Maybe we can grab something out tonight. I'm in the mood for a grouper sandwich."

"Sure. Wherever you want to go."

"We can take a ride into Bonita, maybe the Fish House or the Big Hickory Grille."

"Sounds good."

"All right, let's see how the rest of my day goes."

"Okay. You know, I was talking to Jessica a little while ago. She's thinking about doing a semester in Europe."

Ah, the real reason for the call. There was always a dance before raising a difficult issue. "Europe?"

"Yes, they have a great program where she can study in Florence. She's so excited."

"Let me guess: it's not included in the ridiculous amount of money we're paying for tuition."

"No, but don't forget she's getting a big scholarship."

"How much?"

"It's only about seven thousand."

"Only?"

"It's a once-in-a-lifetime opportunity for her."

"We're pretty stretched, Mary Ann."

"I know, but it'd be a wonderful experience. Can you imagine studying in Italy? In a place like Florence?"

No, it was beyond me. Sipping a Chianti? That was my trip to Italy. "Man, we're setting up kids for disappointment when they get in the real world."

"Maybe we could go and visit when she's there."

It wasn't a question of *if* Jessie was going. The decision had been made. Did this qualify as being bullied? "We'll talk about it later."

"She has her heart set on it."

"I need time to digest this. Okay?"

"Sure, sure. Of course."

We were trying to rebuild our savings and another leak had opened.

Derrick was on the phone. He jumped out of his chair and pumped his fist. Hanging up, he said, "The blood in Lopez's car is Holmes's."

47

DERRICK SAID, "LET'S GET AN ARREST WARRANT GOING. I can't wait to haul his ass in."

Scraping my knees in my first homicide case acted as a moderator. "It might be better to bring him in and talk. See if he changes his tune."

"You don't feel he's guilty?"

"It's not about feeling; it's about the evidence."

"That's bullshit. You're always talking about gut feeling and instincts."

"Hang on. Instincts are crucial, at least the ones filtered by training and experience. That'll point us in a direction, but arresting someone takes more, if you want it to stick."

"You think I don't know that?"

"Of course you do. I'm just saying—"

"Just forget it, then. Do it your way, like you always do."

"What's that supposed to mean? We work cases together and— Hey, where you going?"

"Out."

Playing back what I'd said, there was nothing to trigger his tantrum. He wanted to arrest Lopez, and my suggestion was to talk to him first. It took a couple of attempts to recall exactly how I said it.

It wasn't as if his superior overruled him; it was the prudent thing to do. If it turned out Lopez wasn't guilty, it'd save us both embarrassment.

What was going on? Applying for the top job in Port Charlotte was proof he wanted to run things. Was he so tired of working with me to wait it out? Was my approach too cautious for the next generation?

Or was something weighing on my partner's personal life? It had to be. I closed the office door and called Mary Ann. "Hi, do me a favor and call Lynn."

"Why? What's going on?"

"Derrick is acting like a ten-year-old. Anything I say ticks him off."

"You'd said he was sensitive."

"Make that hypersensitive. Something must be going on with him. Maybe there's trouble with Lynn."

"Oh no. I hope not."

"See if she'll open up."

"I'll let you know if I find out anything."

DERRICK HAD BROUGHT me the morning coffee he'd been getting for years. The unknown was whether it was out of habit or an expression he still cared for me.

It was hard to separate the personal from the business, but we had an interview to conduct. Trying to talk through what Lynn had said he was feeling had to wait.

Derrick kept his cell phone glued to his ear until Ponte and Lopez were in the interview room. I watched the attorney and his young client on the feed, waiting for my parter to get things going.

The college kid couldn't have been antsier if he was sitting on hot coals. Ponte kept a smile plastered to his face to reassure his client.

Hearing footsteps, I turned around. Derrick gave a slight nod. I said, "You going to take the lead?"

Half expecting him to say, *If you want me to*, he said, "Sure."

"Great. It's all yours."

We took chairs opposite Ponte and Lopez. Derrick got the formalities out of the way and thanked them for coming in. My shoulders loosened.

"My client has gone out of his way to cooperate. And now, you've impounded his car, the one he needs to complete his studies. Mr. Lopez wants to get the press off his back and get back to his life. I have to warn you: we're reaching a point many consider harassment."

"Mr. Lopez is a person of interest in a homicide investigation. The search of his vehicle was authorized by the court and contained some interesting evidence."

Fear flashed across Lopez's face. "What are you—"

Ponte placed his hand on his client's forearm. "What evidence are you alluding to?"

"Deborah Holmes's blood."

"No, no. That can't be."

"Where was this supposed blood located?"

"On the passenger door."

"Interesting, but let's not forget my client had a long relationship with the deceased; whatever you claim to have found, could have come anytime they were together."

That would qualify as a coincidence, and not something I

believed in. The kid squeezed his eyes shut. Was he wishing he'd be someplace else when he opened them?

"Mr. Lopez was seen driving the car, where Ms. Holmes's blood was found the night she disappeared."

"It's the only car my client owns."

Lopez turned to Ponte. "I know where it came from. She scraped her knee when we went to the park on Livingston. She fell and cut her knee."

The mention of Livingston brought Ramos to mind.

Derrick said, "And how did she do that?"

"We were fooling around in the kids' playground. They have these big rocks, and she slipped on one."

"And when did this supposedly occur?"

"It did happen. I was there and other people seen it. Even Mrs. Reedy, she saw."

"Mrs. Reedy was at the park?"

"Yeah, she was coming out of a yoga class and saw us. Debbie was bleeding, so we left right after."

I said, "Detective Dickson asked when this happened. What date?"

"Oh, the day after her birthday. I couldn't see her. We had a swim meet, and they'd kick me off the team if I missed a meet."

"How did the blood get on the door?"

"I don't know. She must've hit her leg on the door, getting in. She was, like, hopping around."

The park had cameras. But were they covering the playground? Unless the kid was a good liar—and many psychopaths were—he could be telling the truth.

Flipping open the file, I checked Holmes's birthday. It was March twenty-second. Almost three months before she went missing.

Derrick asked, "How bad was the cut on her leg?"

"Not too bad, but you know girls, they make a big deal out of things."

Last night I stubbed my toe on the bed and did more hopping than in a rabbit's lifetime.

"Where did you and Debbie go the night of May twenty-third?"

Derrick had framed the question to trick Lopez.

Ponte said, "My client is already on record that he did not see or meet with Ms. Holmes on that night."

"Answer the question, Mr. Lopez."

He looked at his lawyer, who nodded. "Like I said before, I didn't see her that night."

"But you were in front of her house that night."

"I just drove past her community."

"And you parked across the street, near the entrance to her neighborhood."

"No. I didn't park anywhere. I already told you that."

Ponte said, "Do you have any new questions? If not, we'll consider this interview over."

Derrick looked at me, and I nodded. He still needed my direction. We had work to do: check the park's video, check with the Holmeses on whether Debbie had scraped her knee, and ask the lab to date the blood sample.

The tests wouldn't pinpoint how old it was, but the range could be all we needed.

48

Talking to Derrick was important, but bringing it up was messy. It was easier to follow up on the Lopez interview.

Walking back to the office, I said, "That went pretty good."

Derrick said, "Stop with the phony accolades."

"What are you talking about? We have actionable threads to follow. We'll find out soon enough if it's Lopez."

He shrugged. "You know the guys at the lab better than me. You want to ask them to date the blood?"

"Sure. Then I'll go talk to the Holmeses, uh, unless you want to."

"Nah, I'll run down to the park, check what they have video-wise."

It felt like walking around in a hall of mirrors; one minute, Derrick wanted the wheel, the next, he was claiming the passenger seat.

Mrs. Holmes answered the door. Her eyes widened. "He confessed?"

"No, ma'am."

She frowned. "Come in."

"I wanted to ask you about a possible injury, a minor one, your daughter may have suffered around her birthday."

"Injury?"

"She may have scraped her knee at the park."

"Oh, right. That. She was with Javier and fell at the water park."

"The water park? Not the children's playground?"

"Oh, maybe it was the playground."

"When did this happen?"

"Maybe, uh, maybe three months ago, or less."

"Was it around her birthday?"

"Hmm." Her lip quivered. "I'm sorry . . ."

"It's fine, ma'am. No problem, it's not important. If you remember, call me. If not, it's not a problem."

Mothers rarely, if ever, forgot when their kid had a hangnail. And birthdays were events that supported memories. But losing a child was a blow few recovered from, especially in the short term.

Mrs. Reedy came to the door, wearing an apron. "Oh, uh, Detective . . ."

"Luca, ma'am. Can I have a word?"

"With me?"

"Yes, it concerns an injury Debbie Holmes got while at North Collier Park. A witness said you were there."

"Yes, but I didn't see it happen or anything. I was leaving the gym."

"She hurt her knee?"

"Yes. Why are you asking?"

"Just one more thing, when was this?"

"I think right around her birthday."

Mr. Reedy came into the room. "Detective Luca. What brings you here?"

"We're following up on something, and we'd like to know about a knee injury Debbie suffered around her birthday."

Mrs. Reedy said, "Remember I told you I saw her bleeding at the park."

"I remember her saying she lost her balance, but it wasn't a scrape or anything. It was a bruise."

"Are you sure?"

"A hundred percent, and it was weeks after her birthday."

"The date could be important. We need to be certain about it."

"I've got a great memory. Right?" Mr. Reedy said to his wife.

"He really does. I don't know how he remembers things, but he does."

My memory was shot from the chemo I'd been soaked in. It bothered me, but the surgery and drugs had saved me. "How's your memory, ma'am?"

"Pretty good."

"Nowhere as good as mine."

Her husband was dominating, making me uncomfortable. If he had a better memory, great. But the difference in dates didn't sit right.

DERRICK WAS STILL OUT. There was no easy way to getting personal. The only decision was whether to discuss the case before we dipped into uncharted waters. Men like to keep their emotional distance, especially with other men.

My partner swept into the office. "You get any video?"

He shook his head. "No coverage on the playground."

"Damn."

"What'd the Holmeses say?"

"The mother wasn't much help. She's still in shock. Started to break down, so I went to see Mrs. Reedy."

"What'd she say?"

"She remembered her scraping her knee around her birthday, but the husband said she was wrong."

"He denied it?"

"Yeah. Said it was a bruise, no blood, and that it didn't happen around her birthday."

"That's weird."

"Sure is. The mother was talking to me, but he cut her off when he came into the room."

"By all accounts, he's domineering."

"I don't know if he's got it in for Lopez because of his son or he's just a know-it-all."

"Maybe he does, but either way, he's a bossy son of a bitch."

Did Derrick describe me to his wife in the same way? "I don't know if it's too late to separate the two of them and see what we get."

"That ship sailed. And we can't ask their son, Jason. He'll toe the old man's line."

"Maybe a friend or neighbor can clear it up."

"What about asking him to take a lie-detector test?"

It was a novel approach. "That's an idea. But, I don't know . . ."

"You always say you learn something when somebody says no."

He still respected me. "True. I like your idea. Let's do it."

Derrick picked up the receiver. "I'll check Franco's schedule."

"Hang on a second." I got up and closed the door. "I wanted to talk to you."

"What about?"

"Us." It sounded like a line out of a romance show.

He leaned back in his chair. "Okay."

"Mary Ann was talking to Lynn the other day, and she mentioned that I, uh, you know, was inconsiderate at times. You have to know it wasn't intentional. I'd never do anything to insult you."

His silence meant the apology wasn't enough. It was a safe bet Lynn told him everything she related to Mary Ann.

"Bilotti and me go back to the day I got here. The whole wine thing was a total accident. I was working this case and went to see him, and you know his office has all those wine-country shots—"

"I've never even been to his office."

"It's no big deal. Anyway, that day, I said I liked the pictures, and he started talking about wine. He wanted to know what wine I liked and I said Italian. Next thing you know, he invited me to lunch, and he had, like, four wines poured out. It was—"

He shook his head. "It has nothing to do with wine, man. You act like I'm not even there when he's around. It's demeaning."

"I'm sorry, bro. I had no idea."

"It's like you two have a secret club or something."

"No, it's not that. I mean, you don't even drink wine; you like beer."

"Come on, man. I told you it ain't the wine. It's insulting

not to be even invited or included. Just make the invite; if I say no, at least—"

"I get it. I'm sorry, really I am. You taught me something here. I didn't even know I was hurting your feelings, and I should have. I feel like a total jerk."

"I wanted to say something, but—"

"It's on me. I screwed up, big time."

He stuck out his hand. "Let get this behind us."

Bypassing his hand, I hugged him. "Trust me, brother. I had no idea."

"It's history, man."

There was a knock on the door, Gesso opened the door. "I hate to break up the *Dr. Phil* show, but there's been another attempted rape."

49

Grabbing our jackets, we headed to the parking lot. Derrick said, "We have eyes on Shaw. If he didn't slip away, we have the wrong guy."

The thought of telling Lisa Ramos we were on the wrong track shot a spray of bile at back of my throat. Punching a number into the phone, I said, "We have to know if we lost sight of Shaw. If somebody screwed up, you'll have to bail me out of jail."

"I'll be in the cell with you."

I hung up. "McCloskey said Shaw was working, and he was parked outside the car wash all day. Said Shaw was outside most of the day but was out of sight for about an hour and a half—"

"Let me guess, the same time the attempted rape took place."

"It was, but he'd have to have been Houdini to slip out, do it, and get back undetected."

"Tell him to check with Shaw's coworkers—"

"Already got that working."

Derrick turned off Golden Gate Boulevard onto Santa Barbara. My phone rang. "Detective Luca."

"Hey, Frank, you have a minute?"

It was Sergio from the lab. "Make it quick, we're heading out to interview an attempted rape victim."

"Geez, another one? What the hell is going on?"

Good question. "What do you have for me?"

"We have the blood results for Richard Shaw."

"Any marijuana or illicit drugs?"

"None."

"Was there any substance in his blood you couldn't identify?"

"Nothing in the normal panels."

"We'd turned over a bottle of pills found during a search of his premises."

"I'm not aware of them. They're probably sitting in evidence."

"I'll call Gesso and get them released. We need to know what they are. There was Chinese writing on the bottle, but it gave us nothing."

"That's above my pay grade. We're going to have to send it out."

"How long is that going to take?"

"Your guess is as good as mine."

"Come on, Serg, this is a rape we're talking about."

"Just an expression, man. I'll press them as hard as I can."

Golden Gate Community Park was on our left, and the victim lived across Recreation Lane, in a neighborhood called The Coast Townhomes of Naples. A long name for a small group of homes.

Derrick said, "Let's leave the jackets behind."

Swallowing a protest, I said, "It is thick out today."

The hum of traffic on the interstate was the only sound hanging in the humid air.

Derrick rang the doorbell, and five seconds later, the door opened. "You with the police?"

"Yes, ma'am. Detectives Luca and Dickson."

She barely looked at our badges. "I'm Lois Weaver. Come on in."

Weaver was built like the other victims and had brown hair. But her demeanor threw me off.

"Tell us what happened, Ms. Weaver."

She wore a blue tank top that showed off an eagle tattoo. "Some frigging nut jumped me and started groping me like crazy. I was, like, what the fuck?"

"Did you get hurt?"

"No, I didn't give the prick a chance."

"Where did the attack occur?"

"Across the street. In the park."

"Where, exactly?"

"By the baseball diamonds."

"Were there any other witnesses?"

"Nah, it's too hot for most people, but not me. The humidity don't bother me none."

"Did he say anything?"

"Not unless you count whimpering. I tossed him off and kicked him right in the balls."

"Do you have any idea who the attacker was?"

"Oh yeah, it's the same punk you guys had in the drawing on the news."

Pulling out my phone, I pulled up the sketch. "Does this look familiar?"

"Yeah, that's the bastard. If he didn't run away, I'd have kicked his ass. I got a black belt in judo."

Mine was in speculation. "Are you certain it's the same man?"

"Believe me, I won't forget that face. It's him."

"Was he carrying anything?"

"He had a bag or something like that."

"Would you be okay with showing us where the attack took place?"

"Sure, why not?"

"Only if you're up to it."

"I'm so wired right now, getting out will do me good."

THE HOUSE SMELLED like garlic and onions. The day had been stressful but it was going to end well.

"Smells good in here. What are you making?"

Mary Ann said, "Cauliflower and macaroni."

"Sounds good. But don't we need cheese?"

"Picked some up earlier."

"Thanks."

"Heard you patched things up with Derrick."

Woman traded information better than confidential informants. "Yeah. Everything is good."

"What did he say?"

"He felt like I was excluding him with wine and Bilotti. But that wasn't the way it was. I'd never do something like that."

She raised her eyebrows. "Frank, you did the same thing to our neighbor Jimmy."

Bingo. It was clear why most archaeologists were women; they loved digging up the past.

"That was different. A misunderstanding."

"No, you were rude."

"No way. We were going to a spring-training game, and he doesn't even like baseball."

"That's not the point. You can't invite one person in front of another; I don't care what the event is. It's common courtesy."

"You're right. I just, you know, figured he wasn't interested."

"Let him decline, then."

There was no way of salvaging this. "I know. If you see me doing anything like that, try and let me know, but don't embarrass me, okay?"

"I'd never do that."

She had. "Thanks."

"Oh, we need to transfer three thousand to cover Jessica's trip."

She was a seasoned negotiator. "Okay, go ahead."

"Jessica is so excited."

"I'll bet she is."

"Thanks, I know you're worried about our finances, but this is a once-in-a-lifetime opportunity."

Parents always put themselves second. "I'm going to get changed."

"Oh, what happened with the attempted rape?"

"This woman was one of the toughest ladies I ever met. She kicked him in the balls."

"Good for her. But who's behind these?"

"I'm going to get changed."

50

Derrick put a cup of java on my desk. "Morning, Frank."

"Morning."

"You're in early. What are you working on?"

"Going over the hotline calls. I'm not convinced it isn't Shaw. We focused on Shaw because his sister called, but there were thirty others that seemed legit."

"So we're looking for Shaw's doppelganger?"

"They say everyone has a look-alike."

"Yours is George Clooney."

"Used to be, but the clock has changed things."

He scoffed. "You still look like him. Give me half the list."

"Here you go. By the way, it's a negative on the park's surveillance cameras."

"No surprise, the way this has been going."

He was right. After each of us made a handful of calls, Derrick stood up. He was on the phone. As he hung up, he said, "Might have something here."

"What?"

"George Eckert. He works at Driftwood on 41."

"The garden nursery?"

"Yeah. A coworker said he looks like the sketch and is one strange dude. And get this, he was off yesterday when Weaver was attacked."

"Where does he live?"

"On Airport Pulling by Orange Blossom."

"Pretty close to the park on Livingston."

"I checked. He got busted for drugs a year ago. He needs to be checked out, and we have time before Reedy comes in for the polygraph."

"Go for it. I don't want to waste manpower or I'd tag along."

"See you later."

Having a lead felt good. I made another call. "Mr. Fernandez?"

"Yes?"

"This is Detective Luca. You called into the hotline about a sketch we put out on a man we're looking to talk to."

He lowered his voice. "Man, you guys must be busy."

Fernandez had a drawl. Was he trying to throw us off? "Crime doesn't take a day off. Tell me who you believe looks like the drawing."

"It's Peter Gatrod. He lives in the building and is a real creep."

"What makes you think it's him?"

"The way he looks at my wife and daughter, I want to punch his lights out."

Tapping the name into the system, I said, "Has he made any advances?"

Before he answered, Gatrod's motor-vehicle picture came up. He did look like Shaw.

"Not directly, but I told them to stay the hell away from the weirdo."

"You live on Derbyshire Court?"

"Yes."

It was steps away from Golden Gate Community Park. "Let me ask you, does Mr. Gatrod have a drawl?"

"Not really."

"Does he live alone?"

"I'm pretty sure he does."

"Do you know what he does for a living?"

"I don't think he works. The creep is probably collecting checks from the damn government."

There was no information in Florida's data base on where Gatrod worked. Maybe the neighbor was right. Time to check it out.

Peter Gatrod lived in a middle unit on the first floor of a six-unit building. His white Ford Focus was parked across the street, under a carport.

The shades were down in all the windows. I parked in front of the next building and peeked inside Gatrod's car. Burger King wrappers and a can of Coke sat on the passenger's seat.

Approaching the door, it sounded like someone was coughing inside. Or was it from another apartment? After ringing the bell three times, I pounded the door with the palm of my hand. Nothing.

Weaver lived nearby. It veered from protocol, but it'd be helpful showing her a picture of Gatrod. She wasn't home. I tucked my card under the door and left.

DERRICK WAS BACK in the office. "How'd you make out with Eckert?"

"He's a weirdo, for sure. Guess what he was doing when I got there?"

"Playing chess?"

He laughed. "They directed me toward the back. And when I saw him, he was following a woman in skimpy shorts. I laid back, and he cut into a row where they have all this pottery. I went around the back, and he's just standing there, staring at this woman's ass."

"Frigging jerk."

"Yeah, and this lady, she must've felt something, 'cause she turned around, shook her head, and left."

"What did he say?"

"He was evasive. When I asked him where he was yesterday, he said he took the day off 'cause his sister was in from Tennessee."

"He have a drawl?"

"Yep, a big one."

"How were his teeth?"

"Not the best but not too bad."

"What about when Ramos was raped?"

"Said he didn't remember exactly, but since it was a weeknight, he said he had to be home. Said the heat from working outside for ten hours knocks him out."

True, if convenient. "How close do you think he looks to Shaw?"

"There's definitely a similarity, but I wouldn't mix them up."

"I know, but we're talking about seeing someone from a distance. Don't forget one of them was a kid and the other is Noon."

"We need to run it by Weaver. She's the only victim who saw him."

"I went by her house to show her a picture of this guy, Peter Gatrod. But she wasn't there. A neighbor called the hotline, saying he looks like the sketch. I gotta say, this Gatrod is a close match."

THE POLYGRAPH OPERATOR was wrapping a belt-like device around Jason Reedy's dad. It was one of the sensors that would measure his respiration, blood pressure, heart rate, and skin conductivity.

Lie-detector test results weren't allowed in court, but the tool had value. At times.

One thing we learned was Reedy quickly agreed to be tested. It signaled he was telling the truth, but that wasn't foolproof either.

The operator, John Hardy, was considered one of the best in Southwest Florida. He finishing hooking up Reedy by placing monitors on two of his fingers and sat beside him, behind the machine.

Hardy said, "Are you ready to begin?"

"Absolutely."

Hardy clicked on the machine and asked, "Are you married?"

"Yes."

"Do you have a son?"

"Yes."

"Is his name Robert?"

"No."

"During this interview, will you answer all the questions

concerning the disappearance and murder of Deborah Holmes truthfully?"

"Yes."

As the graph paper moved forward, Hardy made marks on it.

"Do you know who murdered Deborah Holmes?"

"No."

Hardy made another mark. "Did you see Javier Lopez on Livingston Road the night Deborah Holmes disappeared?"

"Yes."

"Did you have any involvement in Ms. Holmes's disappearance or death?"

Each time Reedy answered, the arm of the machine would move, and Hardy would make a notation. "No."

"Was your son, Jason, involved in any way?"

"No."

"Did you see Javier Lopez parked in a parking lot on Livingston Road?"

"Yes."

Looking at the video feed, Derrick said, "What do you think?"

"It's tough to tell. He seems a little too confident."

"He could be telling the truth."

"Let's see what Hardy says."

Hardy asked Reedy six more questions, and it was over. We thanked Reedy for coming in and waited for Hardy to pack up his machine.

We stepped into the room. Derrick said, "How did he do?"

"He was being deceptive."

51

DERRICK COLLAPSED INTO HIS CHAIR. "INSTEAD OF PROVIDING answers, we got more questions."

I said, "What was Reedy being deceptive about?"

"I don't think he's covering for his son, Jason. Hardy said he wasn't lying when asked if he knew who killed Holmes."

"Could he have it in for Lopez?"

"What could the kid have done? Framing someone for murder because he dated your son's girlfriend would be bizarre."

"Bizarre is the right word, but don't forget the business we're in."

"Amen. How about the nuts who held up the dog-grooming place? They left the cash behind but took the dogs."

"This whole pet thing is getting out of hand. We don't have the time, but it's important to quash it."

"It's the broken-window thing Guiliani used to talk about in New York."

The ex-mayor had turned New York City around. "If you

don't address the so-called little crimes, you'll get bigger ones. But back to Reedy. Why did he agree to take the test?"

"He's got an agenda. But what?"

"I wonder if he may have crossed the line with Holmes."

Derrick leaned forward. "You think he was having an affair with her?"

"It's possible, but it wouldn't be an affair—she was a minor."

"I don't know . . . if she was going to say something, he could've tried to stop her and it went too far—"

"But he didn't appear to be lying when asked if he knew who killed her."

"Yeah. It's got to be about his son and Lopez."

Nodding, I said, "We should've told Hardy to ask Reedy about the scraped-knee timing."

"Damn, I forgot about that."

"We need to circle back to Holmes's friends. Someone might remember the incident."

"I'll start in the morning."

"Okay, I'm going to drop by Weaver's house after dinner. She went to see her mother in Sarasota and will be back around eight. I'll show her pictures of both Gatrod and Eckert."

<hr>

FRESH MARKET WAS PACKED. Looking left, the checkout lines were a cluster of carts. Swiveling around to leave, my stomach took over. Their chicken burgers were good.

Standing in line, my spirits raised. If Weaver could identify either Gatrod or Eckert, we'd know he was responsible for Ramos as well.

But we had nothing to link him to Ramos or Samus.

Gatrod had no priors for sexual assault. If we nailed him for Weaver, the chances of him going away for a long time were slim.

His attorney would argue for a simple battery and assault, and with no major injuries sustained, that's the way it would go. Inching up the checkout line, a solution surfaced.

I cranked up the air-conditioning in the car, sent a text to Mary Ann, and pulled out of the grocer's lot. My idea had merit but required a cautious approach.

The sign outside Wild Pines said they were offering five hundred off selected apartments. It didn't make sense; rents had jumped everywhere.

After backing into a space, I downloaded two pictures of men from the web and added them to an album containing images of Shaw and Gatrod.

Bruce Noon was laying on a yellow chaise lounge by the pool. Fully clothed, he had headphones on. I opened the pool gate and approached.

Noon was rocking his head and jumped when he saw me. Ripping off his headset, he said, "Oh my God. Detective Luca. What are you doing here?"

"Hi, Bruce. What are you listening to?"

"A podcast. You ever listen to *Anatomy of a Murder*? It's all true stuff."

There was enough true crime in my life. "I heard about that one. It's good?"

"Oh man, you gotta listen. The best episode was last week. This—"

"Thanks, but I'm here on official police business."

He pulled back his shoulders. "Is it the sketch? You got the guy?"

"We're closing in."

"Oh man, so exciting. I wish I could come along when you put the handcuffs on him."

"Maybe one day I'll arrange a ride-along for you."

"Really? That would be so cool."

The sheriff's office had a program giving civilians a chance to ride with a patrol on duty. "We'll make it happen."

"Oh man. I can't wait. When?"

"I'll get back to you, but first I wanted to ask you for some help."

"Sure. Anything. What?"

"I'd like you to look at a couple of pictures, see if the man you saw at the park on Livingston is in the mix."

"You see? I told them it wasn't that other guy."

"Here's the first man."

Noon shook his head when he saw the anonymous man. "Nope. Let me see the next one."

Shaw's face appeared. "That's the guy from the last one. It ain't him."

"Okay. How about this one?" It was the other arbitrary male.

"That's not the guy. You got more?"

Swiping to the left, Peter Gatrod's picture appeared.

"That's him. That's the guy."

"Are you sure?"

"Yeah, man."

I swiped back to Shaw's picture. "This man looks very close to the other one."

"No, no. Look here"—he pointed to Shaw's mouth—"the other guy's lips are, like, curved up, and his eyes are closer together."

Going back to Gatrod's image confirmed Noon's assessment. "But you originally said you were far away when you saw him."

"Not that far. It's easy to tell the difference. Look, look at his eyes. See how they're close? Go back to the other one."

There was a difference, but at a distance, it would be hard to discern. If it came down to it, Noon would have to testify in court. Perhaps the prosecutors could have him describe the differences in a couple of people in the back row of the courtroom.

"You've been a big help, Bruce."

His smile was the highlight of the week. "What about the ride-along? When can I do it?"

"I'll set it up. Just give me a couple of days to get this case wrapped up."

The guy who'd tried to help the police countless times had another shot. And if he was right about the Ramos case, we'd have to recommend him for citizen of the year.

52

AFTER THE SCARE WEAVER HAD GIVEN GATROD, THE PERVERT would probably stay home and nurse his bruised nuts. But the assumption was he was dangerous.

Calling Mary Ann, I said, "Hey, I'm not going to make it home for dinner."

"What's going on?"

"I want to keep eyes on a rape suspect."

"You've been working all day. Can't you get a patrol car to cover it?"

"I know, but I was going to go back out after dinner to run a picture of this mutt by a victim. She lives close by. I figured it would be easier."

"What are you going to eat?"

"I'm okay. Just save me a dish of whatever you made?"

"You were supposed to pick up from Jimmy P's, remember?"

"Oh yeah."

"I'll get you a Cobb salad but no bacon for you."

"Hold on, tell them to put a little on, okay?"

"All right."

"Thanks. See you later."

Gatrod's car was in the same spot, and the shades were still down. He had either left on foot or was hiding out.

Backing into a spot in front of the next building, I called Derrick.

"Hey, I wanted to let you know Noon identified Gatrod."

"Wow. It's got to be him."

"Looks like it."

"Let's get an arrest warrant."

"We need to make sure Weaver says it's him before we grab him. I'm sitting outside his place just in case he tries to run."

"I'll come down and sit with you."

We were back on track. "That's okay. It looks like it might be a long night. Gatrod doesn't seem to be home."

"It's all right. I'll bring you coffee."

"Why don't you stay home. I'll call you if Weaver confirms it's him. Then you can get a warrant going and issue an all-points on Gatrod."

"You got it. I'll stand by."

After an hour, it was time to stretch the back. The sky was darkening as I climbed back in the car. In another hour or so, Weaver would be home.

Derrick called, "Hey, Frank, I wanted to let you know I'm heading out to see one of Holmes's friends."

"Which one?"

"Melissa Howser. Dana Foyle turned me on to her, said she was good friends with Holmes. She was visiting family in Austin and just got back today."

"Maybe we'll get lucky."

He laughed. "I thought you said luck doesn't play a part in it."

"It doesn't. You did the work, and if you get something, it's because of the effort not luck."

The phone rang. Weaver was home. Telling myself to drive slowly, I went to her house.

"Hey, come on in."

She was barefoot and had ladybug tattoos on both feet.

"Thanks. Good trip?"

"It was all right. Mom's falling apart. It sucks getting old."

It certainly did. "Sorry. I want you to see a couple of pictures, see if you can identify the man who accosted you."

"Let's do it."

The plan was to show her the same lineup Noon had seen.

"Here's the first one."

"That's not him."

"How about this one?"

"Nope. It ain't him."

"Is this him?"

"That's the bastard. What's his fuckin' name?"

"I'm sorry, but at this point, I'm unable to reveal it."

"That's bullshit!"

"Trust me, ma'am. Just give me a little time to get him into custody."

She shook her head. "Text me the picture, okay?"

"I can't do that."

"Can't I get anything on him?"

"You will. Just give me a day, no more than that."

As soon as I got in the car, I called Derrick, "Weaver ID'd Gatrod. Get a warrant and put out an APB."

"Okay, I'll head for the office."

Crossing over Santa Barbara onto Prince Andrew Boulevard, I gripped the wheel. It took us too long but we had him. He wouldn't hurt another woman.

Pulling into the lot, I surveyed the area. Where was

Gatrod's car? I hit the brakes. It had been parked across from his unit. I slammed my fist on the wheel.

The spot was empty. Gatrod was gone. I'd been keeping my eyes on him. How'd he slip out during the ten minutes I was gone? Was he watching me?

53

After issuing an alert for Gatrod's vehicle, I called Derrick again. "Gatrod might be on the run."

"What? What happened?"

"I don't know. I went over to Weaver's but only for five minutes and when I came back, he was gone."

"Could've just stepped out for something to eat."

"I had the same idea. I'm heading onto Santa Barbara to check the fast-food places."

"Great minds think alike."

"Uh, yeah, right, okay. Look, get the arrest warrant for Gatrod but keep it quiet. Word gets out, he'll be in the wind for sure."

"I'm on it."

"All right, see you later."

"Hold on a second."

"What?"

"I called Melissa Howser, Holmes's friend, to tell her I wasn't going to make it tonight."

I pulled into a McDonald's parking lot. "Okay."

"Well, I asked her if she recalled Holmes hurting herself around her birthday."

"And?"

"She remembered being with her the day after it happened, two days after her birthday."

"So, Lopez was telling the truth."

As I exited the lot, he said, "That's the way it looks."

"Reedy Senior was lying, then."

"We gotta find out why he has such a hard-on for Lopez."

"Don't ask me why it popped in my head, but you think Lopez might have made an advance on Mrs. Reedy?"

"Man, that would be unreal."

"The kid is pretty good looking—"

"And in better shape than Reedy is."

Pulling into a Wendy's lot, I said, "But she's too timid for something like that."

"Maybe she's that way only when he's around."

Though you never really knew someone, it seemed like a stretch. "Could be. We need to ask Lopez about it, see if we can get anything from it."

"We back burning Lopez now?"

There was no sight of Gatrod or his car. "Let's wait until we get the blood dating. If it confirms it's old, we'll lower Lopez on the suspect ladder."

"If the blood is old, then chances are it's not him. We shouldn't waste any more time on him."

Taking chances weren't in the job description. "He lied about his whereabouts and was in the area when she went missing."

"You're right, but—"

"Let's focus on Gatrod. Do me a favor and call the lab, see where they are on dating the blood. Once we know that, we'll grill Reedy."

Circling out of Pollo Tropical's lot, I turned onto Santa Barbara. Where the hell was he? Slowing down as I passed IL Primo Pizza and Wings, I surveyed the area. Nothing.

Gatrod wasn't at any of the restaurants near his apartment. He could be in a bar but was probably on the run. I'd had him in my grasp. Losing him was embarrassing, but the thought of how Lisa Ramos would react, tied my stomach into knots.

Remembering a Mexican bar and restaurant called La Sierra, on Golden Gate Boulevard, I prepared to make a left at the CVS.

As the light turned red, a car shot out of the pharmacy's lot. It was Gatrod.

Grabbing the radio, I called for assistance and put my flashers on. Gatrod didn't slow down. I hit the gas. Swerving into the oncoming lane, I yanked the wheel and pulled in front of him.

Coming to a slow stop, Gatrod veered toward the curb and stopped. The rearview mirror had him with his hands up, palms to the windshield.

Siren in the distance and gun in hand, I got out. "Keep your hands up."

Opening the door, I said, "Get out slowly."

Gatrod complied but said, "What I do?"

He had bad teeth and a drawl as bad as the neighbor who tuned us in to him. "You're under arrest for assault." Cuffing him, a patrol car skidded to a halt.

After handing him off and calling for a tow truck, I put gloves on and checked out Gatrod's car. On the passenger seat were fresh food wrappers. Next to them, a CVS bag.

The sack contained a pack of condoms, a bag of chips, and a box of dish gloves. We'd nailed him just in time.

I called Derrick. "We got Gatrod."

"You did? How?"

After explaining, my partner said, "Grilling this bastard is going be fun."

"It's better if we search his house first. We find something, it'll save us time."

"I'll get a warrant going."

"Good. Look, when Gatrod gets there, record his voice with your phone. I want Ramos to listen to it. We may need her testimony."

"You think the audio could hold up in court?"

"Not much precedent in a situation like this, but if we can't tie him to Ramos with something hard, we might have to use a couple of things to do it."

"We're going find something at his place."

"Let's hope so, but it'll have to be tomorrow. I'm dead tired, and it's going take two hours to do the paperwork on Gatrod."

<hr>

DERRICK PICKED THE LOCK, and we had access to Gatrod's apartment. It was dark and sparsely furnished.

Derrick said, "This place is small."

I hit the light switch. "I'll take the bedroom."

He made a beeline to a magazine-laden table next to a corduroy recliner. "Look at this smut." He held up a publication, with a naked woman tied up on the cover.

"How this crap is allowed, is part of the problem."

"These perverts are flouting the First Amendment."

Flouting? "I'm no lawyer; let's get going."

An unmade, twin-size bed anchored the sleeping quarters. The room's brown rug was two years past replacement time.

Pulling open the nightstand's only drawer, I fished out

two porno magazines. A bottle of Excedrin, and a cheap pair of reading glasses were all that remained.

Opening the accordion closet doors, I surveyed the few items hanging. My gaze went to the shelf. My heart sped up when I saw it.

54

Standing on my tiptoes, I pinched a corner with two fingers and slid it off the shelf. "Derrick! In here!"

Footsteps sounded. "What?"

"This could be it."

"It's got to be. Why else would you have a ski mask in Florida?"

"If we can pull DNA off it, we won't need anything more."

He smiled. "We're overdue for a break."

It was easy to agree. Bagging it, I said, "Let's see what else we can find."

Gatrod was slumped in a chair. Dark circles under his armpits, marred the orange jumpsuit. His body language sniffled defeat.

Brian Getz, a young lawyer I'd worked with once, was assigned to defend him. The only question was whether Getz would face reality and put his idealism aside.

Knocking quickly, I entered. "Mr. Gatrod, Counselor."

Getz offered his hand. His client threw a chin at me. Activating the recording device, I cited the formalities and began.

"I've been authorized to offer a plea if you confess to the assaults."

"We're not interested in pleading. We'll go through discovery—"

"I'm sorry, Mr. Getz, but if your client doesn't accept the offer today, it's going to be pulled."

"Is this a ploy, Detective?"

"Not at all. We have three eyewitnesses, including a victim, who have identified Mr. Gatrod."

"Eyewitnesses are notoriously unreliable."

"Agreed, but we also have an ear-witness. A victim your client sexually assaulted, identified his voice."

"Voice recognition—"

"We're well aware of the limitations, but a jury will find the combination compelling. And then we have the ski mask your client wore, attacking at least one victim. It's at the lab. Forensics is extracting DNA from it. We expect more evidence it was Mr. Gatrod."

"It's early—"

"No, it's late. We get what we think we will from the mask, and there'll be no deal."

"What kind of arrangement are you offering?"

"He pleads guilty to one count of statutory rape, and we'll drop the other assaults."

"What kind of prison term are you expecting?"

"Twenty years." Gatrod turned dishwater gray before I added, "No parole."

Getz said, "But the guidelines are fifteen to forty."

"Take the offer, or we'll go for a habitual-offender conviction, and your client will get life."

WE FOLLOWED Remin into the press room. Derrick and I stood to the side as the sheriff stepped to the podium. Smiling, he was in his element, ready to bask.

"Good afternoon, ladies and gentlemen. We're pleased to confirm the individual who terrorized the women of our community has been brought into custody." Remin paused, and the roomful of reporters applauded.

"Thank you. There's a reason why Naples is the safest town in America; it's the hardworking women and men in our department. They work tirelessly on the public's behalf.

"I'd like to recognize one of them today, Detective Frank Luca who headed up the investigation, leading to the capture of Peter Gatrod.

"Detective Luca, come on up here."

A handful of people clapped. I grabbed Derrick's elbow and whispered, "You're coming too."

Remin backed up, and we stood side by side at the podium. I said, "This is Detective Derrick Dickson. Without his efforts, we wouldn't be here today.

"Like all cases, this one presented several challenges, and I'd like to acknowledge two other individuals whose help were key in identifying Mr. Gatrod.

"These members of the public came forward with vital information. One wished to remain anonymous. The other person was Bruce Noon. The assistance they gave us was invaluable. The department thanks both of you and encourages the public to work with law enforcement to keep Collier County the special place it is."

We walked away from the podium to a smattering of applause.

Derrick whispered, "Thanks. Lynn will get a kick out of it."

"You earned it."

"That was nice to thank Noon. I hope he was watching."

"Oh, he was. I called him."

He chuckled. "He might be calling more than he used to, but it's worth it."

A reporter's comment had Derrick's smile disappearing faster than a dog scarfing up a dropped piece of meat. Remin said, "Well, that's not an accurate depiction."

The *Naples Daily News* reporter continued, "With all due respect, what part is not on point? The fact the person who murdered Debbie Holmes is still free? Or that your department waited too long to focus on her when she went missing?"

Remin's glare was too familiar. He cleared his throat. "We take every missing persons report seriously, especially when it concerns a minor. Let me remind the press and community, that much of the work we do here is accomplished out of view."

"That may be true, but the lack of progress is troubling to say the least."

"Again, I'll remind you that we don't conduct our investigations in the press."

"The public has a right to know, and when an agency fails to be transparent, it's the duty of the press to bring it to light."

Remin's face reddened. "This department is transparent, and progress is being made in the Holmes case. That's all for today."

The attack was unfair, but what was really unfair was Remin's rage would be channeled toward me. We followed Remin into the anteroom as reporters shouted questions.

The sheriff looked at his watch. He turned toward me. "You. My office in twenty."

We retreated to our office. Derrick said, "You better wear your flack jacket."

"He'll calm down. These press people think we're standing around."

"Nobody understands how hard this job is."

"That's true of any job. They all look easy until you have to do it."

My desk phone rang. "Homicide. Detective Luca."

"Hey, Frank, it's Sergio."

"What's cooking?"

"They just finished running the blood from the Lopez car through the Raman spectroscope."

"And?"

"The results age it somewhere between the four-and-seven-month mark."

"How sure are you?"

"We have a a high degree of confidence in the test. They ran it twice."

Hanging up, I said, "Blood from Lopez's car is old. The kid was telling the truth."

"Back to square one."

"We'll develop something. Every suspect eliminated helps focus our attention on other possibilities."

"I know, but I'd like an easy one every now and then."

"Me too. Look, I need to call Lisa Ramos before I see Remin."

"You looking to brag?"

Was I? "No way. I want to make sure she knows, with the plea, she won't have to testify."

Remin's office was ice cold. If he wore short sleeves like most people, he wouldn't have to keep it so low. He motioned to a chair. "Sit down. I want an update on the Holmes case."

"Thank you, sir."

"Where are you in regards to the boyfriend, the one whose car had her blood in it?"

There was no way I'd reveal Lopez was off the hook. "He's still a person of interest, but we're expanding our viewpoint.'

He leaned forward. "Expanding?"

"Yes, there are inconsistencies and leads that just surfaced. It's early, but they're promising."

Remin steepled his fingers. "You heard what we're up against."

"It was uncalled for, sir. We can't rush an investigation."

"Frankly, this one does appear to be taking an inordinate amount of time. Am I missing something?"

Where was a recording device when you needed one? The case was weeks old. "Um, I'm not sure what you're referring to. We may have lost a couple of days thinking it was a kidnapping—"

"I'm not in the mood for excuses. What I want, is for you to apprehend the killer. Is that clear?"

What else would a homicide detective do? Dr. Bruno had said there was no good in escalating, no matter who was wrong. It was solid advice. "We'll get him or her. You can count on it."

The exchange was more proof of why I'd passed up opportunities to move upstairs. It was another thing Dr. Bruno had taught: try to do what makes you happy. Playing politics wasn't it.

Trudging down the stairs, the reality of the decision to

spin the conversation with Remin hit me. It was politics, plain and simple.

It was distasteful but I'd bury it; there was no sense in giving Derrick a reason to take a job in another department.

55

DERRICK SAID, "HOW'D IT GO WITH REMIN?"

"Okay. He wanted to know if we had everything we needed."

"Really? He didn't jump on you?"

Smiling, I said, "No more than usual."

"You tell him about the blood in Lopez's car?"

"No. There's no use in throwing gas on the fire."

"You're not worried he's going to find out?"

"By the time he does, we'll have somebody in our sights." It came out with confidence. Putting on a spin was getting easy.

"I guess we start with Mr. Reedy."

"He has some explaining to do. And after reviewing my notes last night, we might never have followed up with Sammi Cava."

"Cava? I don't recall him."

"It's a she. Jason Reedy said something about Debbie and her getting physical in school."

"I can't believe we missed her."

"We had a lot of balls in the air."

"You know what? I'll run down Cava; you talk to Reedy."

"Sounds good." It was better than good. Walking on eggshells with Derrick's feelings had shred my desire to efficiently use our resources.

The boat and trailer were missing from the side of the Reedy house. He was a planner and rational. If he'd taken off after our phone call, it would be a signal bigger than the ball drop in Times Square.

Knowing people act irrationally all the time, I pressed the bell. Before the ring faded, the door opened. It was Mr. Reedy. Though standing a step below him, I was taller than him.

"Come in, Detective."

"Thank you."

Trailing behind, I passed a side table with a family photo. His son was a younger version of him.

Reedy closed a laptop on the kitchen counter, and we settled around the table we'd spoken to his son over.

"What do you do for a living?"

"I'm a consultant."

"For what kind of business?"

"It doesn't matter. I'm a processes consultant."

"You look at what they do and suggest improvements?"

"Exactly. There's a lot of low-hanging fruit, but it's not easy convincing people to change what they've been doing for years."

"They say the only constant in life is change."

"You have to adapt to the current environment or you're going to lose."

Mary Ann liked to kid me, calling me a dinosaur every now and then. It didn't bother me. Even though forensics and technology revolutionized law enforcement, my job hadn't changed much.

We still had to canvas, search for evidence, make connections, and interrogate in many of the same ways we did twenty years ago.

"I guess you're right; look at Borders or Toys R Us."

"I was just telling Jason this morning, you must have a plan, but when things change, you have to alter the plan or you'll be toast."

"You make it sound easy."

"It's not, but it's doable. Look, no one saw Amazon upsetting the book business, but even if you can't control everything, you can still influence outcomes."

It was a reminder my job wasn't preventing people from harming others—it was catching them after the fact.

"Was that what you were trying to do with Javier Lopez?"

"What?"

He knew what the inference was. "You lied about seeing Lopez the night Holmes went missing."

"No, I saw him on Livingston."

"You also claimed he was parked in a lot for the car condo places on Livingston."

"It was the same car. It had to be him."

Since he lied, it was fair game to do the same. "The surveillance cameras have no record of any car parking on their properties that night."

"It had to be that night."

"You also got the dating wrong on the injury Ms. Holmes suffered. It didn't happen weeks after her birthday."

"That's not how I remember it. She could have had a second injury."

"Who are you protecting?"

"Nobody. What makes you believe I'm trying to protect somebody?"

"You lied during the polygraph."

"No, I didn't. Those machines aren't accurate."

"Were you and Ms. Holmes engaged in an inappropriate relationship?"

"Of course not. She's a kid, for God's sake."

"Sometimes kids misinterpret things, and if they have a crush on an adult, can make an advance. Is that what happened?"

"No."

"Did anything transpire between the two of you?"

"Absolutely not."

"What do you have against Javier Lopez?"

"Nothing."

"Come on, Mr. Reedy. You tried to frame him."

"That's ridiculous. I did nothing of the sort. All I wanted to do was help catch whoever killed Debbie."

"And keep the focus off you and your son?"

"My son? What does Jason have to do with this?"

Reedy had to know those closest to a victim were likely suspects. "We're going to find out."

"Great, I try to help the police—they don't like what I've said and are going after my son, to retaliate?"

"Mr. Reedy, you agreed to take a polygraph and lied during it. What are you hiding?"

"You're forcing me to repeat myself. I'm not hiding anything. I told you what I know."

"I don't think you're telling me everything. You're holding back. If you don't come clean, I'll make it my business to find out what or who you're protecting. And when I do, I'm coming after you for obstruction."

"Obstruction? That's ridiculous. I came to you with information—"

"That doesn't matter, if you misdirected the investigation.

It's a chargeable offense, and we'll make sure it's prosecuted to the full extent of the law."

"This interview is over. I'd like you to leave."

DRIVING BACK TO THE OFFICE, I rolled around who Chris Reedy might be trying to protect. The easy answer was himself. Had he crossed the line with Holmes? There was no evidence Holmes had been sexually assaulted. And she wasn't pregnant.

But if she were about to reveal something had happened between them, Reedy would be ruined, if not imprisoned. That was enough motivation.

Reedy denied it but who wouldn't? He needed a closer look. His son, Jason, was the other person he could be protecting. What parent wouldn't protect their child?

The problem with either was, when asked during the polygraph if he knew who killed Holmes, Reedy said no and appeared to be telling the truth.

Running scenarios, like the chance two people were involved and he couldn't determine who did it, or that he witnessed something but was uncertain how it ended, I pulled into the office parking lot.

56

___

GETTING OUT OF THE CAR, I GRABBED FOR MY KNEE. A SHOT of pain hit the side of my kneecap. Where the heck did that come from?

Every step I took, the pain returned. It wasn't sharp, but it made me limp. Entering the office, Derrick said, "You hurt your leg?"

"Not that I know of. Getting out of the car it started hurting."

"Getting old, buddy."

"Thanks, pal, just what I needed to hear."

He got up. "Where does it hurt?"

I pointed to the inside of my knee. "Right here."

"It's probably your meniscus."

"What's that?"

"A piece of cartilage that's like a shock absorber. You probably have a small tear or aggravated it."

"It heals on its own?"

"Most times, but if there's a big tear, it won't."

"It can't be bad; I didn't do anything to hurt it."

"Just take it easy. It'll be okay. How'd it go with Reedy?"

After briefing him, I said, "Something is there, but he isn't going to give it up. We have to fish around him. We can try to talk to his son. If his father makes him lawyer up, then we can assume he's the one being protected."

Derrick sat on the edge of my desk. "You said he denied having an affair with Holmes. I'm not messing with her reputation, but she was dating Jason Reedy and Javier Lopez at the same time. Maybe she was a little, you know, uh, adventurous."

"It seems like a stretch, but then again, some of the crap we've seen is unbelievable."

"We'll talk to some neighbors—"

"As much as I dislike this guy, we have to be careful what we say. Putting something like that out there will ruin him."

"True. But knowing he cheated on his wife would go a long way."

"Did you get anything out of Sammi Cava?"

"She's a tough kid. I don't think there's anything there, but Cava said we should also be talking to Joey Centro. Apparently, this kid was tight with Jason and Holmes and had a crush on her."

My cell vibrated. "Let me get this. It's Sergio from the lab."

"Hey, Serg, what's going on?"

"The feds just emailed a report on those pills you seized. The ones with the Chinese writing on them."

"And?"

"It's a homemade compound with several components; testosterone, dopamine, vitamins D and E, a bit of L-arginine, and traces of Chinese supplements, like ginger root."

"Would this increase a man's sex drive?"

"Testosterone replacement is a go-to for those with low levels, but the pills only contained fifteen percent of it."

"What's the L one?"

"L-arginine is a blood-flow enhancer and used to treat ED."

Was that in the pills I had taken months ago when I was having trouble? "Did the feds know what this was?"

"No. It's considered unidentified."

"What do you think?"

"I'm not a pharmacist, but based on the testosterone, blood-flow drugs, and supplements, I'd say it's some home-made Chinese potion to increase sex drive."

It was a good call, considering Sergio didn't know Shaw was chemically castrated. We'd been wrong about Shaw, but it was clear he was trying to reverse the effects of the treatment he'd used to get out of prison.

Whether it was enough to put him back behind bars wasn't my decision. My obligation was to report what we'd learned and let the prosecutors and court determine if it violated the terms of his parole.

THERE WERE a couple of ways to find out if Chris Reedy was unfaithful. Asking his wife might not get to the truth, as he was too dominating. Interviewing neighbors was another path, but the easiest was talking to one of the wife's friends.

We'd picked up a couple of names. Derrick was talking to a Charlene Grazi, and I was two doors away, ringing the bell where Gwen Lee lived. A woman in her late forties opened the door.

"Mrs. Lee?"

"Yes. Can I help you?"

Flashing my badge, she placed her hand on her chest. "Oh my God, what happened?"

"Nothing, ma'am. We're conducting routine interviews regarding the Holmes murder."

"What a shame. Janet said Jason is heartbroken."

"You're a close friend of Mrs. Reedy, right?"

"Yes, we met before she moved to the block. It was funny we ended up on the same street."

"That's nice. Is your husband friends with Mr. Reedy?

She winced. "Not really."

"Oh, that's too bad."

"To tell you the truth, Chris is too high strung for my husband."

"Everybody is different."

"It's funny because they're both good friends with James. He lives four houses down."

"What's his last name?"

"Fernwood."

"By the way, anything we discuss is confidential."

"Oh, okay."

"You mentioned Mr. Reedy is high strung. I know what you mean by that. There's no doubt who wears the pants in that house." I chuckled.

"That's the truth."

"How is the Reedys' marriage?"

Her face clouded. "I give Janet a lot of credit. He can't be an easy man to live with."

Had my wife ever said that about me? "She confides in you?"

"Not much. She's private."

"Do you think he's been unfaithful to her?"

"To be honest, it wouldn't surprise me."

Why did people use the expressions "to be honest" and "to tell you the truth"? Was everything said previously a lie? "What makes you say that?"

"Just a feeling, that's all. Why are you asking so many questions about him?" She put her hand over her mouth. "Don't tell me he was involved . . ."

"It's completely routine. We need to build profiles on everyone who knew the victim. But since you brought it up, do you think he could have done it?"

"Chris? You mean, uh, kill someone?"

"Yes."

"I don't think so, but I really wouldn't know."

It was clear this lady didn't like or trust Mr. Reedy. "Do you know their son, Jason?"

"Of course. Why?"

"What can you tell me about him?"

"He's just like his father."

"What do you mean by that?"

"They both kind of, like, think they're superior or something. Especially, Chris."

57

CROSSING THE STREET, I REALIZED MY KNEE DIDN'T HURT. The pain couldn't be from a tear. It was probably strained.

The street was bathed in sunlight. Over the last couple of days, all the curb trees had been pruned back. The green was gone, replaced by stubby limbs that'd be bushy in weeks.

James Fernwood's house had a circular driveway and an island filled with red flowers. Over the gurgle of a fountain off the front door, I heard a man's voice. He was on the phone. But who wasn't these days?

The bell sounded like Big Ben. Ear to his cell, Fernwood's gaze settled on my badge. "Oh, I gotta go. I'll call you later."

Stuffing his phone in a pocket, he said, "What can I do for you?"

"We're conducting background information for the Holmes homicide and talking to everyone on the block."

"What a shocker that was. I seen her around a couple of times, but that's it."

"You didn't notice anything unusual?"

"Not that I'm aware of."

"You're friends with Chris Reedy, right?"

"Yeah, he's a good guy."

"I understand he's, shall we say, intense?"

He smiled. "He can seem that way, but that's just, like, his outside persona."

"What do you mean?"

"When I first met him, I was, like, you know, he's not the warmest person, but then he found out I was having issues with my blood pressure and panic attacks, and he helped me get it under control."

"How'd he help you out?"

"He introduced me to biofeedback and a guy named Wim Hof. This guy is incredible. He can stay in a tub of ice for hours and keep his body temperature normal."

"Wow. But how did that help you?"

"Through breathing and other techniques, I controlled my blood pressure without meds. My doctor couldn't believe it."

"How do you spell that name?"

"W-I-M, H-O-F. I think he's from Holland. He's amazing. You should check out his website. I'm pretty sure he's got a free video up there."

Did Wim have a way to fix my knee and help me drop ten pounds? "How long did it take to learn to control your heart rate and body temperature?"

"It was pretty fast, a couple of weeks, but I just did the heartbeat stuff. Chris took all the classes; he's, like, a top-level guy."

"It sounds very interesting. I should try it."

"You should. You know, Chris said he never gets sick anymore. The whole program strengthens your immune system."

What couldn't it do? "Thanks. I'm going to check it out."

"Some of it seems weird; you just have to stick with it."

"Will do. Say, you're close with Chris; he must've told you about stepping out on his wife."

"You mean having an affair?"

"Yes."

"Not Chris. He's not that type of guy. He and Janet have a good thing going."

"Thanks for your help, sir."

Nobody understood how frequently we received opposing opinions, conducting interviews.

Maybe Reedy wasn't a wife cheater. But it appeared he had the training to fool a polygraph test. Our expert said he was being deceptive. Had he lied when asked if he knew who killed Holmes?

Derrick crossed the street, and we climbed back in the SUV, and Derrick cranked up the air. He said, "This street has zero shade."

"For now Come next month, it'll be a jungle again."

"Something about the weather makes everything grow, including my hair and nails."

"It does. Look, it seems like Reedy knew how to pass the lie-detector test."

"How so?"

"He took courses with a Dutch guy named Hof, on controlling your body with your mind."

"He's some kind of guru?"

"Apparently. One of Reedy's neighbors said he helped him lower his blood pressure without drugs."

"Placebo effect?"

"I don't know, but the guy can stay in ice for hours, and his body temp doesn't drop."

"That's got to be a scam."

Tapping Wim Hof into my phone's browser, I said, "Maybe."

"Got to be. I bet you he's pimping classes—"

"Look at this." I passed my phone to Derrick.

"Holy shit! This dude is climbing Everest in shorts and no shirt."

Taking the phone back, I clicked on a link for breath holding. "This is nuts. It says he held his breath for six minutes."

"He's a freak."

"I don't know, but if he helped Reedy to beat the polygraph, we have to reevaluate. Oh, and another neighbor left me with the impression Reedy was the type to wander on his wife."

"Interesting."

"You get anything?"

"Yeah, but more on his kid, Jason. The woman two houses down had no love for Reedy senior, but this Grazi lady said the main reason she pulled her son out of Baron Collier High was to keep him away from Jason Reedy."

"What happened?"

"According to her, her son and Jason went to summer camp three years ago, and when he came home, he'd changed. She felt like her son was being controlled by Jason."

"How so?"

"She said she thought it was some kind of spell."

I chuckled. "Maybe he took this guy Hof's classes as well."

"Like father, like son."

"What are the chances the two of them killed her?"

"The father and son?"

"Rare but not unheard of."

"Then we gotta look into them."

"We haven't done much on Jason Reedy."

"The Cava girl said Joey Centro was his best friend, and he had a crush on Debbie. We should start there."

"Uh-huh. Did we ever get that list of kids who didn't show up at school the day after she disappeared?"

58

Taking the step up from the garage, a stabbing pain hit my knee. I paused and reached for it just as Mary Ann came out of the laundry with a basket of clean clothes.

"What's the matter?"

"Something is going on with my damn knee."

She set the clothing down. "Where?"

"Here. Derrick said it's probably the meniscus."

"It could be. We have the brace I used that time. You should put it on."

Yeah and telegraph to the world I was getting old? "I don't know."

"You could wear it under your pants. Nobody will know."

Busted. "Let me see how it feels."

She headed down the hallway. "Whatever you want, Macho Man."

"How much time before dinner?"

"About an hour."

"Okay." I ducked into the den and powered up my laptop.

"FRANK!"

"Yeah?"

"We're ready to eat."

Fifty minutes had flown by.

Settling behind a bowl of lentil soup, I looked at the steam rising from the dish. I picked up a spoonful, and instead of blowing on it, wondered if I could will myself not to feel the heat . . .

Mary Ann asked, "Frank? Are you all right?"

"Uh, yeah. Just, uh, thinking of something. Did you ever hear of someone called Wim Hof?"

"No. Is that Scandinavian?"

"Dutch. Anyway, he's a guy who climbed Mount Everest in shorts and can stay in ice for hours without it affecting his body temperature."

"That's weird. It must be something biological."

"Hof claims the ability to control his body with his mind and through breathing. He can hold his breath forever."

"I read something a while ago on biofeedback. People in a clinical trials were able to control their heart rate just by getting the information on what it was doing."

"This guy has a couple of free videos. We should watch them together."

"Let me guess; he has one that can effect your partner's sex drive."

"Now, that's a class I'd sign up for."

We both laughed, and I said, "Seriously, he says they're able to reduce stress. We should give it a try."

DERRICK WAS BEHIND HIS DESK. "Morning, Frank."

"Morning."

"How's the knee?"

"So-so." I lowered my voice. "I'm wearing a brace. Mary Ann made me."

"The support is good. You don't want to make it worse."

Nodding, I said, "We get that list from the school?"

"Let me check my email."

Easing into my chair, I powered up my desktop. Derrick said, "It came in. Want me to forward a copy?"

"Print it."

He handed me a two sheets of warm paper. "Geez, these many kids are out on a normal day?"

"I'm pretty sure there're close to two thousand students going to Baron Collier High."

"There must be fifty kids on this list. That seems like a lot."

"Who knows. Maybe something went around."

"We have to cross-check these, see who is friends with Jason Reedy and who was close with Holmes."

"Why Holmes?"

"No particular reason other than we might get some intel." I ran my finger down the page. "Bingo. Jason Reedy was out that day."

"Interesting."

Flipping to the second page, I said, "And here's that kid you mentioned, Joseph Centro."

"Maybe the both of them played hooky."

"I don't know."

"Don't forget, the mother wasn't home; she was in Orlando."

"True." What kid hadn't taken advantage of a lack of parental supervision. "I'd like to talk to Centro, but Reedy and his attorney are due in under an hour."

59

REEDY AND TOM O'BRIEN WERE HUDDLED IN THE INTERVIEW room. O'Brien was one of the highest-priced defense lawyers in the county. He was tough but fair. I hadn't messed with the room's temperature and wouldn't keep them waiting. I disliked Chris Reedy but didn't want anyone paying a lawyer a penny more than they had to.

They put smiles on as we entered. It was clear O'Brien had counseled his client. Or did Reedy do the breathing exercises Wim Hof recommended?

After the introductions and formalities, I said, "We'd like to thank you for coming in today."

"My client is anxious to clear up any confusion related to his attempt to assist law enforcement in the Holmes investigation."

"Mr. Reedy, when was the last time you saw Deborah Holmes?"

"A day or two before we heard she went missing."

"How do you remember that?"

"Well, it was quite traumatic for our son, when Debbie

disappeared. Jason and her had a long relationship, and well, you remember these things."

"And what date was that?"

"Hmm, let me see . . . Janet went to see her sister . . . yeah, it was a Monday, and Debbie was over that Saturday."

It felt rehearsed, but it was to be expected. "That Monday night, you said you saw Javier Lopez on Livingston Road by your neighborhood, near where Ms. Holmes lived."

"Yes. That's what I saw."

"What were you doing when you saw Mr. Lopez?"

"Me?"

"Yes."

"I was taking a walk."

"Do you walk every night?"

"No, not usually."

"Why that Monday night?"

"My wife wasn't home, and I just felt like going."

"I understand your wife left that morning. So, why that particular time of night?"

"I'd been busy earlier, had a phone call with a client, and wanted to think things through. Walking helps me clear the head."

"But you don't walk regularly?"

"It's sporadic, but I get out there once a week or so."

"How long are your walks?"

"An hour or so."

"You also claimed to see Mr. Lopez parked across the street, in a lot on Livingston Road."

"I think it was him. The car was the same."

"When did you see him? How long after you originally saw him?"

"About a half an hour, maybe longer."

"So, your walk was a short one?"

"Not really, I went on for a while and turned around."

"Where did you turn around?"

"Oh, I don't remember. Probably around Wyndemere."

"You left your house on foot, exited the community, walked along Livingston to somewhere by Wyndemere, and reversed course?"

"Yes, that's about right."

"What we find interesting is, no one we talked to saw you outside your home that night."

O'Brien said, "As was stated, Mr. Reedy's walk took place later that night when people are in their homes doing things like watching TV."

"Mr. Reedy, now is the time to revise your statement. Did you see Mr. Lopez once, twice, or not at all that night?"

"For sure, it was once; the second time, I saw the car and assumed it was him."

"During the polygraph test, the examiner, a recognized expert, said you were being deceptive."

O'Brien said, "Please, Detective, we both know the reason these tests are inadmissible in a court of law is they're not accurate."

"We found it strange your client agreed to take one."

"He was trying to be helpful. The family lost someone they cared deeply about."

"He wasn't being helpful. He was trying to divert attention to Mr. Lopez."

"That's a serious charge you're going to have to back up or recant."

"Your client used techniques from a course he took from Wim Hof to control his heart, breath, and perspiration. They worked to a degree, but you couldn't fool our guy."

O'Brien looked as if Elvis had stepped into the room.

Reedy said, "You don't know what you're talking about. I took the classes years ago, to control anxiety."

His lawyer cleared his throat. "Debating instruction which seriously predates the incident in question is irrelevant."

"What is relevant, is the reason your client lied. Why did he attempt to frame Javier Lopez? Who is he trying to protect? Did he do something to Ms. Holmes, or was it his son?"

Reedy turned to his attorney. "See? They're accusing me of something. What, I don't know."

The lawyer patted his client's forearm and said, "Detectives, with all due respect, casting allegations without evidence is, at best, unhelpful. If you have something tangible to discuss, now would be the time to do so."

"Mr. Reedy is not being truthful. He lied during the polygraph and attempted to frame another man for the murder of Deborah Holmes. If your client wasn't involved in the crime, now would be a good time to clear it up."

"My client has denied involvement in that heinous crime. As far as the charge of framing goes, it could be a simple case of mistaken identify. We're all familiar with the unreliability of eyewitnesses."

"And we're familiar with the type of obstruction we believe your client is engaged in."

O'Brien elbowed Reedy and stood. "Unless you can offer evidence, we're finished here."

60

Derrick said, "That went the way I thought it would. We got nothing."

"I don't know about that. O'Brien wanted to see what we had, and he didn't show it, but we surprised him with the polygraph-training stuff."

"Yeah, but he's right; the timing don't help us."

"That doesn't mean anything. If you trained to be a sniper five years ago, you can still hit the target. It's a skill. Reedy's problem is he wasn't as good as he thought."

"True, but how are we going to use it?"

"Not sure. But we might have enough to get Reedy's phone records. We get a bead on where he was, we'll know for certain whether he was actually out for a walk."

"But if he didn't cross to another cell tower when walking, we won't know where he was."

"The judge won't know about towers. Craft the request, or I can do it, to deal with his location and call data. Reedy may not even have been home, as he claims."

"That's important. I'll get the request going and walk it up."

"Thanks. I've got to update Remin. The interview *WINK* did with Holmes's parents put him on the warpath."

"Good luck with that."

"It'll be okay. When we're done, we'll go see Centro."

———

WE MADE a right off Pine Ridge Road onto Osceoala Trail. Derrick missed the turn onto Cougar Road, and we passed in front of the Osceoala Elementary School.

Pointing to the school's playground, I said, "Look at that."

"What?"

"There's a mother out there wiping down the slide with Clorox wipes."

Making a U-turn, he said, "A sign of the times."

"It's making things worse; if you don't have exposure, you can't build immunities."

We pulled into the lot, and Derrick said, "Remind me to tell you about the immune system and aging."

Aging? Was he referring to me, in particular?

After showing the principal the written consent Centro's mother gave us, we were shown into a conference room. Five minutes passed, and the door swung open. The principal told Centro he'd be outside, and whenever he wanted to leave, he could.

We stood and introduced ourselves. In dark clothes, Centro stared at the table, never meeting our eyes. It was a pet peeve of mine; most teenagers acted the same way.

Centro began cracking his knuckles.

"We know you and Jason Reedy are good friends."

He nodded.

"You knew Debbie Holmes as well."

"Uh-huh."

"Did the two of them get along?"

"Yeah, they were going out."

"You had a crush on her."

"She goes with Jason."

"It's a shame what happened to her."

He frowned.

"The day after Debbie went missing, you didn't go to school."

He stiffened. "I didn't?"

"Not according to the school attendance records."

"Oh, guess not, then."

"What did you do that day?"

"I don't know. I was probably sick."

"That's interesting. Jason didn't attend school either. Was he sick too?"

"I don't remember."

"Where did you two go?"

"Nowhere."

They were together. "Look, I'm not going to tell your mother or the school anything. We're just getting background information for the report we have to file. You wouldn't believe all the paperwork we have to do. I just want to get this off my desk."

Derrick said, "Yeah, they don't tell you in the academy that ninety percent of the time, we're nothing but paper pushers. This case is going to the cold files, so if you could help us a little, we can move on. We have a ton of other cases to work."

"We just hung out, that's all."

"You and Jason?"

"Yeah."

"Where'd you hang out?"

"I don't know, just around."

When my mother used to ask where I was going, I'd just say, 'out,' and leave. "It'd be real helpful if you could give me a place or two. You know, there's a box on the report we have to fill in. Where were the both of you?"

"I'm pretty sure we just hung at Jason's house. His mom wasn't around; she went somewhere with his grandma."

"You were there the whole day?"

"Yeah."

"Was Mr. Reedy there?"

"Uh, some of the time."

"Was Debbie with you?"

"No."

"So all day you hung at his house?"

"Uh, we went to his granny's house to feed the cat."

"Were you guys partying over there?"

He shrugged. "No."

"What did you do there?"

"Nothing, just fed the stupid cat."

"You don't like cats?"

He stood. "Mr. Hitchens said I could leave if I want to and I'm going."

"You sure can. Thanks, Joe."

We hopped in the SUV. Derrick said, "The kid was lying. First, he was sick, and then he was with Jason."

"No doubt, but was it just normal teenager evasiveness or something sinister?"

"They could've been drinking or doing drugs."

"Sure could've."

"We need to talk to Jason."

"We got to go through O'Brien. Call him now, see if we can get together Monday. We can go to them, if it's easier."

"I'll reach out." Palming his cell phone, he said, "You have that wedding tomorrow, right?"

"Yep. I'll let you know how it was. You have plans for the weekend?"

"Nothing big, got to do some touch-up painting."

"Be careful if you're getting on a ladder." I sounded like an old man.

"I'm okay with it. Oh, I wanted to tell you about this drug I researched. It's called Rapamycin. It's called an anti-aging drug."

"Sounds like BS."

"No, that's what they call it, but I read a ton on it, and bottom line, the way it extends life is by strengthening your immune system, preventing age-related diseases from killing you."

"I never heard about it."

"It's worth checking into. The FDA approved it as a transplant anti-rejection drug. But some doctors found out it really helped the immune system. They tested it in mice, and it extended their lives by thirty percent."

"Thirty percent is huge." Did we really want a bunch of hundred-and-twenty-year-olds?

"No doubt, and there's a large-scale trial being done using dogs."

"What about humans?"

"A bunch of doctors are pushing it and using it themselves."

"What are the downsides?"

"They're really not bad, but check them out yourself. I'm looking for a way to get it."

"Make sure it doesn't come from China."

61

The room quieted down as the father of the bride moved aside, and Dr. Bilotti stepped up to the microphone.

Pulling a large sword out of its sheath, he said, "To enhance the toast to such a fine couple, Fred asked me to perform a sabrage. This ritual goes back to the days of Napoleon Bonaparte where the saber was the weapon of choice for his light cavalry.

"Napoleon's spectacular victories across Europe gave them plenty of reasons to celebrate. And they did so opening bottles of champagne with their sabers.

"As a wine drinker, I appreciate Napolean saying, when he won, he drank champagne to celebrate, and when he lost, he drank it to console himself."

As the laughter died down, Bilotti said, "Sabrage is a celebratory act and thus suited to commemorate the beautiful union we witnessed today."

Bilotti was handed an unopened bottle of champagne. He removed the foil and wire hood and located the seam of the bottle. Holding the bottle at a thirty-degree angle, he smiled. "Let's hope this goes as planned."

The doctor placed the edge of his sword on the bottle and in one motion, slid it toward the top, hitting the lip of the bottle's top.

The top of of the bottle crashed to the floor as the room burst into applause. Bilotti held the opened bottle over his head. "The best in life and love to the newlyweds."

I stopped clapping as Bilotti took the seat next to me. "Nice going, Doc."

"It's always a little dicey doing it in public."

"You made it look easy."

"I can teach you how to do it."

Mary Ann said, "Please, don't. He can't hit a nail without smashing a finger."

"Hey, no fair."

A old man with cropped white hair, tapped the doctor on the back with a liver-spotted hand. The men embraced, and Bilotti said, "Frank, this is Johnny Coburn. He used to be in the wine-tasting group."

We shook hands, and Bilotti said, "Frank is the detective I told you about. He's the best detective I've ever worked with, and I've worked with a lot of good ones."

Coburn said, "That's saying a lot."

"He's exaggerating."

"No, I'm not. Frank can find anyone or anything."

"That might be right." I pointed. "I see a couple of bags on the table. I'm betting they contain bottles of great wine. Coburn asked a couple of questions before Mary Ann pulled me away. "We have to dance; it's our wedding song."

My knee ached as we headed for the exit. Mary Ann said, "That was a beautiful affair."

"It was fun, the food was good, and the wine . . . you liked it, right?"

"I only had one glass."

Handing her the car keys, John Coburn ambled up. "May I borrow your husband for a moment?"

"Sure."

We stepped away, and Coburn lowered his voice. "Bilotti told me a lot about you."

"Don't believe half of it."

His eyes and cheeks were sunken. "Seriously, he said you can be trusted."

Trusted? We just met. "I believe that's true."

He nodded slightly, pausing before saying, "It's a long story, and I'm happy to tell you what I know, but I have information regarding something that's been hidden for a long time."

"And what's that?"

He looked both ways before saying, "A large sum of money."

"And how did it go missing?"

"It was hidden, on purpose."

"If this is illegal, I don't want to hear any more."

"It's not. At least, not technically, and according to the lawyers I've consulted."

"And you're telling me, why?"

"Gauging your appetite for a treasure hunt."

Mary Ann took a step toward us. "Come on, Frank. We're the last ones here."

"I have to go."

"Is it okay if I reach out to you to discuss this matter?"

"Sure."

"I assume you'll keep this conversation and any in the future confidential."

I hustled over to Mary Ann. "What did he want?"

"He's a friend of Bilotti's and has a problem."
"Don't get mixed up in other people's business."
Yes, Mom. "I'm not sure what it is; he didn't get into it."

62

"HEY, DOC, HOW ARE YOU?"

"Good, Frank. That was a nice wedding, wasn't it?"

"Yeah, we had a good time, and thanks for bringing the wine. I overdid it. It's been two days, and I'm still feeling the effects."

He laughed. "We don't recover as quickly as we once did."

"Amen. You know, I really liked that one from Washington State. What was its name?"

"Force Majeure. It's one of the few American wines I'm still buying."

"That Sassicaia was nice too. It might be the most expensive wine I ever had."

"Sassicaia is the original super Tuscan, and it costs about three hundred now."

"That's crazy."

"It is. I don't buy them any longer. I think I paid a hundred, when I bought it ten years ago."

"Thanks for sharing it."

"My pleasure."

"Hey, I wanted to ask you about a drug called rapamycin. Do you know about it?"

"It's the new anti-aging drug, though the jury is out on whether it's worth the risks or not."

"But it works?"

"It seems to, but human trials are just getting underway. Everything else is anecdotal."

Did he hear the air going out of my balloon? "Oh."

"I'd recommend against taking it, at this point. If it works, you have time to get some of the benefits."

"Thanks. I appreciate the advice, and thanks again for the wine."

"Anytime. Say, what did you think of the way Johnny Coburn described wine?"

"It was like reading the *Wine Spectator*."

"He used to have an amazing palette when he was younger. He's a good guy."

"He wanted to know if he could trust me. I thought that was weird."

"Johnny has gotten a bit mysterious as the years piled on. I think his brother-in-law, or maybe it was his uncle, was a DEA agent."

"Really?"

"I'm pretty sure he worked in Miami years ago."

"What did Johnny do for a living?"

"He's been retired a long time. I believe he had a couple of retail stores. Why?"

"Just curious. How old is he?"

"Went to his eightieth a couple of years ago."

"That's what I figured."

"Sorry, Frank, but I have to get moving. Have a good one."

Hanging up, my mind ran through the possibility the

money Coburn mentioned came from cash he skimmed out of his retail businesses. He would've avoided declaring the income. It was tax avoidance and illegal.

It wasn't uncommon, but why would he have hidden it and tell me about it? Had he forgotten where he put it? That seemed like a long shot but Coburn was in his early eighties. Was he looking for someone he could trust to piece together where he'd hidden it?

Typing "Johnny Coburn" into the system produced no record of a criminal history. A welcome surprise.

A chance to earn extra income was enticing, but there wasn't enough time or energy left to moonlight. The time to reevaluate would be after the Holmes case was solved.

DERRICK SAID, "Verizon sent Reedy's phone records. I'm printing them out." He jumped out of his seat and the printer hummed.

He passed a document to me. "Here's the cell-tower data."

There were two sections: one for May twenty-third and the next day. "It looks like Reedy never left the area."

"If he had any smarts, he'd have left it behind."

"Where's the map of the tower's coverage?"

"Here."

"Hmm. He could've taken a walk. The next tower is just past Golden Gate."

"Unless he didn't take his phone with him, he was home or walking in the area."

"Let's go over the calls he made or received."

"It's weird. There's no record of him sending or receiving a text."

Pointing to the report, I said, "He called this number

seven times but it never went through. Check who it belongs to."

He tapped the number into a program and said, "Holy shit! It's his son's."

"The calls were made between eleven thirty-nine and twelve eighteen. Either he was way past his curfew, or something was going on."

"Check the other number. He called it four times as well."

After typing it in, I hit find, and said, "It's a landline registered to a Mildred Fenster."

"Could be a girlfriend."

"Maybe. Let me check DMV."

A picture of an gray-haired woman, with deep wrinkles, populated the screen. Derrick said, "It can't be. She's way too old."

"Has to be a relative or friend he was trying to check in with."

"Maybe he thought she'd know where his son was."

Tapping on my keyboard, I navigated to a search of public records. Derrick said, "What are you looking for?"

"This right here. Janet Reedy changed her name from Janet Fenster when she got married. I'm betting this is her mother."

"Probably. But she went with her daughter to—"

"Reedy must have thought his son was at the grandmother's house." I went back to the DMV page. "She lives at 10981 SW Sixty-Sixth Street. Check the cell tower's data for calls made to his son against the address."

Derrick shuffled through a couple of pages. "The cell tower services the grandma's house."

"The father either knew or suspected his son was at the grandmother's. What was he doing there so late?"

"He knew the house was empty. Maybe he was partying with friends."

"Was Debbie Holmes there? Her cell last pinged from the same tower."

"She could've been."

"It fits."

"It sure does. She may have went there willingly."

"She wouldn't have left her bike behind."

"It was hidden. Maybe she figured she'd get it back later."

"Long shot, it wouldn't fit in Jason's trunk. But why not go home, drop the bike and go in the car?"

"Maybe her parents wouldn't have let her go. It was a school night."

"Good point. She went around her parents just like Jason did and ended up dead."

"She could've been murdered in the grandmother's home."

Speculation was the currency of a homicide detective. Whether it was well spent was the question.

63

—————

DERRICK STOOD. "WE HAVE TO ASK REEDY ABOUT THESE calls."

"We will, but he's crafty. We're better off talking to a couple of the grandmother's neighbors. Hopefully, we'll pick up some intel, and if Reedy starts bullshitting, we can back him in a corner."

"You're right. It might save us time. I'll get out there now."

He never said it, but the way he was acting said he'd turned down the Charlotte job. "We'll go together."

Turning onto SW Sixty-Sixth Street, we passed Center Point Community Church. Derrick said, "How old is this lady, Fenster?"

"Eighty-two."

"What is she doing out here? The houses are too spread out. If she needs something, she's in trouble."

It was a good question. "Maybe she's lived out here a long time. It isn't easy convincing somebody to move out of a house."

"Tell me about it. I told my parents to downsize, but they'll never sell their place."

"As long as they're able to, it's better having them make the decision themselves."

"True. They'd be blaming me."

"Slow down." I pointed ahead. "The yellow one is the Fenster place."

"I doubt anyone saw anything. There's no streetlights out here."

"Probably, but we're here. Let's ring a couple doorbells. I'll do the two on either side, and you can take the two across the street."

Walking away from the first house, I gave Derrick a thumbs-down. I cut across what passed for grass and headed toward a one-story, blue home with a metal roof.

Ten feet from the front door, a pair of dogs began barking as if I'd broken in.

An elf of a man, with a ponytail, answered the bell. I showed him my badge as he shooed the dogs. "Macy! Garmin! Stop!"

"I'm sorry. Once they know ya, you won't be able to stop them from licking you."

"They look like twins."

"Brothers. Had him since the litter."

"They're cute."

"We're attached at the hip. How can I help you?"

"I'd like to see if you saw anything at the Fenster home."

"Did something happen to Mildred?"

"No, she's fine. But a couple of weeks ago, she was away, and we're interested in any activity at the house during that time. The days in question are Monday and Tuesday, the twenty-third and twenty-fourth of May."

"Was it a break-in?"

"No. Do you remember seeing anything?"

"You know, I did. I was walking the boys, my dogs, and it was just before midnight; we go out every night that time."

Another reason not to have a dog. "What did you see?"

"Well, a car was in the driveway that wasn't there when we went out around five. We walked past the house, but I just figured she had a visitor; her family lives in town."

"What kind of car?"

"It was white, is all I know."

Reedy drove a white Honda.

"Were the lights in the house on?"

"A couple were. But when we turned around, we go down to the canal, another car came up and turned in the driveway. A young guy got out, and by the time we got to the house, he was getting back in his car and he drove off."

"You think it was a food delivery?"

"Maybe. He had a bag when he got back in the car."

"Was he carrying anything when he first got there?"

"Can't say. Me and the boys were too far down."

"How long you think he was at the house?"

"Five, ten minutes?"

"Did you see a young woman around seventeen?"

"No."

"And you're certain of the time?"

"Ah-huh. The boys got their routine. I don't take 'em on time, they get restless."

"Thank you. Can I have your number in case I have a question?"

Back in the car, Derrick said, "Struck out completely. How'd you do?"

I filled him in. He said, "Looks like Jason was here. The other guy could've been making a delivery."

He pulled away from the curb as a truck turned onto the

street. I said, "We have to assume Jason Reedy was here. There's no other explanation for the father to call the house."

"Agree."

The truck rumbled by. I said, "Turn around."

"What?"

"That's a landscaper. Maybe he saw something the next day; today's a Tuesday."

"During the day?"

"You never know."

The Paradise Landscaping truck stopped in front of a house Derrick had gone to. Pulling behind, we got out as a man rode a mower down a ramp. Another man was pulling a cord on a Weedwacker.

"Excuse me! Can we have a word?"

The man on the mower shut it off. "What's up?"

"You cut this lawn every Tuesday?"

"Yeah, why? We do something?"

"No, no. A couple of Tuesdays ago, May twenty-fourth, did you see anything at that house?" I pointed to Fenster's home.

"I think an old lady lives there, right?"

"Yes. Do you remember seeing anything?"

He started talking Spanish to the other man, then said, "That was like, six weeks ago?"

"Yes."

"We're not sure, but we think it could've been the day there was a boat on a hitch."

"You saw a boat pulled by a car?"

"Yeah."

"What kind of car?"

"Oh, I don't know. I think it was a white one, a foreign job."

"You sure?"

He spoke Spanish again before saying, "Luis thinks it was silver, maybe a Ford."

Here we go with eyewitnesses. "Okay. But, the boat, you're both sure that you saw it in the driveway of that house?"

"Yeah, we said so. It was backed up to the garage."

"What time was that?"

"Around now, we come the same time."

It was just before four in the afternoon. "Thanks."

We got back in the car. "It looks like the next day, Reedy or his son came back to the house."

"Maybe the old man had been out fishing and on the way back stopped over, looking for his son."

"I don't buy it. He would have come first thing in the morning if the kid didn't come home."

"Maybe he did and came back."

"It could be, but I'm betting that's not the case."

64

SKIPPING DOWN THE STAIRS TWO AT A TIME, I CAME OUT ON our floor and trotted into the office. "We have enough for a warrant on the grandmother's house."

"I thought they were going to shoot it down."

"This case has brought a lot of pressure. I thought we were light but they're green-lighting it."

"What the sheriff say?"

"He bounced it off Wilner. Among the things he said were the boyfriend being one of the last, if not *the* last person to see her, and the fact her phone last pinged from the same area at the house, that we had enough."

"A judge who's helpful. Who'd a thunk it?"

"It is nice."

"I'm thinking the father and kid are in it together. Why else would he keep calling him every couple of minutes?"

Derrick's child was too young for him to understand when your kid left the house, a parent couldn't rest, especially if you were out of contact. "Maybe, but it's also possible he was just worried about where his kid was."

"So why'd he lie about Lopez, and Holmes's knee?"

"He and the son are at the top of the list. Let's polish this request and get it signed off."

My phone rang. It was Mary Ann. "Hi, I figured I'd see how you're doing."

She was bored. "I'm good. We're going for a warrant on a house we think is connected to the Holmes case."

"Sounds exciting."

She must have forgotten all the paperwork she was required to file when on the force. "We'll see. What are you doing?"

"Nothing."

"Did you do your laps?"

"Yes."

"You know, I was thinking maybe we should take a trip to Savannah. You always said you wanted to go."

"That would be fun, but when?"

"As soon as this case is over."

"Oh."

"But why don't you do some research, find a hotel, and things to do over a long weekend?"

"You want to stay in the city itself?"

"Wherever you want."

"I should have recorded that."

I laughed. "I'll deny it, especially if it's expensive. I'll see you later."

Putting my phone away, I noticed a text. It was from Johnny Coburn. He wanted to meet. I deleted it.

NEXT TO NOTIFYING someone about the death of a loved one, pulling an innocent person into a case they had zero knowledge of, was disturbing.

"Everybody has to lay back. This is an older lady, an innocent bystander."

"You tell us when to take over."

"Will do, and please be gentle. Do your job, but I don't want this house tossed. Is that clear?"

"No problem, Luca."

Shirt plastered to my back, I rang the bell and stepped away from the door. Ready to ring it again, the door opened. Mildred Fenster had a pleasant smile and erect posture. "Hello, there. Can I help you, young man?"

Young man? It was impossible not to like her. "Sorry to bother you, ma'am, but we're from the sheriff's office."

"The sheriff's office?"

I held out the warrant. "Yes, we're going to have to search your home."

"Why on earth would you do that?"

"A judge believes there may be evidence inside your home?"

"Evidence? Of what? You must have the wrong address. I've lived here for nearly thirty-two years."

"I'm sorry, ma'am. This is the correct home. We have to ask you to step outside. It's warm out; you may want to wait in one of our cars."

"I don't understand what is going on? May I call my daughter?"

"Yes, but you'll have to do it outside."

Derrick said, "Come with me, Mrs. Fenster. My car is comfortable. You can wait there and make your calls."

I waved to the search team, and the five approached. "Get whatever you can find but be gentle."

Always uncomfortable going into a stranger's house, walking into Fenster's bedroom was painful. It was a throwback to the seventies. Debating whether to open the drawers of her brown nightstand, I knew she wasn't hiding anything.

In a compromise, I slid out the top drawer and closed it. If there'd been something, it would have been the biggest surprise of my career.

Closing the bedroom door behind me, I went into the family room. A forensic tech was on his knees collecting fibers and hairs from the rug, while another was examining the couch.

Derrick came into the house from the garage. He waved me over. "Over here. They think there's blood in the garage."

Two techs were kneeling down near the back of Fenster's car. "What do you have?"

"We sprayed luminol, and this area lit up."

It was a liver-shaped stain. "It's brown. Got to be old."

"Might be, but it's been scrubbed, and detergents would discolor it."

"We need a sample for a DNA analysis. Can you do that?"

"It's tricky, but we've done it before."

"How you do that?"

"The best way is to cut out a section of the concrete."

"What else can you do?"

"Use an adhesive tape, and we'll back it up with scraping some of the material up."

"Will it be accurate?"

"Yes."

"Go for it."

I turned to Derrick. "You go over the rest of the garage?"

"Yeah, nothing but a bunch of moldy stuff. Half the crap in here should be tossed."

"You know people and their 'stuff.'"

"She's got more tools than me."

"Probably held on to them when her husband passed."

"What sentimental value does a drill have?"

He had a point. "Mary Ann is looking for something to do. Maybe she can help her sell some of this stuff on eBay."

"Who'd want it?"

"You'd be surprised what people buy."

"Mary Ann is itching to get back to work?"

"She knows it's not good for her. She needs to find something to keep busy with. Let's talk to Fenster about the blood. She's a nice lady, so be gentle. I don't want her more upset than she already is."

"I feel bad for her, especially if it turns out her son-in-law or grandson was involved in Holmes's murder."

65

Derrick came back into the office. "The neighbor with the dogs said he thinks the guy he saw getting into the car was Joe Centro."

"We knew Centro was lying, but about what?"

"The neighbor kept to his story; he didn't think Centro had gone in the house."

"Why was he there, then?"

"Jason Reedy was there. Maybe his father called Centro and asked him to check on his son."

"There were no calls from the father's phone to Centro."

"Yeah. Then Jason called Centro."

"What for if he didn't go in the house? Did Jason change his mind?"

"Centro could've known he was there and was concerned about what was going on with Holmes."

"I'm going to call the lab. They should be able to tell us if any of the hairs collected match Holmes's. We can wait on the DNA, but the color should be a good indicator. I can't see Fenster having a ton of visitors."

"Ask them about the blood."

"A DNA workup takes time."

"Can't Remin push them?"

"I asked, but you know what they say about line jumping."

"Do you believe the old lady saying she didn't know anything about the blood?"

"I do. Fenster is in her eighties. When she's pulling into the garage, she's focused on not hitting anything. Then she goes in the house. She's not going to putter around the garage."

"What about when she gets her groceries out of the trunk. It wasn't bad, but I'd notice it."

I reached for the ringing desk phone. "Look, if she's involved in a cover-up, or worse, I'll hand in my badge."

"Detective Luca, Homicide.

"Oh, hello.

"Okay.

"Yes, I understand. Goodbye, Counselor."

Hanging up, I said, "That was O'Brien. His firm is representing Jason Reedy and Fenster."

"Fenster? Why would she need a lawyer if she wasn't involved?"

Good point. "They may be trying to limit access; they don't want her saying something that hurts the Reedys."

"Welcome to America, where everybody has a mouthpiece."

"Not far from the truth." I picked up the phone. "I'm calling the lab."

"Serge, it's Luca."

"Hi, Frank. I was about to call you. We have the blood results."

"And?"

"It's not human."

"What do you mean?"

"It's animal blood. Possibly a rodent or possum."

"Are you sure about that?"

"Yes. The cell-type ratios aren't human."

"Damn it."

"Sorry, but there is good news."

"What? Tell me."

"Four of the hairs collected from the Fenster residence materially match the known sample."

"They match Debbie Holmes's?"

"Yes."

"You said 'materially.' What does that mean?"

"The questioned hair exhibits the same microscopic characteristics as the Holmes hair sample. It's consistent with coming from the same source."

"So, it's Debbie Holmes's hair?"

"We believe so."

"Are you doing a DNA test on them?"

"No."

"Why not?"

"There were no follicles on the recovered hairs. They fell out naturally."

"Thanks, Serge."

Derrick was standing in front of my desk. "It's Holmes's hair?"

"Yep."

"She was at the house. What about the blood?"

"It's from an animal."

"Man, I thought—"

"We have to bring in Jason Reedy."

Derrick picked up the phone. "I'll call O'Brien."

"Hold on."

"Why?"

"I'm thinking maybe we should talk to Centro first. See what he says."

"Really?"

"We have nothing to lose, and we might get something we can use with Reedy."

"You want to do it here?"

"No. We don't want to alarm him at this point. He'd get a lawyer."

WE WERE SHOWN into the same conference room we'd been in. Five minutes later, Joey Centro entered. Dressed in black again, I thought of the movie *Groundhog Day*.

Eyes on the table again, he shifted his weight when I said, "We have a couple more questions."

"I didn't do anything."

"We haven't said you did. We're interested in your friend Jason Reedy. Sit down."

He scraped a chair back and plopped onto it. "Remember our little chat a few days ago?"

He nodded.

"Well, it seems you weren't telling us the truth."

He squirmed like a five-year-old. "I told you everything, everything I remembered."

Ah, the hedge came early. "Since you've had the time to think it over, we can set the record straight."

Derrick said, "Lying to a police officer is called obstruction, and you could go to jail for it."

The kid's shoulders slumped.

He slid farther down the chair when I followed with, "He's right. You don't want to get into the criminal justice system; you'll carry it with you your entire life. Now, the night that Debbie Holmes was reported missing, May twenty-third, to be exact. What did you do?"

"Nothing. I was home."

"Didn't you just hear Detective Dickson say lying is a jailable offense? Where did you go that night?"

"I don't think anywhere."

"I'm going to give you a little help: we know you went to Jason Reedy's grandmother's home."

His eyes widened. "Oh yeah, I forgot that."

"Why did you go there?"

"Jason called me and asked me to come."

"It was late."

He shrugged.

"What did you do there?"

"Nothing. We just hung."

"Debbie Holmes was there, wasn't she?"

"Uh, I don't know. I didn't see her."

We knew he hadn't gone in the house. "You were hanging out and didn't see Debbie?"

"I didn't."

"How long were you there?"

"Not long."

"Five minutes? An hour?"

"It was just, like, a quick drop-in, you know?"

"We have a witness who saw you there."

Color drained out of his face.

"What were you carrying?"

"Nothing."

"You had a bag."

"Uh, my backpack."

"What was in it?"

"Nothing."

"Then why carry it?"

"I, uh, I had beer in it."

"Why didn't you drink it with Jason?"

"He said he had to go, so I left."

"And you never saw Debbie Holmes when you were there?"

"No."

"Did you hear her voice?"

He shook his head.

"Are you sure?"

He nodded.

"All right, thank you for cooperating. Get back to class."

Derrick said, "I'm surprised you ended it so early."

"I have an idea that might work."

66

Mary Ann popped a pod in the coffee maker. "You taking lunch today?"

"I don't know. It's going to be pretty busy."

"Take a yogurt with you."

That wasn't lunch. Did they even have yogurt when I was growing up? "Maybe."

"What do you have today?"

"We're bringing in Jason Reedy and his friend at the same time. We'll separate them and see where the cracks in their stories lead us."

"Remember we did once. With the Freeport brothers, remember?"

"That was when we first got paired up."

"And you didn't trust me for anything."

"That's not true."

Mary Ann raised her eyebrows. "Really?"

She was right. "I had to keep you on your toes."

I smelled her coffee breath as she drew next to me. "It took me a while to soften you up. I like this version of you better."

I kissed her cheek. "I guess I aged well, then. What are you up to today?"

"Going to lunch with Brittany, and I'm going keep sniffing around those dognappers. I got a hunch on them."

"What?"

"I'll let you know if it has promise."

"You miss the job, don't you?"

"Some of it. Boy, it'd be nice to do it two days a week."

"Maybe we can reopen the private practice when I hang it up."

PEERING OVER HIS MONITOR, Derrick said, "Morning, Frank."

"Morning. It's going to be a good day."

"It would have been better if Chris Reedy was in a room as well."

"O'Brien is too sharp to let that happen. We keep the pressure on, we'll find out what his involvement was."

"Looks like Centro is coming in with his mother. I think the kid has nothing to do with it."

"He lied repeatedly—"

"He's protecting a friend."

"I doubt he's just being loyal."

"You're probably right."

"Crime aside, it'd be nice if people stuck up for each other every now and then."

"Keep dreaming."

Looking at the video feed, I wondered if the Centro family were color blind. His mother had a black cane and wore a long, black dress. Her son was in jeans and a dress shirt, both black.

Derrick said, "If she had gray streak, she could be

Morticia from *The Adams Family*."

"Maybe Goth?" I knocked and opened the door. "Do you folks need anything? A water?"

"No, thanks."

"Sorry about the delay, we'll be with you in a bit."

We went around the corner to room 5. O'Brien and Jason Reedy were chatting amicably. The Reedy kid was smiling like he was with a buddy in a pizzeria. We didn't believe Reedy and Centro had talked before coming in.

I said, "Let's do it."

"You going soft on me?"

"What are you talking about?"

"You didn't monkey with the room temperature."

"Aw, O'Brien's okay, and it ain't right making the mom uncomfortable. She's got a cane . . ."

He smiled. "Yeah, right." He knocked on the door and threw it open.

Derrick advised them the interview was being recorded and stated the attendees and time.

O'Brien said, "We're anxious to cooperate and bring my client's involvement to a close."

I said, "Let's get going, then. Jason. May I call you Jason to avoid any confusion in the record with your father?"

"That is my name."

As I recalled what my dad used to say, about wiping the smirk off someone's face, Derrick said, "We'd like to start with the night of May twenty-third of this year, the day Deborah Holmes was last seen alive."

I said, "What did you do that night?"

"Nothing special. I was home, if I recall correctly."

"The entire evening?"

"Yes."

"Then why did your father keep calling your cell phone?"

"How would I know? If I answered, it would be speculating."

Was this kid taking law classes? "He was looking for you. Isn't that why?"

"Maybe."

"Why would he do that if you were home?"

"Again, I can't answer that."

"You were at your grandmother's house. Weren't you?"

O'Brien realized we knew and whispered in Jason's ear. The kid said, "I had completely forgotten about that. My grams was away with my mom, and her cat, Felix, needed to be fed."

"Who did you go to your grandmother's home with?"

"I went by myself."

"Your girlfriend, Deborah Holmes, wasn't with you?"

"No."

"That's interesting, because during the search of her house we collected four of her hairs."

O'Brien said, "My client and the deceased were a couple for a over a year. She'd been to the grandmother's home on a number of occasions. The hairs could have been shed anytime over the time they were together."

"We have a witness who said she was there."

Jason leaned forward. "Who said that?"

"Your friend Joseph Centro. He said you called him to come over."

A flash of anger ran across his face. "I never called him, but Debbie was there."

"Why were you hiding it?"

"For multiple reasons: one, her parents would get mad if they knew she'd gone out against their wishes, and after what happened, it would cast me as a suspect."

"You said, 'after what happened.' Tell us what happened."

"Nothing. We were messing around, and, uh, she wanted to go home and she left."

"Why didn't you drive her home?"

"I'd been drinking, probably had six beers. As painful as it is to think things would be different if I took her home, I was in no condition to drive."

"You let her walk home?"

"I realize it sounds crazy after what happened but the neighborhood is safe. Or used to be."

"Why not ask your friend to drive her home?"

"She didn't want to leave when he came by."

"You called him to come over, and yet he left after a brief visit?"

"I didn't call him. He knew I was there and popped over. I'd been drinking, and then before he arrived, Deb started to come on to me, and we started messing around. Then Joey got there. I told him what was going on and he left."

"How soon after did Debbie leave?"

"Shortly thereafter. Joey broke the mood, and, uh, she wanted to go."

"What do you believe happened?"

"I'm not one to speculate, but it's possible, and I hate to say it, probable that Joey saw her and grabbed her. He's always had a crush on her, and he's made several unsolicited advances on Debbie."

"You think your friend had something to do with her death?"

"It's certainly possible. What else could have occurred?"

"Rather than have you come back, can you wait here for fifteen, twenty minutes?"

Jason rolled his eyes, but I knew O'Brien, at six hundred an hour, wouldn't complain. "That's fine. Just have someone bring us water."

67

COMING INTO THE ROOM WITH TWO WATER BOTTLES, I SAID, "We're sorry to keep you waiting.

I handed Ms. Centro and her son a bottle of water. Ms. Centro winced and shifted in her chair. "Do you have a more comfortable chair? I have spinal stenosis."

"I'm sorry, ma'am. We don't, but if standing is more comfortable . . ."

She shook her head and inched to the front of her seat as Derrick turned the recording device on and recited the formalities.

I said, "Mr. Centro, we're going to be very direct, and I urge you to do the same. Your friend Jason Reedy and his lawyer are in another room down the hall."

Ms. Centro said, "Oh my God. Did Jason kill that poor girl?"

"We're conducting an investigation, and your son may have information to clarify the roles of several individuals."

"Joey, help the police. It's your duty."

Derrick said, "No dancing around this time. If you played

a part in this crime, tell us now. If you cooperate, we'll do our best to help you."

"Detective Dickson is right. Whatever happened has happened. We can't change the past but if you're straight with us, we can make life easier for you."

"Oh my God. Joey, did you do something?"

"No, Mom. Don't worry."

"Tell us what happened the night of May twenty-third."

"I told you already. Jason called me, and I went over there—"

"On the the night of the murder?"

"Ma'am, you have the right to be here, but please no interruptions."

"Okay, I'm sorry."

"You went to Jason Reedy's grandmother's house."

"Yeah."

"And what did you do there?"

"Nothing. I left right away."

"Why?"

"I just did."

"Did you see Deborah Holmes?"

"No."

"Did you have a crush on her?"

"Not really."

"Did you see her leave?"

"No, I told you already."

"Your friend Jason said Debbie left the house around the time you did. He said she was walking home and that you grabbed her and killed her."

"What the fuck?"

"Joey! Watch your language."

"Ma! Jason's lying."

"Tell us what really happened."

"Am I gonna get in trouble?"

"Did you hurt Ms. Holmes?"

"No."

"Did you detain her?"

"No."

"Then you have nothing to worry about. If you're straight with us, we'll forget your obstructive efforts."

"Joey is a good boy. He wouldn't harm anyone."

"It's in your son's interest to tell us the truth, everything he knows."

"Go ahead, Joey. Tell them."

Centro sighed. "I feel bad, but if he's trying to dump on me, then I gotta say what I gotta say."

"Go ahead."

"He called me and asked me to come to his grandma's. I was tired and didn't want to go. He kept saying I had to, that he needed help. I asked him with what, but he said he'd tell me when I got there."

Ms. Centro said, "You have to stop listening to him. You have your own mind; you don't want to do something, don't do it. See where it got you?"

She was right, and interrupting her might diminish the lesson she was trying to impart.

"Come on, Ma."

Derrick said, "Continue. Jason Reedy called you and said he needed help. Then what?"

"I went out and drove to his grandma's."

"What happened when you got there?"

"He called me on the way there, I was like five minutes away. He was real nervous, said not to make noise when I got there."

"Did he tell you why?"

"No."

"Please continue."

"Well, I got there and rang the bell. J opened the door and looked stressed, you know. I took a step to go inside, but he said, 'No, stay there,' and closed the door. A minute later, he opened the door and said, "Take this and ditch it. I don't want anybody to find it. I had to take a pee but he wouldn't let me in. It was weird, he just told me to go and get rid of the bag as fast as I could."

"What did he give you?"

"A plastic bag."

"What was in it?"

"I don't know. I didn't look in."

"What did you do?"

"I said, what's in it? And J said, "None of your business, and you better not look inside."

"Are you sure you didn't check what was in the bag? I would've."

"No. You don't know Jason; he'd get really pissed if I did."

"How would he have known? He told you to dump it."

"Believe me, he would've known."

"Okay. What kind of bag?"

"It was black, like the ones used for garbage bags."

"Could you tell what was in it?"

"Not really, maybe clothes?"

"Where is the bag?"

Centro frowned. "I got rid of it."

"How?"

"I tossed it in the water."

"Where?"

"By the bridge to Marco."

"You threw it in the bay?"

"Yeah."

"Did it sink?"

"Yeah, I put the iron tire thing, from our car, inside."

The mother hadn't stopped shaking her head. The pain on her face wasn't from her back.

"And when you placed the tire iron in, you didn't see what was in it?"

"It was dark. Maybe there was a shirt or something."

"You remember where on the bridge you put it in the water?"

"Yeah, kind of at the beginning. I was scared and wanted to get out of there."

"We may need you to show us where. Can you do that?"

"Yeah, I know where."

"Take us through this again. You received a call from Jason Reedy, asking you to come to his grandmother's house."

"That's right and I went. But when I got there, he wouldn't let me in. He told me to wait, and then he gave me a bag and told me to ditch it."

"Those were his exact words?"

"Yeah."

"When you were driving from your house to his grandmother's, did anything happen?"

"What do you mean?"

"Did you stop anywhere? See anyone?"

"No, I went straight there, but J called me and told me to be quiet when I got there."

"Okay. He gives you this bag and then what?"

"I took off. I was nervous and trying to think of where to get rid of it. I was going to burn it, but I couldn't think of where, and somebody could see the fire."

"When you left, did you see anybody?"

"There was this guy walking a dog, two dogs. He was passing the house."

"Did you talk to him?"

"No. I got in the car and went out the other way."

"Other way?"

"I came down the street from Golden Gate but went back so I didn't have to pass him."

"Why were you so careful avoiding people if you didn't do anything wrong?"

"I don't know. It felt like Jason did something bad."

"What gave you that feeling?"

He shrugged.

"It's okay to tell us. You won't get in trouble."

"Just the way J was."

"Did you tell Jason Reedy what you did with the bag?"

"Yeah, he asked me and I told him."

"What did he say?"

"Nothing, just thanks for helping him out, and he wouldn't forget it."

68

———

We released Centro and his mother and headed to the interrogation room holding Jason Reedy and his lawyer. I said, "Hold on a sec."

Derrick said, "What's going on?"

"We need to impound the Reedy boat. If he used it to move Holmes's body, he's going to be spooked and try to clean any evidence."

"For sure. As soon as we're done, we'll draft a warrant."

"I'm afraid we can't wait, or he'll have a head start. It's going to take several hours at best to get a seizure approved."

"You finish the interview; I'll write up the request and run it upstairs."

"Thanks, pal."

We parted ways, and I entered the interview room. "Sorry to keep you waiting. Something came up."

O'Brien said, "We understand. Do you have anything further for us?"

"Yes. We'd like to know what your client gave to Joseph Centro, the night of May twenty-third, while at his grandmother's house."

The kid's eyes widened. "I didn't give him anything."

"That's not what Mr. Centro said. He said you gave him a plastic bag, instructing him to get rid of it."

"Oh, that. It was garbage. I asked him to throw it out."

"And you didn't want anyone to know?"

O'Brien said, "Please clarify the question."

"When you handed the bag to Mr. Centro, you told him to keep it quiet, not to look in the bag or tell anyone about it."

"It was a bunch of empty beer cans. Plus, I'd thrown up in it. It smelled horrific."

"Why didn't you throw it out?"

"He was at the door. Grandma keeps the cans on the side of the house, I didn't have shoes on."

This kid had an answer for everything. Whether they were true was the one question we couldn't ask him.

"You didn't go to school the next day."

"I wasn't feeling well from overdrinking."

"Yet you went back to your grandmother's house the next day. Why?"

"Felix needs to be fed every day."

"Why did you take the boat?"

"I went out for a ride after feeding Felix."

"Where did you go?"

"Fishing."

"Catch anything?"

"They weren't biting, and being on the water made me nauseous."

"You washed the boat when you got back?"

"I always do. You have to stay on top of it, or the crud turns into cement."

"The day after your girlfriend goes missing, you go fishing?"

"I called Deb but she didn't answer."

"Did you go looking for her?"

"A little. I checked the area around my grandma's."

"You didn't go out of your way, did you?"

O'Brien said, "That's unnecessary, Detective. As I recall, when Ms. Holmes was reported missing, everyone, including law enforcement, believed she'd run away."

"Fair enough, Counselor. Did you do anything else to try and locate Ms. Holmes?"

"I checked with friends to see if anyone knew anything, but since the police were involved, we felt you'd find her."

I counted to three. "And all the time she was in Marco Bay."

He frowned.

"You can be sure we're going to find who put her there."

DERRICK WAS TAPPING on his keyboard. "How'd the rest of the interview go?"

I briefed him and said, "Where's Jason Reedy's phone records?"

"In the murder book, on the credenza."

Picking it up, I said, "You almost finished with the request?"

"It's upstairs already. I'm writing the report on the Centro interview."

"Thanks. You know, Jason didn't call Centro from his cell phone. You think he called him, or is Centro in deeper than we think?"

"They've both lied. Maybe they're playing us, together."

"Centro said he went to the bridge to dump the bag. Maybe he tossed the body from there."

"He could've."

"We need to find that bag. What's in it could go a long way in seeing who is telling the truth."

"That's going to require a bunch of resources. Marco Bay is huge."

"Remin will be all over us if we retrieve the bag and it turns out to be full of vomit."

Derrick chuckled. "I can see it now on *WINK News*: 'Bumbling Department Fishes for Upchuck.'"

"You know, if we find it and Centro didn't tie a tight knot, who knows what we'll find. Crazy as it seems, I remember being on a party boat out of Sheepshead Bay in Brooklyn. It was rough seas and a couple of guys got sick. They started throwing up over the side of the boat. Man, you should've seen the fish coming to the surface to eat it."

"That's disgusting."

"It almost made me lose my lunch."

"Well, you killed my appetite."

Laughing, I dialed a number. "Sophia Livoti."

"Hi, Sophia, It's Frank Luca."

"How are you?"

"Good. I wanted to check and see how Lisa Ramos is."

"Lisa's got a ways to go, but she's doing much better."

"That's good to hear. Say hello for me."

"I will. Thanks for checking in."

"Thanks for everything you do for her and all the others you work with."

"Thank you, Frank."

THE SMELL of rosemary was in the air. I kissed Mary Ann on the cheek. "You making red potatoes?"

"No, I'm doing branzino they way you like it at La Pescheria."

"Al Forno?"

"Yes, with red onions and sliced potatoes."

"Olives?"

"Yes, I hope it comes out good."

"It will, and it'll be a heck of lot cheaper."

"You got lucky. I was by Wynn's Market and remembered they had branzino on sale."

I came up behind her. "You planning to take advantage of me later?"

"You're not that lucky."

"Hey, no fair."

"We'll see. How'd those interrogations go?"

"Pretty good. Got the Reedy kid to admit Holmes was there that night, and he pointed the finger at his friend."

"When they start turning on each other, the end is in sight."

"Hope so. What did you do?"

"Remember I told you about these people selling dogs on Craigslist?"

"Yeah?"

"I checked around and think they could be behind it. I asked for photos of this Yorkie. She was so cute—"

"We don't need a dog."

"I know, but I'll show you later; she's adorable. But anyway, in one of the pictures, in the room where the guy was taking the photo, was a mirror, and he looks like one of the thieves in that *WINK* video. Remember, the two guys?"

"Yes."

"One of them looks like the dog seller. I'm going to ask for more pictures and check if *WINK* has the video on their website."

Keeping the chance for some lovemaking alive, I said, "You still have good instincts."

69

———

APPROACHING THE JUDGE JOLLEY BRIDGE TO MARCO Island, my cell rang. "Hey, Sarge, what's up?"

"Wanted to let you know, the Reedy boat is secure and on its way in."

"Great. Appreciate the heads-up."

"No problem. Hey, good luck with finding that bag."

My gaze drifted toward the wide expanse of East Marco Bay. "We're going to need it; there's a ton of territory to cover."

Hanging up, I said, "They grabbed the boat. It's on the way to the lab."

"Good."

I slowed to a stop halfway to the highest point. Derrick said, "Look, there they are." He pointed to four boats flying the sheriff's flag.

"Let's hope the guy at Gulf Coast University is on the money with the current for that night."

The boats motored away from each other and slowed down. "The divers are getting ready."

Derrick said, "I'm feeling lucky." He clicked the handheld

radio. "This is Detective Dickson. Take your time out there and be safe. Stick to the grid as best you can."

A crackled reply came through, "We've got one boat at the target site, and the others are working from mid-bridge to the beach."

As a diver flopped overboard, I said, "I forgot my hat."

"The sun is strong."

"It's peaceful out here. But every time I cross this bridge, I'm going be thinking about this poor kid."

"Let's get out of the sun for a while. They find something, they'll radio."

Climbing into the car, Derrick said, "Look at that guy on the paddleboard. He's got a dog with him."

"That's crazy."

"He's just sitting there, so well-behaved."

"By the way, Mary Ann's got a line on who might be behind the dognapping."

"What's she got?"

The radio came to life. "One of the divers just brought something up. Looks like we found it."

"We're on the way. Meet us at Bear Point."

We pulled onto a sandy area, got out, and pulled gloves on. The flotilla cast anchors twenty feet offshore.

Derrick and I walked to the edge of the water as a diver hopped off the boat. He was handed a black plastic bag. Waist deep, he held the bag high and waded toward us.

Glistening beads of water rolled off the plastic. "We found it quicker than expected."

My gaze focused on the top as he handed it off to my partner. "Well done. Thanks."

Derrick said, "Looks like a pretty tight knot."

"It does but water finds its way everywhere."

I patted the bottom of the bag. "Not much, if any, water."

We opened the rear door of our SUV and set the bag down. My stomach turned. "This could be bagful of vomit or the ticket to solving the Holmes case."

Derrick said, "Fingers crossed."

Gently tugging on the knot, it slowly loosened. "Here we go."

Spreading the wrinkled top open, I took a sniff. "Not too bad."

Heads an inch apart, we looked inside. Derrick said, "What's that? A sheet?"

"A pillowcase. Probably the one used to suffocate her."

"Let's take pictures before we move anything."

We snapped five shots. Slowly, I lowered my hand inside the bag. Pawing at the fabric, I felt something hard. "Holmes's phone."

"Probably, she had an iPhone."

What kid didn't? As I pulled the pillowcase out, a leather strap became visible. "Here's her pocketbook." I handed the bedding to Derrick and took the small purse out. It was wet.

"It's one of those belt bags."

"She started the night out on her bike."

Holding the edges of the pillowcase, he unfurled it. He pointed. "Look at this: it's lipstick."

It felt like someone sat on my chest. "Sounds crazy saying it, but it's likely the murder weapon. Be careful, whatever is on there, we need to preserve."

"I'm bagging it."

Tinted brown, I shoved a bunch of tissues to the side, revealing crushed beer cans, two purple snack wrappers, and the tire iron.

Separating the items, I bagged them separately before focusing on what we thought was Holmes's pocketbook.

Unzipping the purse, I pulled out her school ID. Holmes

had a bright smile on. Shaking my head, I laid out the remaining contents: two packs of gum, a compact mirror, lipstick, and a key.

"So, there were beer cans and vomit, like Jason Reedy said."

"Yep, he just forgot to tell us about the pillowcase and Holmes's phone and purse."

"You think his old man was involved?"

"He did lead us astray. Why?"

"We'll find out."

"Let's bring this into forensics."

Derrick was behind the wheel and said, "You think forensics can pull DNA off the pillowcase?"

"Yes. They should be able to get Holmes's DNA from the lipstick."

"It's amazing what can be done today."

"We need to see if there were any fibers from it in Holmes's throat."

"That should've been on the autopsy, but I don't recall it."

Chemo was known to intermittently affect one's ability to recall. "Me neither. But it looks like we have what was used to kill her. What we need is to tie Reedy to it."

"We'll get his DNA off the pillowcase as well."

"He handed off the bag to Centro, instructed him to dump it, and admitted Holmes was with him at the grandmother's house."

"I'd say it's time to pop the champagne."

A video of Bilotti using a sword to open the bottle at the wedding ran through my head. "We're not celebrating. A young woman has been murdered. What we're doing is mopping up."

"I know, man, but this one's been tough."

"We still have to drag it over the line."

"It's up to the lab now."

"To a degree, but never leave your fate in another's hands."

"Getting philosophical?"

Emotional was more accurate. "No, maybe just tired of this whole scene. It ain't exactly uplifting."

"Hang in there, buddy."

"Yeah, right. Look, I hate to do it, but we need to rush another warrant through on the grandmother's house. We have to match the pillowcase and where the garbage bag came from to tie it to the Reedy kid."

70

Hanging up the phone, I said, "Remin wants me at the weekly press conference."

"Again? What's up with that?"

"I don't know. Maybe he knows I hate doing media and wants to torture me."

"He likes you, man. You don't think so, but he does."

"It's not about liking; he finds me useful, at times. I'll see you later."

"I'm gonna take a ride to the forensics garage, see what's up with the boat."

I was hoping they'd find something to tie Reedy senior to the murder but knew how that would sound. "Let me know what's going on."

Remin was wearing a light-gray suit. He looked weird. It was hard not speculating what the calculation was, deviating from dark blue?

He stepped to the podium. "Good to see everyone. I'd like to start on the traffic front. In an effort to reduce speeding, which contributed to a fatality this past week, we're going to increase enforcement. We don't enjoy ticketing residents or visitors, but we have no choice.

"Beginning Monday, major arteries throughout the county will be patrolled by both marked and unmarked vehicles.

"A raid in Golden Gate late last week resulted in eight indictments. We believe that particular drug gang was responsible for a quarter of the meth in the county.

"Additionally, we're pleased to announce the members of a burglary ring hitting the homes of part-time residents have been apprehended. This operation, not previously made public, involved a dozen officers and uncovered a connection with a Miami-based gang. Working with our counterparts in Miami-Dade, we believe we've shut them down completely.

"That's it for today. Questions? Let's start with Cynthia."

The *Naples Daily News* reporter stood. "Sheriff, can we have an update on the Deborah Holmes murder? The department seized a boat, and various items were recovered from Marco Bay."

"The investigation is continuing, and I'm confident we'll close this case soon."

"Is an arrest imminent?"

"I can't say at this time."

"The boat you seized belongs to a Christopher Reedy. His son, Jason, was in a relationship with Debbie Holmes. Are they suspects?"

"Persons of interest, is all I can say."

"At what point can you assure the community that the killer is off the streets?"

"Within days, we expect to make an announcement."

"What is taking so long?"

"Getting justice right, takes time."

It would be nice to regurgitate that line on Remin the next time he pressed me.

Remin pointed at a *WINK* reporter, "Melissa?"

"Thank you, Sheriff. I realize you're reluctant to name the Reedy family as suspects, but other than them, is there another suspect?"

"Detective Luca and his team are leading the investigation. Frank, would you like to say anything?"

And just like that, Remin tossed the grenade to me. Was saying no an option?

"As Sheriff Remin mentioned, we're close bringing this case to a conclusion. It may have taken longer than everyone wanted, but we have a system of justice and need to get it right."

"And you think you've got it right?"

"Yes, ma'am. We just need a little time for forensics to provide additional evidence."

"You sound confident you'll wrap this up shortly."

"Yes, ma'am."

"Do you have the Reedy family under surveillance?"

"We don't comment on whether an operation is live."

Remin said, "We're going to have to leave it there for today. We'll advise you when we're ready to make an announcement."

I followed the sheriff into the anteroom, knowing the press wanted something interesting to report. He said, "We gave them as much as we could. They'll fill in the rest."

"As soon as the lab is finished, you can announce the arrest, sir."

"I authorized forty hours of OT yesterday. They should have it tomorrow, at the latest."

"Thanks."

Walking back to the office, a text from Derrick hit my phone. Steps away, I shoved it back in my pocket.

As soon I entered the office, Derrick said, "How'd it go?"

"Actually, pretty good. They know it's a Reedy, but we didn't give them anything."

"Good, because the boat had nothing."

"Really?"

"Yep. Sprayed it with luminol as well, and nothing."

"That's weird. Luminol picks up one part out of a million. They fish; there had to be some blood."

"Reedy must've went crazy cleaning it."

"We should check with his neighbors, see if they saw him washing it."

"We won't need it."

"We don't need it now, but the prosecutors will want it to build a narrative in court."

My desk phone rang. "Homicide."

"Frank, it's Sergio."

"We can confirm the the plastic bag matches the roll of bags from the grandmother's house."

"Excellent. How'd you figure that out?"

"The gauge and coloring are identical and the blade at the bag factory used to serrate the edges matches."

"You guys are the best."

"Yeah, we know that."

"Get me the DNA on the pillowcase and I'll buy you lunch."

"Lunch with you is Wendy's."

"You don't like their roast beef?"

"Goodbye, cheapo."

Hanging up, I told Derrick and he said, "We got the kid."

"Yeah but it don't feel good. Teenagers killing teenagers; what has the world come to?"

"You don't want an answer, do you?"

"No. Let's get the paperwork going for the arrest."

"I'm gonna take a piss, and then I'll get started."

My cell buzzed.It was Mary Ann. "Hey, Mare, what's going on?"

"You're having a good day."

"Why do you say that?"

"I saw the news. They said you were about to arrest Jason Reedy."

"We're a hair away. In fact, we're just getting started on the arrest warrant."

"Congrats."

"I don't know if that's in order." I lowered my voice: "Maybe I'm getting too old for this, but nailing a kid for killing a kid, doesn't ring my bell anymore."

"I know it's hard, but you're doing your job, and it's an important one."

My desk phone rang again. "Hey, I gotta go. I'll see you later."

"Homi—"

"Frank, it's Sergio."

"What do you have for me?"

"A problem, a big one."

71

I GASPED AS IF MIKE TYSON PUNCHED MY GUT. "WHAT DO you mean, the pillowcase doesn't match?"

"We ran fiber comparisons on the pillowcase extracted from Marco Bay, against the ones seized from the Fenster residence. They're not the same; the colors are even slightly off."

"What about the DNA?"

"We're in the midst of testing it. Should have something soon."

"All right. But you're sure on the pillowcases?"

"A hundred percent."

"Okay." I slammed the phone down as Derrick came back.

"What's the matter?"

"Serge said the pillowcase doesn't match any from the grandmother's house."

"Really?"

"Yep."

"Maybe the kid brought it with him."

"That would mean it was premeditated. I don't think it was, otherwise, why bring her to your grandmother's?"

"Nobody was home."

"The kid is too smart for that."

"Maybe it was a one-off case, the last one in a pair. It was old."

"Yeah. And the guest room had a single bed in it."

"That could be it." He slid onto his chair. "Yeah, it's got to be."

"He could've asked his father. Nah, that's crazy."

"What about Centro? He could've brought one."

"That's far-fetched. It probably came out of the guest room. He figured she'd never miss it, or when she did, it'd be long forgotten."

"Yeah, I'm sure the old lady has memory issues, and it's not going to get better as time goes on."

It was easy to be cavalier about aging when in your early forties. In another decade, he'd realize Father Time was coming for him as well.

I flipped through a binder. "I have the summary Bilotti sent, but where is the full autopsy report?"

"Should be in the murder book."

"It's not."

"I hope I didn't misplace it."

"Don't worry, I'll call Bilotti and get another copy."

The doctor answered on the second ring: "Medical Examiner Bilotti."

"Hey, Doc. It's Frank."

"How are you?"

"Okay. I hate to say it, but it looks like we misfiled the Holmes autopsy. Can you email me a copy?"

"There's a first time for everything. I'll send it right over."

There was no need admitting I couldn't remember something from the report. "Thanks, you're a lifesaver."

He chuckled. "Actually, I come in after the life is gone."

"Not much different from what we do here." I lowered my voice. "Does it ever get to you?"

"It's not easy, especially with younger victims. A little too close to home."

He'd lost a daughter, and I regretted bringing it up. "Amen. Hey, how's your buddy Coburn doing? He called me, but I haven't had a chance to call him back."

"Must have been a couple of days ago because he had a massive stroke."

"Oh no. How's he doing?"

"With the brain, you never know, but it doesn't look good."

"I'm sorry, Doc."

"At the wedding, he said he wasn't feeling right, felt a little unbalanced. I told him to go to a doctor but didn't think he'd suffer a stroke."

It was natural to ignore aches, pains, and feeling off. But this time it had serious consequences. "When it's your time, it's your time."

"I don't know about that. There are plenty of ways to increase the odds of a long life."

It was an inconsiderate thing for me to say. "I know. I have to get moving. Send the report when you have a chance."

"It's on its way."

"Bilotti sent it." I opened the attachment and skimmed through the first five pages. The information was on page six. "Here it is: 'Minuscule particles of a cotton fiber were lodged deep in the larynx and in upper trachea. The filaments likely originated from the material used to suffocate the victim.'"

"No surprise there. The kid was fighting for her life."

The reminder wasn't needed. "Just trying to line things up for the prosecutors."

"What's the hurry?"

"I'd like to take some time off when this one is over."

"Taking a trip somewhere?"

"No, just a staycation."

"The new word for hanging around the house. Just make sure to relax and not do a bunch of odd jobs around the house."

He was right. "I'm all thumbs anyway. Anything more than a loose screw, and Mary Ann won't let me near it."

He laughed.

"It's not funny. Remember the mess I made doing touch-up painting?" I'd put a can of paint on the ladder, and when I moved the ladder, it fell over."

"Now, that was something out of a slapstick comedy."

Except it was real, and I stood there so shocked, it took me a few minutes to start cleaning it up. Before I could agree with Derrick, the phone rang.

"Homicide, Detective Luca."

"Frank, it's Sergio."

"Hey. What do you have for me?"

I listened for a moment. What he said made my body rumble. Was it diarrhea or vomit? I said, "I'll call you back." I took off for the bathroom, unsure whether I'd make it in time.

72

After rinsing my mouth, I splashed cold water on my face. The fog began lifting. I trudged back to the office.

Derrick met me at the door. "You all right? You're white as a ghost."

"All four of their DNA are on the pillowcase."

"Which four? What happened?"

"The lab found Holmes's DNA as well as both Reedy's and Centro's."

"That's crazy. It has to be Jason. There's got to be a reason."

"It could be a secondary transfer of DNA."

"It has to be it. Centro said he didn't look in the bag, but he had to've."

"He put the tire iron in. The transfer could have happened then."

"That's it, then."

"But that doesn't explain Reedy senior's DNA on the pillowcase."

"It's his mother's house. Maybe he slept on that pillow recently."

"They didn't find any hair on it. And if it wasn't laundered, there would have been skin cells all over it."

"What if all three of them were in it together? That would explain it."

"It's possible, but conspiracies are tough to keep quiet."

"The old man is a control freak. Maybe he's pulling the strings."

The image on the cover of Mario Puzo's *The Godfather* came to mind. "He's got a teenage son; he knows how difficult it is to control what they do."

"Why don't we bring them in, see what they say?"

"Hang on." I dialed a number. "Serge, it's Luca. We're going to need you to recover DNA off every item in the bag and on the bag itself. As well as the amount of DNA found."

"We can do that."

"How long is that going to take?"

"Normally, I'd say a week minimum, but the sheriff gave us a block of OT. I hate to use it on one case."

"You have to; a young girl was murdered."

"We'll get on it."

Derrick said, "Can we get that level of detail to make sense of it?"

"I have no idea, but whatever we get has to help or we're dead in the water."

"Isn't it just like life? We get a great tool like DNA, and now the collection kits are so sensitive, it picks up everything."

"The only constant is change. I'm going to call Bilotti; he went to a forensics conference in Tampa a month ago. This secondary-transfer thing is becoming an issue for everybody; they had to've talked about it."

He answered on the first ring. "Hey, Doc, you have a minute?"

"Anytime, Frank. What's on your mind?"

"The Holmes case. We have the pillowcase used to suffocate her; it matches the fibers found in her throat."

"I recall extracting filaments."

"Well, forensics discovered the DNA of three persons of interest on the pillowcase."

"You believe all participated in the murder?"

"That's a possibility, but I'm wondering about the chances one or two of their DNA got there in a secondary-transfer situation."

"Items handled by the others came in contact with the pillowcase?"

"They were in the same bag. What do you know about telling the difference between primary and secondary transference?"

"It's an area of growing interest. With the increased sensitivity of DNA kits, the absence or presence of DNA is not sufficient to determine whether the DNA found is primary or secondary. Therefore, DNA results need to be described more precisely, in terms of quantity and quality, to highlight characteristics to help discriminate activities."

"Doc, my eyes are glazing over. Can you simplify this?"

"Essentially, the goal is to examine trace amounts of DNA and determine if they can be classified as secondary."

"How do they do that?"

"The quantity is one factor. But that would depend on where the DNA is found. As one can imagine, if an item comes into contact with an article of cloth, the transfer has an easier time than if it were a piece of plastic."

"We're dealing with a pillowcase. The other items were beer cans, a tire iron, tissues, and candy wrappers."

"Interesting. At the conference they referenced an exhaustive study to help technicians make determinations."

"What did they say?"

"Give me some time. I'll pull the material. I recall they had a couple of graphics that'll make it easy to understand."

"Thanks, Doc."

Laying out the photos I'd taken when the plastic bag was recovered, I tried to envision how DNA transfers might occur. I exhaled. "Without knowing if Centro pawed through the bag, or what happened when he tossed the bag in the water, it's impossible to speculate."

"We may have to rely on seeing if one of them breaks. If they're in it together, one of them might bite if we offer a deal."

"Maybe." My cell buzzed. It was the wife. "Hey, Mary Ann, what's going on?"

"You busy?"

Nah, sitting here, sipping a glass of Chianti. "What's up?"

"I was following up with that man who claims to be a breeder. The puppy I told him I was interested in, is gone. When I said I had my heart set on it, he said not to worry, he'd get another in a couple of days."

"Okay."

"Don't you see? They're stealing to order."

"They could be, but I can't check into it right now. I'm up to my neck in the Holmes case. Give me a couple of days, and we'll run it down."

"Okay."

"Hey, I have to go. Dr. Bilotti just walked in."

I stood. "You didn't have to come down. I would've gone to you."

"I had a meeting with HR. I can't figure out which new health plan we should take."

It was reassuring a doctor couldn't navigate the complexities of health plans. "We took the one with the lowest premium."

Derrick said, "Us too."

"You're both a couple years younger than us, and the missus takes two expensive meds. It looks like neither plan covers both, which seems crazy. It's one or the other."

Derrick was much younger, but I'd had bladder cancer. "Good luck with it."

"Thanks." He set a binder on my desk. "This is what I wanted to show you. I think it's going to be helpful."

73

HUNCHED OVER MY DESK, WE PORED OVER THE DATA ON THE forensics report. I pointed. "See, these two places have the highest concentration of DNA."

"It's a wider spread than you'd think, if you were holding a pillow over her mouth."

"Holmes had nothing in her system; she'd have fought back. Whoever suffocated her had to keep the pressure on for six to ten minutes as she tried to free herself."

"True."

"And the chart Bilotti shared said applying pressure to cloth transferred as much DNA as friction did. It's proof of suffocation. We can use it to get a confession."

"His lawyer will rebut it as an inexact science, and with this discovery, they'll know two other persons of interest were on the pillowcase as well."

"That's for the courtroom. Remin said he ran it by the prosecutors, and they said the limited quantities left by the others, strongly suggest secondary transfers."

"I hope it's enough."

"Remin said they considered the supporting evidence we developed. They felt it was enough and green-lighted it."

I SLAMMED THE PHONE DOWN. "That was O'Brien. He said he's on his way with Jason Reedy, but Reedy senior isn't coming. He said he's no longer representing him. Said it's a conflict of interest."

"We were waiting for that. But why pull it at the last minute?"

"O'Brien is good. He knows it'll throw us off."

"Probably."

"We didn't even get started, and the plan is coming apart."

Derrick stood. "It'll be okay. I'm going to grab a coffee. You want one?"

"No, thanks."

Visualization was a practice I was trying to implement. The number of successful people using the technique prompted me to try.

I closed my eyes. Running through an optimum interview, my desk phone jangled. "Homicide, Detective Luca."

"Hello, Frank, it's Marjorie. The sheriff would like to see you."

"Now?"

"Yes. He said immediately."

"I've got interviews kicking off in minutes."

"That's the subject he wants to discuss."

I jotted a note to Derrick and hustled upstairs.

Marjorie smiled as I breezed into the sheriff's office.

"Sir, you needed me?"

"Have a seat."

"We have interviews to conduct . . ."

He nodded and I sat. "The prosecutors have raised concerns about going into a courtroom with the DNA evidence."

"I don't understand; they green-lighted it."

"You've been around; you know lawyers change their tune after their bravado wears off."

Or once they signed a client. "What's the concern?"

"The reality of trying the case, dependent on a science under development."

I shifted in the chair, and the pain in my knee returned. "We have him at the scene on the night she was murdered. His DNA is all over the murder weapon. What more do we need?"

"They'd like a confession to remove the secondary-transfer issue. Otherwise, they feel it'll raise reasonable doubt."

And just like that, there was another problem, and the pressure ratcheted up.

As soon as I hit the doorway, Derrick said, "Where'd you go?"

I told him about what Remin said. "That's bullshit. We busted our asses getting what we have. What do they want us to do, try the case too?"

A good question. Sweeping up three files off my desk, I said, "Let's get going."

Walking down the hall, I said, "It's bothering me the kid is here and not the old man? I'd never put my son ahead of me."

"He's probably hiding something. Again."

"And bailing at the last minute. Every time I discount the old man orchestrating the murder or concealing it, a flag goes up."

"O'Brien is the top guy in the county. The old man knows the kid needs the help more than he does."

O'Brien had a fresh haircut. His white shirt stuck out of his suit the same amount on each sleeve. Jason, pumping his leg like a jackhammer, wore a tie six inches too long.

Derrick breezed through the boilerplate and thanked them for coming in.

I said, "Counselor, why did you drop representation of Jason's father?"

"Conflict of interest."

"You believe the two of them are at odds?"

"My beliefs are irrelevant. The fact is, no lawyer will represent two individuals in the same case."

"Understood, but why not represent Mr. Reedy? What was behind the decision?"

"I'm not here to answer questions regarding my practice. Move on, Detective."

Nodding, I said, "Your client, Jason Reedy, misled us previously. I'd strongly suggest he come clean during this interview."

"We're here to clear up remaining misunderstandings."

"Your client was with the deceased the last night of her life—"

"You don't know that. The time of death is never definitive."

"The range of hours in the TOD puts him with her."

"If this ever goes to court, we'll have our experts examine your claim."

"Okay, Jason, let me remind you, we know you handed a bag to your trusted friend, Joey Centro, instructing him to get rid of it immediately."

"I told you I'd drank too much and puked. When I cleaned up, I put the tissues in a bag I was keeping for the beer cans."

"What was the urgency to have Mr. Centro get rid of the bag?"

"I just asked him to put it in the trash cans."

"You had a snack at your grandmother's?"

"I brought a couple of energy bars with me."

"Did you eat them?"

"Yes."

"What did you do with the wrappers?"

"I threw them in the bag."

"You were trying to eliminate any evidence you were at your grandmother's."

"I didn't want her to know we were hanging out, that's all."

"Your grandmother was away and you took your girlfriend there, with alcohol, I might add, and removed evidence so nobody would know you were there."

"I guess so."

"Deborah Holmes didn't drink that night, did she?"

"No, she didn't want to."

"So you had, what, five, six beers?"

"Something like that."

"You had a pretty good buzz on."

"I wasn't drunk."

"Then why did you tell us you were too drunk to drive Ms. Holmes home?"

He shrugged. "I didn't want to take a chance."

"By staying overnight, you were creating more evidence you were there."

Another shrug.

"So you're drunk and looking to have sex with Ms. Holmes."

"It wasn't like that."

"You told your friend to leave because you were in the middle of 'fooling around' with Ms. Holmes."

"So? That's not against the law."

"It isn't, but pushing yourself on her without consent is rape."

"I didn't rape anyone!"

"Detective, there is no evidence Ms. Holmes was sexually assaulted."

"True, but it's our belief your client became frustrated, possibly under threat Ms. Holmes would reveal he tried to force himself on her. Things got out of hand, and he suffocated Ms. Holmes."

"I didn't do anything. I'd never hurt Deb!"

"Detective, I understand your need for a narrative, but where is the evidence?"

"Glad you asked, Counselor. Inside the bag your client admits to handing to Mr. Centro, with specific instructions to get rid of it, was the pillowcase used to suffocate Ms. Holmes."

"If that is true, it means nothing. Mr. Centro could have placed it in the bag."

"The pillowcase had Jason Reedy's DNA on it."

"I didn't do it."

"Then tell us, who did?"

74

Derrick and I shook Bill Hartman's chubby hand, and we got the formalities out of the way.

The button on the defense attorney's shirt was poised to pop with the next sip of water. Hired to defend Centro, Hartman wasn't in the same league as Reedy's lawyer. He was probably two hundred an hour cheaper, but Centro's mother was in no position to be milked, at any rate.

Centro chewed on a thumbnail. Maybe it was the fluorescent lighting, but he had a cadaver's skin tone.

"Mr. Centro, you were at the same house as Deborah Holmes on the last night of her life."

"Yeah, I told you that I went there."

"You did. However, you said that Jason Reedy summoned you with a phone call."

"That's right."

"A search of your phone records failed to verify your claim."

"That's not true. He called me."

"You also said Jason Reedy called you while you were en

route to his grandmother's house. But you were the one who made the call."

"He told me to call."

"Upon your arrival, you said Jason Reedy wouldn't let you in the house."

"That's right. He was acting weird."

"He gave you a bag of trash and asked you to put it in the garbage can on the side of the house."

"No. He told me to get rid of it so nobody could find it."

"What was inside the bag?"

"I don't know. I didn't open it."

"What did you do after he gave you the bag?"

"You know; I took you there—to the Marco Bridge where I threw it in the bay."

"You didn't open it?"

"No."

"But you put the tire iron from your car inside to weigh it down."

"Oh yeah. I forgot. I put it in there, yeah."

"Why did you feel the need to put something inside to keep it under water? So it wouldn't be found?"

"Yeah. Jason was acting weird and said to hide it. I just figured I should do it. I wasn't really thinking about it."

"My client took you to the place where he discarded the bag. If he was concerned for himself about someone discovering it, he would have taken you elsewhere."

That made sense. "Mr. Centro, what else did you put in there?"

"Nothing."

"You sure about that?"

"Uh-huh."

"Ms. Holmes's pocketbook and phone were inside the bag."

"I keep telling you, I didn't know what was in it."

"You know what's strange? If Ms. Holmes was inside the home when you left, why would her pocketbook be in the bag?"

"Detective, I think that clearly points the finger at Jason Reedy, not my client."

"Hang on, Counselor." I looked Centro in the eyes. "Joey, you know what else we found?"

He shook his head.

"We found a pillowcase inside the bag."

Hartman's belly hit the table. "My client has repeatedly stated he did not view the contents of the bag. Placing a tire iron in doesn't mean he looked inside. He simply dropped it in, closed the bag, and discarded it."

"A reasonable explanation, except the pillowcase had Mr. Centro's DNA on it."

"Come on, Detective. You know DNA transfers of a secondary nature happen all the time. Mr. Centro's DNA was on the tire iron, and it simply transferred to the pillowcase."

"That doesn't explain it."

"Explain what?"

"The pillowcase had two heavy concentrations of your client's DNA on it. Fittingly, they match the positions where hands would be while suffocating someone."

"That's rampant speculation."

"No, it's backed by science. The transfer of DNA is very high when pressure and friction are applied, especially on cloth."

"We'll produce our own experts to counter your claims."

I put up a hand. "We're going to make a one-time offer; if Mr. Centro confesses to suffocating Ms. Holmes, we'll guarantee not to go for the death penalty."

Centro put his hands over his face.

"Hold on, now. You have no proof—"

"At this time, the vehicle owned by Ms. Centro and driven by your client that night, is being seized, and a search of the Centro home is being conducted."

Centro wailed, "No! No! My mom, she didn't do nothing. What happened was an accident. I didn't mean to hurt her."

DERRICK FIST-BUMPED ME. "We finally got all the pieces to the puzzle."

There was nothing to cheer about. "If Centro didn't have to take a pee, Holmes would be sitting in a classroom."

"Or a million other ifs, like Reedy not drinking, or—"

I shook my head. "Holmes being afraid to call her parents for a ride is the one that gets me."

"I know, but end of the day, Centro was a time bomb waiting to explode. Holmes rejects his advance, she threatens to tell Jason, and he kills her? Insane, is what it is."

"That's an understatement. Society's got to figure out how to get kids to handle the emotions from rejection. This isn't a damn video game."

"Amen. Hey, how about Reedy senior? You think he was trying to run interference for his son?"

"Probably. People do all kinds of stupid things when trying to protect family. I can't see myself doing anything like that, but I can see the conundrum."

Derrick smiled. "Nice word choice."

My desk phone rang. "Homicide, Detective Luca."

"Detective Luca, you caught the killer."

"Hello, Bruce. How are you?"

"Tell me how you got the killer?"

"How about I tell you what I can, when we do the ride-along?"

"When?"

"How about tomorrow?"

"Oh man! That's so great."

"I'll see you in the morning. Say, ten o'clock?"

"I'll be ready."

Derrick said, "That was Noon?"

"Yeah. He got worked up over the ride-along."

"Hope you didn't get yourself into something you'll regret."

"Nah, it'll be good for both of us." I picked up our report on the signed confession, "I'm going to run this upstairs."

Instead of going to see the prosecutor, I stepped into the parking lot and punched a number in my cell. "Jessie, it's Dad."

"Hi, Dad. How's it going?"

"Good. How are you? You busy?"

"I'm good. Just heading over to the student center. Is something wrong?"

"No, everything is fine."

"How about Mom?"

"She's great. I just called to tell you something."

"What?"

"That no matter what, if you're in trouble or not, if you need something or a ride somewhere, if something is uncomfortable, you call me."

"Where's this coming from?"

"Nowhere. I just want you to know you can count on me. I promise, no questions or judgments. I just want you to be safe."

"I am, Dad."

"I know, but remember, you can call me for anything, and I mean *anything*, and I'm there, no questions."

"Thanks, Dad. I know, but you don't have to worry about me."

"Say what you want, but Mom and I are always going to worry. Just use your head, and if you're in a jam, don't try to solve it, call me."

"Okay, Dad. I hear you. I gotta go, love you."

"Love you too."

Closing my eyes, I turned my face, and soaked up a minute of sunshine before running upstairs.

75

THE NEXT MORNING, DERRICK AND I STEPPED OUT OF A briefing with prosecutors. I said, "So, that's it; we're done with the Holmes case. But the parents will be living with it forever."

"Yeah, that sucks. But we did what we could. Now what's going to take our time up?"

"I'm going take a ride east."

"What's going on?"

"The dognapping ring. Mary Ann said there's a breeder in Immokalee who doesn't line up."

"In what way?"

"A couple. The business-formation docs were two months old, and they're selling the dogs on Craigslist. She made like a buyer on that site. They had different account names but were the same seller. Plus, the prices were too low compared to other breeders. I was surprised at what she uncovered."

"She was a detective."

"Sometimes, I forget that. I'd like you to come along, but if two of us show up, they're likely to get suspicious."

"No problem."

I stopped in front of a yellow home. A Kia SUV and an old pickup truck were parked to the right.

Gravel crunching underfoot, I went to the front door of the cinder-block home. The bell was drowned out by a chorus of barking.

"Shush! Shush!"

The door was opened by a man in a logo-less, red baseball cap. I said, "I'm Peter, my wife, Maureen, called about the terrier."

"Oh yeah, come in. She fell in love with her."

Over the barking, I said, "She wanted to come, but she's in a wheelchair and it's a project."

"She told me. Let me get Missy."

He disappeared down a hallway, and I surveyed the living area. A double reclining couch sat in front of a TV the size of a bedsheet.

"Here she is."

He handed off a gray puppy. "Boy, she is cute. How you doing, little girl?" The terrier licked my finger like a Popsicle. "How much you want for her?"

"Fifteen hundred. Cash only."

"Cash is not a problem." I held the dog in front of my face. "She's a keeper." I handed her back. "Can I see her pedigree papers?"

"You want to hold her while I get them?"

"No, it's okay."

A minute later, he returned. "Here they are."

I examined the certificate of pedigree. It appeared fresh. The lineage listed a sire named Kokopelli Cup of Joe, and the dam as Maggie Mae Stewart. "Looks good."

"As much as I hate to let her go, you got the cash, she's yours."

"You know, we've had Malteses before and they're easy." I

pulled my phone out. "Maureen said you have this one as well. Can I see him?"

"Sure. You know males are easier, too, just like in real life." He smiled, revealing a missing tooth.

I laughed along with him as he left to get the puppy.

"Here's Mr. Sam."

"Oh, you're handsome, Sam." The white ball of fur was shaking. "It's okay." I rubbed his belly. "How much?"

"Nineteen hundred."

"Can I see his papers?"

"Sure."

I exchanged the Maltese for another pedigree certificate. "Where'd he come from?"

"A breeder of ours in Ohio."

The dog's sire was listed as Sexy Rod Java and the dam as Hot Legs Jane. I wasn't a big music fan, but the Rod Stewart connection was impossible to miss. I handed them back. "Even though it's more money, I'd rather have the little guy, but I got to make sure Maureen is on board. You know what they say, happy spouse, happy house."

"Okay, man. Just know, we got other people interested, so hurry up."

I hopped back in the car and drove away. A half mile away, I pulled over and called Gesso. "Sarge, I dropped in on the guys Mary Ann developed, the ones I told you about."

"The dognappers in Immokalee?"

"Yes, I'm certain it's them. The documents are forgeries."

"I'll get some cars going, and we'll shut 'em down."

Passing Oil Well Road, I was about to call Mary Ann when my cell rang. I didn't recognize the number, but it had a 239 area code, and I answered, "Detective Luca."

"Oh, hi. You don't know me, but I'm a nurse taking care of Mr. Coburn. He insisted I call you."

"What about?"

She lowered her voice. "I think he may be losing it; he said to tell you to check into a DEA agent named Withers."

The name rang a bell. The details were fuzzy. "Anything else he said?"

"That was it. He said it would be enough."

Using the voice command, I called Mary Ann. "Hey, you still got it, kid."

"What happened?"

"The paperwork was a tiny bit off; the AKC logo wasn't right, and the lineage was fabricated. These guys need a course in creativity."

"I knew it."

"Good work. I turned it over to Gesso, and he's going to take them down today."

"What about the puppies?"

My heart sank. I hadn't thought of them. "I'll make sure they get Animal Control involved until they can get the rightful owners identified."

"They were cute, right?"

"Especially that terrier. Hey, you got your iPad handy?"

"Yes. What do you need?"

"Remember that DEA agent Withers?"

"Not really."

"It might have been before your time. See what comes up on him."

She clicked away. "Oh geez. He committed suicide."

Right. "What else?"

"He was working a big case where a hundred million in cash went missing."

"I forgot it was that much. They ever find the money?"

"Doesn't look like it. Oh, it says here the money was never recovered. Why you asking about him?"

"Friend of a friend mentioned it, and I couldn't remember the story."

"A hundred million. Wow. I wonder where it is?"

Good question. "Who knows? The drug dealers probably grabbed it."

"Be nice to find it, wouldn't it?"

"You'd have to give it back to the owners."

"Not in Florida. I don't remember exactly, but there's a finders-keepers law, had to do with looking for sunken treasures from the pirate days."

"I didn't know that." It was an interesting twist. But was I up to a hunt?

THE NEXT BOOK IN THIS SERIES IS UNDERWAY, LOOK FOR IT 2023.

HAVE YOU READ THE PREQUEL, THE BARROW CASE?

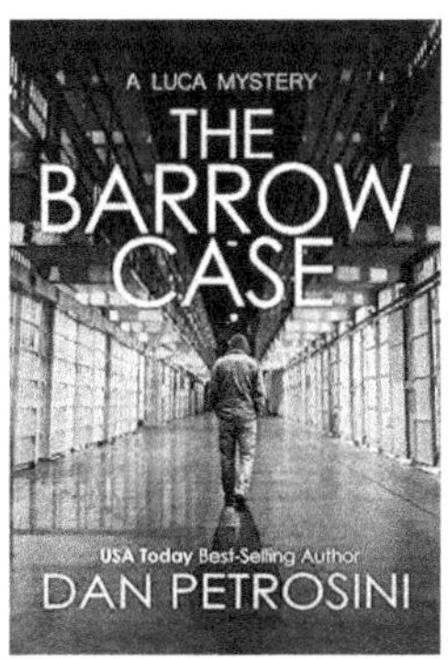

WHILE YOU WAIT FOR BOOK 16, START READING BOOK ONE OF SUSPENSEFUL SECRETS,

CORY'S DILEMMA.

His big music career break . . . was because of a lie.

I hope you enjoyed reading *No On Is Safe* as much as I enjoyed writing it. If you did, I'd appreciate it if you would write a quick review on Amazon or your favorite book site. Reviews are an author's best friend and even a quick line or two is helpful. Thanks, Dan

OTHER BOOKS BY DAN

<u>**THE LUCA MYSTERY SERIES**</u>

Am I the Killer

Vanished

The Serenity Murder

Third Chances

A Cold, Hard Case

Cop or Killer?

Silencing Salter

A Killer Missteps

Uncertain Stakes

The Grandpa Killer

Dangerous Revenge

Where Are They

Buried at the Lake

The Preserve Killer

No One is Safe

<u>**SUSPENSEFUL SECRETS**</u>

Cory's Dilemma

Cory's Flight

Cory's Shift

OTHER WORKS BY DAN PETROSINI

The Final Enemy

Complicit Witness

Push Back

Ambition Cliff

You can keep abreast of my writing and have access to books that are free of discounting by joining my newsletter. It normally is out once a month and also contains notes on self- esteem, motivational pieces and wine articles.

It's free. See bottom of my website: www.danpetrosini.com

ABOUT THE AUTHOR

Dan is a USA Today and Amazon best-selling author who wrote his first story at the age of ten and enjoys telling a story or joke.

Dan gets his story ideas by exploring the question; What if?

In almost every situation he finds himself in, Dan explores what if this or that happened? What if this person died or did something unusual or illegal?

Dan's non-stop mind spin provides him with plenty of material to weave into interesting stories.

A fan of books and films that have twists and are difficult to predict, Dan crafts his stories to prevent readers from guessing correctly. He writes every day, forcing the words out when necessary and has written over twenty-five novels to date.

It's not a matter of wanting to write, Dan simply has to.

Dan passionately believes people can realize their dreams if they focus and act, and he encourages just that.

His favorite saying is – "The price of discipline is always less than the cost of regret"

Dan reminds people to get the negativity out of their lives. He believes it is contagious and advises people to steer clear of negative people. He knows having a true, positive mind set makes it feel like life is rigged in your favor. When he gets off base, he tells himself, 'You can't have a good day with a bad attitude.'

Married with two daughters and a needy Maltese, Dan lives in Southwest Florida. A New York native, Dan has taught at local colleges, writes novels, and plays tenor saxophone in several jazz bands. He also drinks way too much wine and never, ever takes himself too seriously.

He puts out a twice-a-month newsletter featuring articles, his writing and special deals and steals.

Sign up at www.danpetrosini.com

9 781960 286154